THE BEATLES

TELL ME WHAT YOU SEE

Peter Checksfield

Copyright © 2019 Peter Checksfield

All rights reserved.

The editorial arrangement, analysis, and professional commentary are subject to this copyright notice. No portion of this book may be copied, retransmitted, reposted, duplicated, or otherwise used without the express written approval of the author, except by reviewers who may quote brief excerpts in connection with a review.

FOR HEATHER

ALSO FOR MY BROTHER ROBERT

WITH A LITTLE HELP FROM MY FRIENDS

Unlike with my previous books, I haven't asked anyone else for help in research. However, this book still wouldn't have been possible without the help of a great many archivists and music historians over the years. These include James Ross, Gordon Irwin, Jock Barnson, Bobby Baity, Gary Quinn and Alex Radov.

Like any book on The Beatles, this wouldn't have been possible without the groundbreaking work that went on beforehand. These authors / researchers include, but are certainly not limited to, Hunter Davies, Mark Lewisohn, Spencer Leigh, Keith Badman, Doug Sulpy, Chip Madinger, Mark Easter, Richie Unterberger, Bamiyan Shiff and Mike Carrera. See the Bibliography at the back of this book for a fuller list of important books and websites.

Lastly, I'd like to thank my better half Heather. Without her love and support I wouldn't even be an author, let alone write three books.

CONTENTS

1 Introduction 1
2 **THE BEATLES** 3
3 **JOHN LENNON** 73
4 **PAUL McCARTNEY** 101
5 **GEORGE HARRISON** 213
6 **RINGO STARR** 235
7 Bibliography 275
8 About the author 280

Peter Checksfield

INTRODUCTION

PAPERBACK WRITER

'The Beatles – Tell Me What You See' is my third book, following 2018's 'Channelling The Beat – The Ultimate Guide to UK '60s Pop on TV', and 2019's 'Look Wot They Dun – The Ultimate Guide to UK Glam Rock on TV in The '70s'. I never initially planned a book on The Beatles, but in late 2018, following unexpected but fortunately temporary health issues, I visited the moving and life-affirming 'John and Yoko: Double Fantasy' exhibition in Liverpool, as well as (for the first time) The Cavern, The Beatles' childhood homes, etc. I then *knew* what my next book had to be about.

WHAT GOES ON

I've attempted to list all complete or near-complete professionally-filmed musical performances by The Beatles, John Lennon, Paul McCartney, George Harrison and Ringo Starr, whether that is on TV shows, in Promo Videos, as live concert footage, and in movies. NOT usually mentioned are movies that don't feature musical performances (such as 'How I Won The War' and 'The Magic Christian', excellent though they are), documentaries (unless they include full-length, exclusive, performances), interviews, news reports, and amateur footage filmed from the audience.

YOU KNOW MY NAME (LOOK UP MY NUMBER)

For TV shows, I've used broadcast dates, adding taping dates when known. For concerts, I've usually listed them by date of performance, adding broadcast dates when known. For Promo Videos, I've rounded up release dates to the nearest month; these often coincide with the release dates of the corresponding singles, though occasionally videos wouldn't be made until sometime later. Additionally, to give the footage some context, I've listed both UK and US chart positions throughout the book.

NOT A SECOND TIME

Also, I've mentioned when *alternate Promo Videos* were made. Everyone has a different opinion on what constitutes an 'alternate': Some, such as the 3 best-known versions of 'Hello Goodbye', Paul's 2 very different 'This One' and George's 2 'Got My Mind Set On You' videos, are very different. But what about when just a few seconds of different footage is featured, or a live vocal is replace by the studio recording, or a 4:3 picture is cropped to 16:9? These things are generally mentioned, but are not usually regarded as 'alternates' for the purposes of this book. Also, please be aware that what you see on YouTube and bootlegs are often elaborate fakes rather than officially sanctioned promo videos.

YOU WON'T SEE ME

A number of performances, mainly from the 1962 – 1966 era (but sometimes well into the '70s), sadly no longer exist on video or film, though occasionally they do survive as audios. All details of these 'lost' performances have been listed when known.

ALL TOGETHER NOW

There are 5 main sections to this book: The Beatles, John Lennon, Paul McCartney, George Harrison and Ringo Starr. For the sake of simplicity, The Plastic Ono Band is under John Lennon, Wings is under Paul McCartney, The Traveling Wilburys under George Harrison, etc.

I hope, in researching and writing this tome, I've done John, Paul, George and Ringo's TV & video careers justice. Enjoy the book, and if you've any serious comments or further info, let me know.

PETER CHECKSFIELD

www.peterchecksfield.com

THE BEATLES

22-08-62 – **The Cavern, Liverpool (UK)**

Some Other Guy

This incredible footage isn't the earliest filmed performance of The Beatles: that honour goes to a 39-second silent colour 8mm film of the boys performing at St. John's Presbyterian Church Hall in Birkenhead on the 10th of February 1962. However, this live performance of The Beatles performing Ritchie Barrett's 'Some Other Guy' remains THE most historically important footage ever of The Beatles. Not only is it the earliest professionally filmed performance of the band to feature original audio, but it is also the only footage of them filmed in The Cavern, capturing the band just a week after Pete Best was replaced by Ringo Starr, with feelings still running high enough for someone to heckle 'We want Pete!' at the end of the song. Although originally taped by a Granada TV crew for a programme called 'Know The North', it was deemed unsatisfactory, so wasn't actually screened until 06-11-63, when it was broadcast on 'Scene At 6.30'. Also performed for the cameras at the time was 'Kansas City – Hey-Hey-Hey-Hey', as well as some silent 'inserts'; the former only survives on audio, but the latter, as well as an alternate audio of 'Some Other Guy', still survive. This has resulted in at least four different edits of this performance, each with alternate visuals and/or audio. One of these was released on the 'Anthology' official VHS and DVD box-sets. The only official audio release of a performance of the song by The Beatles though, was from the radio show 'Easy Beat', taped on 19-06-63 and broadcast on 23-06-63, and issued on the 'Live At the BBC' album in November 1994.

17-10-62 – 'People and Places' (UK) – *MISSING/LOST*

Some Other Guy / Love Me Do

Between two performances at The Cavern on this day, The Beatles made their debut in a TV studio, for viewers in the northern Granada TV area only. Performing live in the studio, the band plays their current concert favourite 'Some Other Guy', and the A-side of their debut single (discounting the earlier 'My Bonnie' where they anonymously backed Tony Sheridan), 'Love Me Do'. Unfortunately, like a great many of their early TV appearances, this footage no longer survives, though an audio, taped from in front of the TV by a fan, does still exist, and they put in a strong performance. 'Love Me Do' peaked at No. 17 in the UK charts, and, following their breakthrough in early 1964, No. 1 in the US charts.

02-11-62 – 'People and Places' (UK) – *MISSING/LOST*

Love Me Do / A Taste Of Honey

The Beatles' second appearance on the show, this time they pre-taped on 29-10-62, probably due to the fact that they were due to fly out to Hamburg on 30-10-62 for a 14-night residency at The Star Club. As well as more TV promotion for their single, The Beatles perform Lenny Welch's 'A Taste Of Honey', a song that would be issued on the 'Please Please Me' album over 4 months later. For 'Love Me Do', John didn't have a guitar, but instead sat down singing in front of all the others, while Paul and George stood behind him playing their usual instruments alongside Ringo on drums. This no longer exists on video, but an audio of 'A Taste Of Honey' survives.

03-12-62 – 'Discs A Go Go' (UK) – *MISSING/LOST*

Love Me Do

'Discs A Go Go' was a TV show made by TWW (Television Wales and the West), and only broadcast in that area. Making their only ever appearance on the show, the band mime to their current hit single.

04-12-62 – 'Tuesday Rendezvous' (UK) – *MISSING/LOST*

Love Me Do / P.S. I Love You

At last appearing on TV in the London area, the band mime to both 'Love Me Do', and the B-side, 'P.S. I Love You', the only time they performed the latter song on TV.

17-12-62 – 'People and Places' (UK) – *MISSING/LOST*

Love Me Do / Twist and Shout

The day before flying to Hamburg for their final, 13-night, residency at The Star Club, the band returned to 'People and Places' for the 3rd time. Yet again performing 'Love Me Do', they also perform a song that they'd learnt via The Isley Brothers, Twist and Shout. Forever associated more with The Beatles than anyone else following the song's release on the 'Please Please Me' album, it would also become the title track of a chart-topping UK EP, as well as a No. 2 hit in the USA.

08-01-63 – 'Roundup' (UK) – *MISSING/LOST*

Please Please Me

Although not released until 3 days later, The Beatles mime their next single 'Please Please Me' for their only appearance on this Scottish TV show. The record would go on to just miss the UK top spot at No. 2 – or did it? It was listed as No. 1 on both the 'New Musical Express' and 'Melody Maker' charts, yet it got to No. 2 on the 'Record Retailer' charts, a far less-seen and allegedly less-accurate chart at the time. However, it is this chart that is now generally recognised as the official one for much of the '60s and early '70s, so, latter day history records the single as stalling at No. 2. Whatever, it was a big achievement, propelling the group to the big time, as well as giving a huge shove to the whole "Mersey Beat" scene, with such acts as Gerry and The Pacemakers, Billy J. Kramer with The Dakotas, The Swinging Blue Jeans, The Searchers and Cilla Black following The Beatles to the top of the charts within the next year or so. A US flop on its initial release, 'Please Please Me' eventually got to No. 3 on the US Billboard charts.

16-01-63 – **'People and Places' (UK) – *MISSING/LOST***

Ask Me Why / Please Please Me

Performing live on their 4th and final appearance on the show, this time the band play both sides of their current single. This was to be the only time 'Ask Me Why' was performed on TV.

19-01-63 – **'Thank Your Lucky Stars' (UK) – *MISSING/LOST***

Please Please Me

Prior to 'Ready, Steady, Go!' starting in August 1963 and 'Top Of The Pops' debuting in January 1964, the UK's top music TV shows were 'Juke Box Jury', a show that didn't actually feature acts performing, and this one, 'Thank Your Lucky Stars'. So, despite only miming to one song, this was a very important TV appearance for the band. It was pre-taped in Birmingham on 13-01-63.

23-02-63 – 'Thank Your Lucky Stars' (UK) – *MISSING/LOST*

Please Please Me

Making their 2nd appearance on the show, and miming to the same song as before, this was taped on 17-02-63 in ABC's Teddington Studios in London.

09-04-63 – 'Tuesday Rendezvous' (UK) – *MISSING/LOST*

From Me To You / Please Please Me

Performing on this London-based show for the 2nd time, The Beatles mime to their new single 'From Me To You', as well as, over the closing credits, a brief excerpt of 'Please Please Me'. Topping the UK charts, from now onwards it would be No. 1's (nearly) all the way in their homeland, though at this point the band still meant almost nothing in the USA, where 'From Me To You' got to just 116. A year later, as the B-side to the re-promoted 'Please Please Me', it would become a US No. 3.

16-04-63 – 'The 625 Show' (UK) – *MISSING/LOST*

From Me To You / Thank You Girl / Please Please Me

Up till now, all of The Beatles' TV appearances had been on the various ITV (Independent Television) channels, but now even the staid old BBC were waking up to this new phenomenon, with the group appearing on one of their TV shows for the first time. Pre-taped on 13-

04-63 and with the band playing live, this included the only TV performance of 'Thank You Girl', the B-side to 'From Me To You', while 'Please Please Me' was a finale with the entire cast of the show, including compere/singer Jimmy Young, Rolf and Tino, Hank Locklin, Wout Steenhuis, Micky Greeve, Johnny Pearson and Edwin Braben.

16-04-63 – 'Scene At 6.30' (UK) – *MISSING/LOST*

From Me To You

By now Granada TV's 'People and Places' had been replaced by a new show, 'Scene At 6:30', and while the programme's news and magazine format was much the same, the big difference is that bands now tended to mime instead of play live, with The Beatles being no exception. Here they perform their new single.

20-04-63 – 'Thank Your Lucky Stars' (UK) – *MISSING/LOST*

From Me To You

Taped on 14-04-63, the band returns to London's ABC studios to plug their new single. After the taping, The Beatles all go to London's Crawdaddy Club to see and meet, for the first time, their future rivals The Rolling Stones.

16-05-63 – 'Pops and Lenny' (UK) – *MISSING/LOST*

From Me To You / Please Please Me / After You've Gone [with entire cast]

A BBC TV show starring puppet Lenny The Lion along with host Terry Hall, for this performance the band play, live, their two biggest hits to date. Afterwards they are joined by Terry, Lenny, The Raindrops and

Patsy Ann Noble for the grand finale of 'After You've Gone', an old standard from the '20s. All that survives of this show is a poor quality, incomplete, audio of 'From Me To You'.

18-05-63 – 'Thank Your Lucky Stars' (UK) – *MISSING/LOST*

From Me To You / I Saw Her Standing There

By now, The Beatles were deemed too important to perform just one song on the UK's premiere music show, so, taped in Birmingham on 12-05-63, they perform both their biggest hit and the opening song to their No. 1 'Please Please Me' album.

29-06-63 – 'Lucky Stars – Summer Spin' (UK) – *MISSING/LOST*

From Me To You / I Saw Her Standing There

For the summer season, 'Thank Your Lucky Stars' was given a new title 'Lucky Stars – Summer Spin', and this edition, taped in Birmingham on 23-06-63, was a 'Mersey Beat' special. Headlining over Gerry and The Pacemakers, The Searchers, Billy J. Kramer with The Dakotas, The Vernons Girls, Kenneth Cope and The Breakaways, The Big Three and Lee Curtis, The Beatles reprise the two songs they performed on the show the previous month, 'From Me To You' and 'I Saw Her Standing There'.

14-08-63 – 'Scene At 6.30' (UK)

Twist and Shout

Not including the yet-to-be-broadcast footage from The Cavern, The Beatles had performed on TV 16 times to date, with every one of them lost, almost certainly forever. Now, at last, here's a performance that survives. Dressed casually in black roll-neck jumpers and jeans, The Beatles mime to the closing track of their 'Please Please Me' album and the title track of their best-selling EP, 'Twist and Shout'. Frustratingly included on the 'Anthology' telecast/VHS/DVDs as part of a montage (along with clips from 'The Mersey Sound', 'The Royal Variety Performance', 'Drop In' and 'Pathe News – The Beatles Come To Town'), it was finally officially released in full on the '1+' DVD set in 2015.

19-08-63 – **'Scene At 6.30' (UK) –** *MISSING/LOST*

She Loves You

Taped on the same day as the 'Twist and Shout' performance on 14-08-63, here they perform, for the first time anywhere on TV, their new single, 'She Loves You'. Another UK No. 1, it would also, eventually in 1964, get to No. 1 in the USA.

22-08-63 – **'Day By Day' (UK) –** *MISSING/LOST*

She Loves You

A regional TV show in the south, here the band mime to their new single in a Southampton TV studio, before heading back to Bournemouth to perform 2 shows, the 4th of a 6-day residency in the town's Gaumont Cinema.

24-08-63 – **'Lucky Stars – Summer Spin' (UK) –** *MISSING/LOST*

She Loves You / I'll Get You

Taped in Birmingham on the morning of 18-08-63, en route to Torquay where they performed two shows that evening, The Beatles mime to both sides of their current single.

07-09-63 – 'Big Night Out' (UK)

From Me To You / She Loves You / Twist and Shout / I Saw Her Standing There

Taped on 01-09-63, and miming on a set that unconvincingly attempts to recreate The Cavern, The Beatles perform their two biggest hit singles plus the opening and closing tracks of their top selling album. During 'I Saw Her Standing There', the other acts on the show dance in front of the band, including hosts Mike and Bernie Winters, Patsy Ann Noble, Billy Dainty, Sally Barnes, Bobby Beaumont and The Lionel Blair Dancers. Excerpts from this show appear in 'Anthology'.

04-10-63 – 'Ready, Steady, Go!' (UK)

Twist and Shout / I'll Get You / She Loves You

Making their debut on the swinging '60s most famous TV show, The Beatles mime to both sides of their current single and their album closer, as well as all but Paul making amusing cameos during Helen Shapiro's performance of her current single 'Look Who It Is'. The band are introduced by Dusty Springfield (fresh from leaving The Springfields), who also interviews the band, while Paul judges a dance competition (bizarrely, the winner Melanie Coe later inspired the song 'She's Leaving Home' after Paul read about her running away from home). Although all three of The Beatles appearances on 'Ready, Steady, Go!' survive, no footage was included on either 'Anthology' or '1+'. This was, reportedly, because the tapes' owner Dave Clark (of

The Dave Clark Five fame) wanted too much money. All three appearances (though not all of the interview segments or the Helen Shapiro song) were issued across three VHS sets of 'Ready, Steady, Go!' in the mid '80s, but collectors have since then been waiting in vain for official DVD sets.

09-10-63 – 'The Mersey Sound' (UK)

Twist and Shout / She Loves You / Love Me Do

Taped at The Little Theatre in Southport on 27-08-63, as part of a full-length documentary on the Mersey Beat phenomenon, the first two songs are played live to an empty theatre (with the screaming audience overdubbed and intercut later), as was 'Love Me Do', though the footage for this latter song was overdubbed with the studio recording for the telecast. Both 'Love Me Do' and an excerpt of 'Twist and Shout' was included in the Anthology releases, while 'Love Me Do' was also included in '1+', as well as being the basis for the 1982 reissue Promo Video. Apart from a brief excerpt during a medley (see 06-05-64), no other footage of the band performing 'Love Me Do' is known to survive.

13-10-63 – 'Sunday Night At The London Palladium' (UK) – *MISSING/LOST*

From Me To You / I'll Get You / She Loves You / Twist and Shout

In 1963, there was no TV show more prestigious than 'Sunday Night At The London Palladium', and for The Beatles to perform 4 songs while topping the bill was an indication of just how far they'd come in a relatively very short time. Sadly, the footage no longer survives, but

an audio tape does still exist, and gives us a real indication of just how exciting things were that night. It was at this performance that the UK national press finally noticed the hysteria that had been sweeping the country for months, with some genius – and it's debateable exactly whom – dubbing the ensuing chaos 'Beatlemania'. This show doesn't exist on video, but an audio does survive, with 'I'll Get You' appearing on the 'Anthology' CDs.

18-10-63 – **'Scene At 6.30' (UK)** – *MISSING/LOST*

She Loves You

A return to the relative calm of Manchester's Granada TV studios, where The Beatles mime their current hit 'She Loves You'.

26-10-63 – **'Thank Your Lucky Stars' (UK)** – *PARTIALLY MISSING/LOST*

All My Loving / Money (That's What I Want) / She Loves You

Taped on 20-10-63 in Birmingham, the producer of the show got quite a scoop, as amongst the 3 songs they mimed to, both 'All My Loving' and 'Money (That's What I Want)' wouldn't be released until 22-11-63 when they appeared on 'With The Beatles'. Only 'Money (That's What I Want)' is known to survive though, and only in less than perfect quality, which is probably why it wasn't included in 'Anthology'.

03-11-63 – **'Drop In' (Sweden)**

She Loves You / Twist and Shout / I Saw Her Standing There / Long Tall Sally

Although there are other performances such as The Ed Sullivan Shows and Shea Stadium that are far more famous, no other performance shows just how great The Beatles could be when playing live. Taped on 30-10-63 at the end of a short Swedish tour, the band were originally scheduled to play just two songs, but were persuaded by the shows' hosts to add two more. Both 'I Saw Her Standing There' and 'Long Tall Sally' from this show were in 'Anthology', while 'She Loves You' was included in '1+'. Although long part of the group's repertoire, this was the first time 'Long Tall Sally' was performed on TV. It would later be the title track of a No. 1 UK EP.

10-11-63 – 'The Royal Variety Performance' (UK)

From Me To You / She Loves You / Till There Was You / Twist and Shout

Long regarded as the pinnacle of performers' careers in the '60s, this was another very important TV appearance indeed for The Beatles. Taped on 04-11-63 in the presence of both The Queen Mother and Princess Margaret, this fine live performance is infamous for John Lennon's 'rattle your jewellery' remark. This was the first time 'Till There Was You' had been performed by the band on TV, but, as with 'Long Tall Sally' on 'Drop In', it had long been a part of their repertoire, with the band even including it on their Decca audition tape on 01-01-62. How long ago that date must've seemed on this night! All songs with the exception of 'She Loves You' were included on 'Anthology', while 'From Me To You' is also on '1+'.

20-11-63 – 'Pathe News - The Beatles Come To Town' (UK)

She Loves You / Twist and Shout

Filmed live on-stage at the ABC Cinema, Ardwick, Manchester, this superb footage captures Beatlemania at full pelt, though, unbelievably, things would become even more out of control later. The earliest professionally-filmed colour performance footage of The Beatles, it was shown in cinemas for a week from 22-12-63 onwards, and also re-used a year later in the Jimmy Savile-hosted movie 'Pop Gear', re-titled 'Go Go Mania' in the USA. 'She Loves You' and part of 'Twist and Shout' are included in 'Anthology', while both songs, in a slightly different edit, are on the bonus disc for 'Eight Days a Week: The Touring Years' DVD.

27-11-63 – 'Late Scene Extra' (UK)

I Want To Hold Your Hand

Taped on 25-11-63, and miming on a set featuring a mock up of 'The Daily Echo' with Ringo on top of a huge camera, The Beatles perform their latest single, 'I Want To Hold Your Hand'. It was repeated on 26-12-63, along with 'This Boy' – see the 20-12-63 entry. Another UK No. 1, it was this record that finally broke the band in the USA, reaching No. 1 on the Billboard charts on February 1st 1964. This performance is featured on both 'Anthology' and '1+'.

07-12-63 – 'It's The Beatles!' (UK) – *PARTIALLY MISSING/LOST*

From Me To You / I Saw Her Standing There / Roll Over Beethoven / Boys / Till There Was You / She Loves You / This Boy / I Want To Hold Your Hand / Money (That's What I Want) / Twist and Shout / From Me To You (Reprise)

Taped on the afternoon of 07-12-63 in The Empire Theatre, Liverpool, and broadcast later the same day, 'It's The Beatles!' was the only time that a full-length UK Beatles concert was professionally filmed. Unfortunately, this was marred by some technical faults, with 'Boys' sounding particularly bad. Only 'I Want To Hold Your Hand', 'Money (That's What I Want)', 'Twist and Shout' and 'From Me To You (Reprise)' survive on video, though the complete show exists as an audio. Although out of the scope of this book, also worth mentioning is that a complete special edition of 'Juke Box Jury' was both taped and broadcast on this same date, featuring all 4 Beatles on the panel. This no longer survives on video, but, again, it still exists on audio.

20-12-63 – **'Scene At 6.30' (UK)**

This Boy

Taped on 25-11-63, the same day as the 27-11-63 'Late Scene Extra' performance of 'I Want To Hold Your Hand', this features The Beatles miming to the single's B-side on the same set. Both songs were repeated on a 'Scene At 6:30' special on 26-12-63. This performance is on 'Anthology'.

21-12-63 – **'Thank Your Lucky Stars' (UK)**

I Want To Hold Your Hand / All My Loving / Twist and Shout / She Loves You

For the 2nd time, following the 29-06-63 show, a full episode of 'Thank Your Lucky Stars' is devoted entirely to 'Mersey Beat' groups. Taped on 15-12-63, and featuring an unprecedented 4 songs, also on the bill was Gerry and The Pacemakers, The Searchers, Billy J. Kramer with

The Dakotas, Cilla Black, Tommy Quickly and The Breakaways. Unusually for 'Thank Your Lucky Stars', the whole show still survives.

01-01-64 – 'Top Of The Pops' Video (UK) – *MISSING/LOST*

I Want To Hold Your Hand

On 01-01-64, a brand new pop show was broadcast in the UK by the BBC, and it was called 'Top Of The Pops'. Very quickly surpassing 'Ready, Steady, Go!', 'Thank Your Lucky Stars' and every other music TV show in popularity, for this first edition the show included an unofficial video for 'I Want To Hold Your Hand'. Very cheaply produced, these videos often featured archive or specially-shot footage that didn't feature The Beatles on film, and sometimes they'd use no more than photo montages of the group. Mostly lost, these videos are listed throughout this book for the sake of completion.

12-01-64 – 'Sunday Night At The London Palladium' (UK) – *MISSING/LOST*

I Want To Hold Your Hand / This Boy / All My Loving / Money (That's What I Want) / Twist and Shout

The calm before the storm, if appearing on the UK's most watched TV show with all the mayhem that accompanied it can be called calm. This would be the last time the Beatles appeared on the show, despite frequent requests for them to do more. Again no longer existing on video, the show does survive as an audio, albeit in rather ropey sound quality.

09-02-64 – 'The Ed Sullivan Show' (USA)

All My Loving / Till There Was You / She Loves You / I Saw Her Standing There / I Want To Hold Your Hand

Although booked months in advance, no-one could have guessed or even dreamt that The Beatles would be topping the US charts by the time they appeared on this show. A sort of American version of 'Sunday Night At The London Palladium' though with far pizzazz and millions of more viewers, 'The Ed Sullivan Show' was like-wise regarded as the pinnacle of success by state-side entertainers. The 1st of three weekly appearances on the show, this was the first time most US TV viewers had seen The Beatles in action, and the band literally changed US music, fashion and culture overnight. 'All My Loving' from this performance is on the 'Anthology' DVDs, while the whole show is on the 2010 'The 4 Complete Ed Sullivan Shows Starring The Beatles' DVDs.

11-02-64 – **The Coliseum, Washington D.C. (USA)**

Roll Over Beethoven / From Me To You / I Saw Her Standing There / This Boy / All My Loving / I Wanna Be Your Man / Please Please Me / TIll There Was You / She Loves You / I Want To Hold Your Hand / Twist and Shout / Long Tall Sally

An at times shambolic but undoubtedly joyful performance, this, the band's debut US concert, features the band playing on a stage surrounded by an audience, which the stage-hands attempt to overcome by repositioning the microphones, amplifiers and drums after every few songs. 11 of the 12 songs were shown in selective US cinemas a month later, the exception being 'Long Tall Sally', which didn't surface until the mid-'90s. 'I Saw Her Standing There', 'Please Please Me' and 'She Loves You' are all on 'Anthology', while a colourised 'I Saw Her Standing There' is on 'Eight Days a Week: The Touring Years'.

16-02-64 – 'The Ed Sullivan Show' [Dress Rehearsal] (USA)

She Loves You / This Boy / All My Loving / I Saw Her Standing There / From Me To You / I Want To Hold Your Hand

Although it wasn't unusual for The Beatles to do a full dress rehearsal for a TV show, what is unusual is for that footage to survive today, though the performance is plagued by technical problems.

16-02-64 – 'The Ed Sullivan Show' (USA)

She Loves You / This Boy / All My Loving / I Saw Her Standing There / From Me To You / I Want To Hold Your Hand

'The Ed Sullivan Show' was usually broadcast live from New York, but this one, The Beatles' 2nd appearance on the show, came from Miami. Although only sounding slightly better than the dress rehearsal, it was another exciting performance. 'This Boy' is on 'Anthology', and the whole broadcast is on 'The 4 Complete Ed Sullivan Shows Starring The Beatles' DVDs.

23-02-64 – 'The Ed Sullivan Show' (USA)

Twist and Shout / Please Please Me / I Want To Hold Your Hand

Although this was The Beatles' 3rd appearance on 'The Ed Sullivan Show', it was pre-taped back on 09-02-64, the same day as their debut. Probably the most polished of their appearances on the show,

'Please Please Me' is on both 'Anthology' and '1+', while the whole show is on 'The 4 Complete Ed Sullivan Shows Starring The Beatles' DVDs.

29-02-64 – 'Big Night Out' (UK) – *PARTIALLY MISSING/LOST*

All My Loving / I Wanna Be Your Man / Till There Was You / Please Mr. Postman / Money (That's What I Want) / I Want To Hold Your Hand

Taped on 23-02-64, the day after returning from the USA, this mimed show is notable for including the only TV performance of 'Please Mr. Postman'. When this show was sold overseas, 'Money (That's What I Want)' was omitted, and this song no longer survives, though fortunately the other 5 songs do still exist. 'I Wanna Be Your Man' and 'Please Mr. Postman' are both on 'Anthology'.

20-03-64 – 'Ready, Steady, Go!' (UK)

It Won't Be Long / You Can't Do That / Can't Buy Me Love

By now The Beatles were in the middle of shooting their first movie 'A Hard Day's Night' and even filmed some scenes earlier this day, but, despite this, they still continued with other commitments. This mimed return to 'Ready, Steady, Go!' is notable for the inclusion of 'It Won't Be Long', a song they never played on TV again and never performed live. As with their other two appearances on the show, this was available on a '80s VHS tape, albeit without 'It Won't Be Long'.

25-03-64 – 'Top Of The Pops' (UK) – *PARTIALLY MISSING/LOST*

Can't Buy Me Love / You Can't Do That

Taped on 19-03-64, this was The Beatles debut on this long-running TV show, though only the 16-06-66 show featured the band actually in the 'Top Of The Pops' studio, as all of the other appearances including this one were in the form of pre-recorded 'inserts'. 'Can't Buy Me Love' has recently surfaced among collectors, albeit as a poor quality and badly-dubbed filmed-from-TV video.

01-04-64 – **'Top Of The Pops' (UK)** –*MISSING/LOST*

You Can't Do That

This is a repeat of the 25-03-64 performance.

08-04-64 – **'Top Of The Pops' (UK)** –*MISSING/LOST*

Can't Buy Me Love

This is a repeat of the 25-03-64 performance.

15-04-64 – **'Top Of The Pops' Video (UK)** – *MISSING/LOST*

Can't Buy Me Love

Instead of repeating the 25-03-64 performance again, the 15-04-64 edition of 'Top Of The Pops' used a video.

18-04-64 – **'Two Of A Kind' (UK)**

This Boy / All My Loving / I Want To Hold Your Hand / On Moonlight Bay [with Morecambe and Wise]

'Two Of A Kind' is a TV show starring comedy duo Eric Morecambe and Ernie Wise that ran throughout most of the '60s, and is often erroneously called 'The Morecambe and Wise Show', a title that wasn't actually used until 1968. Although the show often featured top

pop acts of the day, it was usually taped months in advance, in this case as far back as 02-12-63. The result was that acts ending up 'plugging' an old record, as The Beatles did here, but they do put in a fine live performance. 'On Moonlight Bay' is an old standard first published over 50 years earlier, here performed, complete with straw boaters and striped jackets, as an amusing duet with the show's hosts. The entire performance was repeated on 24-07-65, with 'On Moonlight Bay' on the 'Anthology' DVDs, and 'This Boy', 'I Want To Hold Your Hand' and 'On Moonlight Bay' on the 'Anthology' CDs.

26-04-64 – 'The N.M.E. Poll Winners Concert', Wembley Empire Pool, London (UK)

She Loves You / You Can't Do That / Twist and Shout / Long Tall Sally / Can't Buy Me Love

Although The Beatles performed at this annual concert in 1963, 1964, 1965 and 1966, the 1963 show wasn't televised, and both The Beatles and The Rolling Stones disallowed their 1966 performances to be filmed. In a show noted for its poor sound balance, The Beatles put on an exuberant but slightly sloppy performance. The Beatles' performance was broadcast in 'Big Beat '64 Part 2' on 10-05-64, part of 'Can't Buy Me Love' can be seen in 'Anthology', and a colourised 'Can't Buy Me Love' is on 'Eight Days a Week: The Touring Years'.

06-05-64 – 'Around The Beatles' (UK)

Twist and Shout / Roll Over Beethoven / I Wanna Be Your Man / Long Tall Sally / My Boy Lollipop [Performed by Millie Small] / Medley: Night Train – Lover Please – I'm Movin' On – Forty Days – Money

(That's What I Want) – Hit The Road Jack [Performed by Long John Baldry and Jean Owen of The Vernons Girls] / Brontosaurus Stomp [Performed by Sounds Incorporated] / Walking The Dog [Performed by P.J. Proby] / Tom Hark [Performed by Millie Small] / Detroit [Performed by Sounds Incorporated] / Only You Can Do It [Performed by The Vernons Girls] / Got My Mojo Working [Performed by Long John Baldry] / Saved [Performed by Cilla Black] / Medley: Cumberland Gap – The Rock Island Line [Performed by P.J. Proby with The Vernons Girls] / I Believe [Performed by P.J. Proby] / You're My World [Performed by Cilla Black] / Heat Wave [Performed by Cilla Black] / Medley: Love Me Do – Please Please Me – From Me To You – She Loves You – I Want To Hold Your Hand / Can't Buy Me Love / Shout

Miming to specially made studio recordings, taped at London's IBC Studios on 19-04-64, here The Beatles host their first TV special. Taped on 28-04-64, this show is noteworthy for the unique medley of their first 5 UK hits, and the only ever performance of 'Shout', a song that features all 4 of The Beatles taking turns to sing lead vocals, as well as a Shakespearean spoof comedy sketch. Soon after this, Jean Owen would pursue a solo career under the name Samantha Jones, while both P.J. Proby and Cilla Black would benefit from donated Lennon-McCartney songs. The entire Beatles performance (minus the sketch and guests) was issued on a '80s VHS tape (misleadingly titled 'Ready, Steady, Go! – Special Edition'), 'Roll Over Beethoven' is on the 'Anthology' DVDs, 'Can't Buy Me Love' is on '1+', and 'I Wanna Be Your Man', 'Shout' plus the unused outtakes 'Long Tall Sally' and 'Boys' are all available without audience noise and in glorious stereo on the 'Anthology' CDs.

24-05-64 – 'The Ed Sullivan Show' (USA)

You Can't Do That

Ed Sullivan visited London to interview The Beatles on the set of 'A Hard Day's Night' on 17-04-64, and was also given footage of the group performing 'You Can't Do That' in the movie, to broadcast exclusively on 'The Ed Sullivan Show' on 24-05-64. It turned out to be far more exclusive than he thought, as the song was cut from the final edit when the movie was released in July. The song was taped along with 'Tell Me Why', 'If I Fell', 'I Should Have Known Better', 'She Loves You' and possibly other, unreleased songs, at London's Scala Theatre on 31-03-64.

06-06-64 – Veilinghal Op Hoop Van Zegan, Blokker (The Netherlands)

I Saw Her Standing There

On the eve of a summer world tour, Ringo collapsed, and was quickly diagnosed as suffering from tonsillitis. George Harrison in particular didn't want the tour to go ahead without him, but instead the group quickly recruited session drummer Jimmie Nicol. While of course he could never replace Ringo as a personality, he played the songs surprisingly well, as witnessed by several surviving audios, and the footage here.

08-06-64 – 'The Beatles In Nederland' (The Netherlands)

She Loves You / All My Loving / Twist and Shout / Roll Over

Beethoven / Long Tall Sally / Can't Buy Me Love

Taped along with a lengthy interview in Treslong on 05-06-64, and still with Jimmie Nicol on drums, unusually The Beatles play along to the records but will their microphones live, resulting in double-tracked studio/live vocals throughout. There is a stage invasion by the mostly male audience during the final song 'Can't Buy Me Love', so Mal Evans, Neil Aspinall and Derek Taylor quickly usher John, Paul and George off the stage, but, rather comically, the song carries on with just Jimmie playing along. The show was repeated on 18-07-64, and 'Long Tall Sally' is on 'Anthology'.

17-06-64 – **Festival Hall, Melbourne (Australia)** – *PARTIALLY MISSING/LOST*

I Saw Her Standing There / You Can't Do That / All My Loving / She Loves You / Till There Was You / Roll Over Beethoven / Can't Buy Me Love / This Boy / Twist and Shout / Long Tall Sally

By now rejoined by Ringo, and with Jimmie Nicol returning to obscurity, this superb performance features The Beatles playing at their best, despite the constant screaming that must've made it impossible for them to hear themselves. Only 'You Can't Do That', 'All My Loving', 'She Loves You', 'Can't Buy Me Love', 'Twist and Shout' and 'Long Tall Sally' survive in their entirety, though excerpts of other songs also exist, as does footage of support acts Sounds Incorporated, Johnny Chester and Johnny Devlin. 'You Can't Do That' and 'All My Loving' are in 'Anthology', and 'You Can't Do That' is also on the bonus disc for 'Eight Days a Week: The Touring Years'.

01-07-64 – 'Top Of The Pops' Video (UK) – *MISSING/LOST*

Long Tall Sally

A specially made video for this song was broadcast on the 01-07-64 edition of 'Top Of The Pops'.

06-07-64 – 'A Hard Day's Night' movie (UK)

A Hard Day's Night / I Should Have Known Better (version #1) / If I Fell (version #2) / Can't Buy Me Love / And I Love Her / I'm Happy Just To Dance With You / Tell Me Why / If I Fell (version #2) / I Should Have Known Better (version #2) / She Loves You

Although not the first great UK pop movie (Cliff Richard and The Shadows' 'Summer Holiday' is a good contender for that title), 'A Hard Day's Night' is undoubtedly one of the most original, influential and entertaining. It was filmed from 02-03-64 to 24-04-64 in London's Twickenham studios, as well as at various locations in London, Surrey and Devon, and received its world premiere in London's The Pavilion Theatre on 06-07-64. 'Can't Buy Me Love' and 'A Hard Day's Night' topped the charts in both the UK and USA, with 'And I Love Her' also extracted as a US single, where it reached No. 12. 'A Hard Day's Night', 'I Should Have Known Better', 'If I Fell' and part of 'Can't Buy Me Love' are all in 'Anthology', and, of course, the entire movie is available on DVD. See also the 24-05-64 entry.

08-07-64 – 'Top Of The Pops' (UK) – *MISSING/LOST*

A Hard Day's Night / Long Tall Sally / Things We Said Today

These mimed 'inserts' for 'Top Of The Pops' were taped in London on

07-07-64, though, like all of their July 1964 TV appearances, none of them survive today.

11-07-64 – 'Lucky Stars - Summer Spin' (UK) – *MISSING/LOST*

A Hard Day's Night / Long Tall Sally / Things We Said Today / You Can't Do That

Usually pre-taped several days in advance, for this edition of the show The Beatles broadcast their mimed performance live.

19-07-64 – 'Blackpool Night Out' (UK) – *MISSING/LOST*

A Hard Day's Night / And I Love Her / If I Fell / Things We Said Today / Long Tall Sally

For this summer replacement for 'Big Night Out', The Beatles perform 5 songs live, not mimed, as well as comedy sketches with hosts Mike and Bernie Winters. Although lost, this show does survive as an audio, and reveals how the Beatles had to re-start 'If I Fell' after John and Paul got the giggles, a song that, for some unknown reason, often got them laughing.

22-07-64 – 'Top Of The Pops' (UK) – *MISSING/LOST*

A Hard Day's Night

This is a repeat of the 08-07-64 performance.

29-07-64 – 'Top Of The Pops' (UK) – *MISSING/LOST*

Things We Said Today

This is a repeat of the 08-07-64 performance.

23-08-64 – **The Hollywood Bowl, Los Angeles (USA)**

Twist and Shout / You Can't Do That / All My Loving / She Loves You / Things We Said Today / Boys / A Hard Day's Night / Long Tall Sally

Although the footage, sourced from various newsreels, is in highly variable quality, the soundtrack, sourced from Capitol's stereo audio tape, has been dubbed to surprisingly good effect. 'All My Loving' is on 'Anthology'.

07-10-64 – **'Shindig!' (USA)**

Kansas City – Hey-Hey-Hey-Hey / I'm A Loser / Boys

There were several major US TV pop shows in the mid '60s, and these include 'Hullabaloo', 'Shivaree', and 'Hollywood A Go Go', but none were quite as exciting as 'Shindig!'. Taped especially for the show in London's Granville Theatre on 03-10-64, this is a fine live performance, though the choice of the 19-month-old 'Boys' (rather than, say, 'Honey Don't') is a surprising one. 'Kansas City – Hey-Hey-Hey-Hey' is featured in 'Anthology', while, unlikely as it seems, a short rendition of 'The House Of The Rising Sun' was apparently performed at the show's taping, and is rumoured to survive in a private collection.

16-10-64 – **'Scene At 6.30' (UK)**

I Should Have Known Better

Taped on 14-10-64, this mimed performance is the only instance of 'I Should Have Known Better' being performed on TV. The original multi-angle footage is long lost, but fortunately, this survives via a 'B-

roll' camera in the studio gallery, as does brief rehearsal footage.

21-11-64 – 'Lucky Stars Special' (UK)

I Feel Fine / She's A Woman / I'm A Loser / Rock and Roll Music

By now it was such a scoop getting The Beatles on 'Thank Your Lucky Stars' that they renamed this edition 'Lucky Stars Special'. Taped without an audience on 14-11-64, this mimed performance was the only time the group played 'Rock and Roll Music' on a TV show. 'I Feel Fine', was another No. 1 hit on both sides of the Atlantic, and this song is on 'Anthology'.

27-11-64 – 'Ready, Steady, Go!' (UK)

I Feel Fine / She's A Woman / Baby's In Black / Kansas City – Hey-Hey-Hey-Hey

For The Beatles 3rd and final appearance on 'Ready, Steady, Go!', they pre-taped their appearance 4 days earlier, on 23-11-64. As with the 04-10-63 and 20-03-64 appearances, this was issued on a long-deleted VHS tape.

03-12-64 – 'Top Of The Pops' (UK) – *MISSING/LOST*

I Feel Fine / She's A Woman

Miming to both sides of their current single, this was pre-taped as far back as 16-11-64.

10-12-64 – 'Top Of The Pops' (UK) – *MISSING/LOST*

She's A Woman

This is a repeat of the 10-12-64 performance.

24-12-64 – 'Top Of The Pops' (UK) – *MISSING/LOST*

A Hard Day's Night / Everybody's Trying To Be My Baby / I Feel Fine

'A Hard Day's Night' is a repeat from 08-07-64, and 'I Feel Fine' is a repeat of the 03-12-64 performance. Some sources also list 'Everybody's Trying To Be My Baby' for this date, so if this is true, then it was probably taped on 16-11-64, the same day as 'I Feel Fine' and 'She's A Woman'. Incidentally, to promote 'I Feel Fine' on the 07-01-65 edition of the show, artist Tony Hart did drawings to accompany the music.

03-04-65 – 'Thank Your Lucky Stars' (UK) – *MISSING/LOST*

Eight Days A Week / Yes It Is / Ticket To Ride

Despite being in the middle of shooting their 2nd movie 'Help!', The Beatles somehow found the time to make several, mimed, UK TV appearances in April 1965 to promote both sides of their new No. 1 single, 'Ticket To Ride' b/w 'Yes It Is', as well as a live concert performance. Taped on 28-03-65, this show also includes 'Eight Days A Week', a song that was only performed this one and only time, despite it being issued as a US single, where it once again made No. 1.

11-04-65 – 'The N.M.E. Poll Winners Concert', Wembley Empire Pool, London (UK)

I Feel Fine / She's A Woman / Baby's In Black / Ticket To Ride / Long Tall Sally

The Beatles first live performance in 3 months, this is, like their 1964 appearance on the same show, an enthusiastic though slightly slap-

dash performance. This was broadcast on 'Poll Winners Concert Part Two' on 25-04-65, while both 'I Feel Fine' and 'She's A Woman' are on the 'Anthology' DVDs.

11-04-65 – 'The Eamonn Andrews Show' (UK) – *MISSING/LOST*

Ticket To Ride / Yes It Is

Performed and broadcast the same day as their 'The N.M.E. Poll Winners Concert' appearance earlier that afternoon, this mimed performance was the only time The Beatles appeared on this popular chat and music show.

15-04-65 – 'Top Of The Pops' (UK) – *PARTIALLY MISSING/LOST*

Ticket To Ride / Yes It Is

Taped on 10-04-65, this was the final time that The Beatles pre-taped 'inserts' for 'Top Of The Pops', though they would make one further appearance on the show in 1966. Although the complete footage is long lost, a brief excerpt of 'Ticket To Ride' was, perhaps surprisingly, rebroadcast on 22-05-65 as part of an episode of the popular sci-fi series 'Dr Who', and this 25-second clip still survives.

22-04-65 – 'Top Of The Pops' (UK) – *MISSING/LOST*

Yes It Is

This is a repeat of the 15-04-65 performance.

13-05-65 – 'Top Of The Pops' Video (UK) – *MISSING/LOST*

Ticket To Ride

For the 13-05-65 edition of 'Top Of The Pops' a video was apparently shown. As The Beatles themselves had yet to make an official video (they wouldn't do so until 23-11-65), this was probably yet another specially commissioned, low budget, affair.

20-06-65 – **Palais De Sports, Paris (France)**

Twist and Shout / She's A Woman / I'm A Loser / Can't Buy Me Love / Baby's In Black / I Wanna Be Your Man / A Hard Day's Night / Everybody's Trying To Be My Baby / Rock and Roll Music / I Feel Fine / Ticket To Ride / Long Tall Sally

Performing to a largely male crowd, The Beatles can actually hear themselves play, so, consequently, this performance is far tighter than most of their shows at the time, with the band putting on a genuinely inspired performance. 'I'm A Loser' and 'Everybody's Trying To Be My Baby' both appeared on 'Anthology', while 'A Hard Day's Night' is on '1+'.

00-07-65 – **Promo Video # 1**

Help!

The first officially-sanctioned Promo Videos by The Beatles are more often than not cited as those that were made in late 1965, but this one was made a full 7 months earlier. Taped on 22-04-65 and miming on a simple stage set-up, the video was broadcast on 'Thank Your Lucky Stars' on 17-07-65, 'Discs A Go Go' on 26-07-65 and 'Top Of The Pops' on both 29-07-65 and 19-08-65. The same video was used during the opening sequence of the 'Help!' movie, where the character 'Clang' (played by Leo McKern) threw darts at the band. Part of the video was also used in the opening sequences of every episode of the 'Anthology' TV series and DVDs. The song was another world-wide No. 1 smash hit.

29-07-65 – 'Help!' movie (UK)

Help! / You're Going To Lose That Girl / You've Got To Hide Your Love Away / Ticket To Ride / I Need You / The Night Before / Another Girl

Looking more expensive than their debut and having more of a plot, The Beatles' 2nd movie 'Help!' was another big success, and stands up well today. Filmed in The Bahamas, Austria and the UK from 23-02-65 to 11-05-65, it was the inspiration for every episode of 'The Monkees', though it doesn't seem to have been quite as loved as 'A Hard Day's Night' by The Beatles themselves. 'Another Girl' was broadcast on 'Top Of The Pops' on 19-08-65, 'You're Going To Lose That Girl', 'You've Got To Hide Your Love Away', 'The Night Before' and 'Another Girl' are all on 'Anthology', and the whole movie is available on DVD.

01-08-65 – 'Blackpool Night Out' (UK)

I Feel Fine / I'm Down / Act Naturally / Ticket To Ride / Yesterday / Help!

Unlike on the earlier 'Big Night Out' shows, The Beatles were expected to perform live for 'Blackpool Night Out', and they rose to the occasion admirably here by singing and playing extremely well throughout. 'I'm Down' (featuring John on keyboards, as with all 1965 performances of the song), 'Act Naturally', 'Yesterday' (making it's TV debut here and performed solo by Paul), 'Help!' and part of 'Ticket To Ride' are all on the 'Anthology' DVDs, while 'I Feel Fine', 'Ticket To Ride', 'Yesterday' and 'Help!' are on the 'Anthology' CDs, and a colourised 'Help!' is on 'Eight Days a Week: The Touring Years'.

15-08-65 – **Shea Stadium, New York (USA)**

Twist and Shout / I Feel Fine / Dizzy Miss Lizzy / Ticket To Ride / Act Naturally / Can't Buy Me Love / Baby's In Black / A Hard Day's Night / Help! / I'm Down

Although they taped better live performances such as 'Drop In' in 1963, Melbourne in 1964 and Paris in 1965, it is Shea Stadium that remains the best known and most seen live footage by the Beatles. Filmed in glorious colour for a future TV special, during later editing the audio for 'Twist and Shout' was replaced by a recording from The Hollywood Bowl on 30-08-65, 'Act Naturally' was substituted by the original studio version, and all other songs in the film received vocal and/or instrumental overdubs, made by The Beatles in a London studio on 05-01-66. This has long led to speculation that the original performance must've been poor, but a few years back the complete, uncut and un-dubbed, audio from the show surfaced in unofficial circles, proving that it was overdubbed largely due to technical shortcomings (for example Paul's harmony vocal is inaudible during 'Act Naturally') and that their actual performance was fine. Along with off-stage footage and clips of the support acts Sounds Incorporated, King Curtis and Brenda Holloway, the documentary 'The Beatles At Shea Stadium' was first broadcast in the UK on 01-03-66, and repeated on 27-08-66, while the USA had to wait until 10-01-67 for the show's TV debut. Additionally, 'I Feel Fine', 'Help!' and 'Can't Buy Me Love' were shown in the UK as part of 'Pop Go The '60s' on 31-12-69, while 'Twist and Shout', 'I Feel Fine', 'Baby's In Black',

'Help!' and 'I'm Down' are on the 'Anthology' DVDs, and the outtake 'Everybody's Trying To Be My Baby' was on the 'Anthology' CDs. A DVD of the show redubbed with the original un-altered soundtrack is available in unofficial circles.

12-09-65 – 'The Ed Sullivan Show' (USA)

I Feel Fine / I'm Down / Act Naturally / Ticket To Ride / Yesterday / Help!

Taped on 14-08-65, The Beatles perform the same 6 songs, and in the same order, as they did on British TV a couple of weeks earlier. This performance is by no means bad, but they sounded much tighter on 'Blackpool Night Out', and during 'I'm Down' Paul manages to get the verses mixed up. 'Yesterday' is on '1+', while the full show is on 'The 4 Complete Ed Sullivan Shows Starring The Beatles' DVDs.

00-11-65 – Promo Video #1

I Feel Fine

The Beatles had been making 'inserts' for such shows as 'Top Of The Pops' and 'Thank Your Lucky Stars for years, but now, tiring of doing TV shows, they decided to go one step further, and make Promo videos that could be used on shows world-wide. Ten such films were made on 23-11-65, varying from straight mimed performances to the use of various props laying about the studio. For this first 'I Feel Fine' video, The Beatles are surrounded by gym equipment, and while John, Paul and George play their regular instruments, a drum-less Ringo rides an exercise bike. This video was first broadcast on 'Top Of The Pops' on 25-12-65, and is available on '1+'.

00-11-65 – **Promo Video #2**

I Feel Fine

Still surrounded by gym equipment, for this video, bizarrely, the group spend the entire time eating bags of fish 'n' chips, while making only occasional cursory efforts to mime the song. Though circulating unofficially for years, this wasn't shown on TV at the time, receiving it's 1st official release on the '1+' DVDs.

00-11-65 – **Promo Video**

Ticket To Ride

Sitting down to play their usual instruments (this time including Ringo on drums), The Beatles do a straight mime to the song against a backdrop of large tickets. This was shown on 'Top Of The Pops' on 25-12-65, while part of the song is on 'Anthology' and it can be seen complete on '1+'.

00-11-65 – **Promo Video #2**

Help!

For this 2nd video of 'Help!' (following the one made for the movie of the same name 7 months earlier), the group all sit astride a workman's bench, with Ringo holding an umbrella while the others play their usual instruments. Again, this was on 'Top Of The Pops' on 25-12-65, and is on '1+'.

00-11-65 – **Promo Videos #1 and #2**

Day Tripper

These first two videos are both very similar, and feature The Beatles dressed in black while doing a straight mime with their usual instruments. At least one of them was broadcast on 'Top Of The Pops' on 02-12-65, 25-12-65 and 26-12-66 and on 'Thank Your Lucky Stars' on 04-12-65, while a montage of difference performances are featured on 'Anthology' and one of these is on '1+'. 'Day Tripper' got to No. 1 on both sides of the Atlantic, along with 'We Can Work It Out' as a double A-side in the UK.

00-11-65 – **Promo Videos #3**

Day Tripper

For this 3rd video, The Beatles wear their famous light 'Shea Stadium' jackets while miming among props of a railway carriage and aeroplane, though Ringo quickly dispenses with his drumsticks and starts cutting away at the railway carriage with a saw. This video was broadcast in the USA on 'Hullabaloo' on 03-01-66, and can also be seen on '1+'.

00-11-65 – **Promo Videos #1 and #2**

We Can Work It Out

Like the 1st and 2nd 'Day Tripper' videos, the first two performances of 'We Can Work It Out' are very similar, featuring straight mimes by the group while dressed in black, all playing their usual instruments with the exception of John, who plays an organ. One of these videos was shown on 'Top Of The Pops' on 02-12-65, 09-12-65, 30-12-65 and 26-12-66, on 'Thank Your Lucky Stars' on 04-12-65, and on 'Hullabaloo' on 03-01-66. A montage of different performances is on 'Anthology', *while a complete performance is on '1+'.*

00-11-65 – **Promo Videos #3**

We Can Work It Out

Playing the same instruments as on the first two videos, the big difference here is that they wear their 'Shea Stadium' jackets. The video can be seen on '1+'. Incidentally, on The Beatles' final tour of the UK in December 1965, it was Paul, not John, who played organ on 'We Can Work It Out', as well as, strangely, on 'Yesterday'. Frustratingly, no professionally-filmed videos and no audios are known to exist from this tour.

16-12-65 – **'The Music Of Lennon and McCartney' (UK)**

I Feel Fine [Performed by The George Martin Orchestra] / A World Without Love [Performed by Peter and Gordon] / I Saw Him Standing There [Performed by Lulu] / A Hard Day's Night [Performed by Alan Haven and Tony Crombie] / Medley: She Loves You – I'll Get You [Performed by Fritz Spiegl's Barock and Roll Ensemble] / Day Tripper / Yesterday [Clip only by Paul McCartney, then Performed by Marianne Faithfull] / She Loves You [Performed by Antonio Vargas] / Things We Said Today [Performed, in French, by Dick Rivers] / Bad To Me [Performed by Billy J. Kramer] / It's For You [Performed by Cilla Black] / Ringo's Theme (This Boy) [Performed by The George Martin Orchestra] / If I Fell [Performed by Henry Mancini] / And I Love Him [Performed by Esther Phillips] / A Hard Day's Night [Performed by Peter Sellers] / We Can Work It Out

Taped on 02-11-65, and hosted by both (John) Lennon and (Paul)

McCartney, this is an enjoyable, albeit mimed, TV special. Admittedly some of the guests are a little tedious, but Lulu, Cilla Black, Peter and Gordon, Billy J. Kramer, Esther Philips and Peter Sellers are all more than worthy guests. The Beatles themselves take the opportunity to plug both sides of their current single, and Paul also performs a snippet of 'Yesterday' preceding Marianne Faithfull's rendition of the song. 'Day Tripper' from this show is on the '1+' DVDs.

19-05-66 – **Promo Videos #1, #2, #3 and #4**

Paperback Writer

Following the success of the 23-11-65 session, when then they taped no less than 10 different promo video in a day, they decided to repeat the exercise for their forthcoming single. Doing straight mimes while playing their usual instruments, they cut 4 similar videos for 'Paperback Writer', one of them in colour, and three in black and white. The colour video, along with a specially taped message from the group, was shown on 'The Ed Sullivan Show' on 05-06-66, while in the UK, where there was no colour TV yet, black and white videos were shown on 'Ready, Steady, Go!' on 03-06-66, and the final episode of 'Thank Your Lucky Stars', re-titled 'Goodbye Lucky Stars', on 25-06-66. The colour video can be seen on '1+'. 'Paperback Writer' b/w 'Rain' was another UK and US No. 1.

19-05-66 – **Promo Videos #1, #2 and #3**

Rain

As with 'Paperback Writer', several similar videos for 'Rain' were made, this time one of them in colour and two in black and white. The colour video was shown on 'The Ed Sullivan Show' on 05-06-66, while black and white videos were broadcast on 'Ready, Steady, Go!' on 03-06-66, and 'Goodbye Lucky Stars' on 25-06-66. A montage of different videos was shown on 'Anthology', while one of the black and white videos is on '1+'.

20-05-66 – **Promo Video #5**

Paperback Writer

If any videos are the true precursor to those from the late '70s onwards, then it is the two that were shot on location at London's Chiswick House today, in particular the one they made for 'Rain'. For 'Paperback Writer', the band mime while playing their usual instruments, with the exception of Ringo, who simply sits around looking a little bored. This was shown on 'Top Of The Pops' in black and white on 02-06-66 and 23-06-66, and can be seen in full colour on both 'Anthology' and '1+'.

20-05-66 – **Promo Video #4**

Rain

Again at Chiswick House, this is a surreal combination of intercut shots, sometimes playing instruments and sometimes without, sometimes sitting and sometimes walking, and sometimes wearing shades and sometimes without. It was first shown, in black and white, on 'Top Of The Pops' on 09-06-66, and can be seen in all its colour glory on '1+'. Incidentally, on all of the May 1966 videos Paul looks a little different from usual, as he'd recently broken a front tooth in a moped accident (it was repaired in time for the summer '66 world tour). Despite this, the band never looked cooler than on here.

16-06-66 – 'Top Of The Pops' (UK) – *MISSING/LOST*

Rain / Paperback Writer

Despite deciding in late 1965 that they didn't want to perform on TV anymore, for this show The Beatles agreed to make an appearance, their first time ever in the actual 'Top Of The Pops' London studio. Broadcast live, they mimed to both sides of their current single. A few years back, much excitement was made when footage of The Hollies performing 'Bus Stop' on this very episode surfaced. Sadly, this didn't mean that The Beatles' only true appearance on the show was imminent, though a poor quality, 11-second clip, filmed from the TV screen, did surface recently.

24-06-66 – Circus Krone, Munich (Germany)

Rock and Roll Music / Baby's In Black / I Feel Fine / Yesterday / Nowhere Man / I'm Down

Judging by surviving videos and audios, up until 1965 The Beatles remained a great live act, despite an unfair later reputation to the contrary. By their final trek around Germany, the Far East and the USA in the summer of 1966 however, it was becoming clear that The Beatles clearly didn't want to do this anymore, and they made little effort to disguise it. Despite this apathy towards performing and clear under-rehearsal, they still seem to be genuinely pleased to be back in front of a German crowd for the first time since their pre-stardom days, though 'I'm Down' is particularly messy. A US No. 3 single, 'Nowhere Man' can be seen on 'Anthology'.

30-06-66 – **'Top Of The Pops' (UK)** – *MISSING/LOST*

Paperback Writer

This is a repeat of the 16-06-66 performance.

30-06-66 – **Budokan Hall, Tokyo (Japan)**

Rock and Roll Music / She's A Woman / If I Needed Someone / Day Tripper / Baby's In Black / I Feel Fine / Yesterday / I Wanna Be Your Man / Nowhere Man / Paperback Writer / I'm Down

Long gone down in history as examples of the band performing at their very worse, these Japanese concerts aren't THAT bad, though they can't be compared to the live peaks of 'Drop In' in 1963 or in Melbourne in 1964. It is easy to identify the difference between this show and the footage the next day thanks to the dark suits and red shirts worn here. 'Paperback Writer' from this show is on 'Anthology'.

01-07-66 – **Budokan Hall, Tokyo (Japan)**

Rock and Roll Music / She's A Woman / If I Needed Someone / Day Tripper / Baby's In Black / I Feel Fine / Yesterday / I Wanna Be Your Man / Nowhere Man / Paperback Writer / I'm Down

Now wearing light striped jackets, this performance is a little better than the previous one, though, again, it's the more recent material such as 'If I Needed Someone', 'Day Tripper' and 'Paperback Writer' that comes off worst. 'Rock and Roll Music' and 'Yesterday' can be seen on 'Anthology'. Following these shows, there would be some final concerts in the USA, culminating in San Francisco's Candlestick Park on 29-08-66, and then The Beatles as a group would never perform on a concert stage again.

11-08-66 – 'Top Of The Pops' Video (UK) – *MISSING/LOST*

Yellow Submarine

The Beatles' 1966 album 'Revolver' is rightly considered one of the finest collection of songs ever made, not only by the group but by anyone. So, it is ironic that The Beatles as a group never performed any of the songs from it, whether in concert, on TV or as Promo Videos. There were cartoons, both in the US TV series 'the Beatles', and, a couple of years later, in the movie 'Yellow Submarine', but the closest there were to Promo Videos were two unofficial and low budget films made for 'Top Of The Pops', and they are long lost. The first of these specially commissioned videos was this one, broadcast on 11-08-66, and repeated on 25-08-66 and 01-09-66. It features no direct involvement from The Beatles, instead incorporating aqua club divers in a London swimming pool. As for the single it was promoting, 'Yellow Submarine' b/w 'Eleanor Rigby' was another double A-side, and was a UK No. 1 and a US No. 2.

08-09-66 – 'Top Of The Pops' Video (UK) – *MISSING/LOST*

Eleanor Rigby

Again made for 'Top Of The Pops', and broadcast just the once on 08-09-66, this features a montage of still images of an actor dressed as a priest while in a Manchester churchyard. Even at the time, viewers must've found this underwhelming, despite the undoubted high quality of the accompanying soundtrack.

26-12-66 – **'Top Of The Pops' (UK)** – *MISSING/LOST*

Paperback Writer

This is a repeat of the 16-06-66 performance.

00-02-67 – **Promo Video**

Penny Lane

Since the beginning, The Beatles had developed at an unbelievable rate, but even by their standards, 'Penny Lane' b/w 'Strawberry Fields Forever', their first single since they gave up touring, is extraordinary, and this is equalled by the accompanying Promo Videos. Taped in Stratford, London, on 05-02-67, and in Sevenoaks, Kent, on 07-02-67, this colourful footage also had filmed inserts (without the band) from Liverpool, giving the illusion that they were actually in the real Penny Lane. Famously 'only' getting to No. 2 in the UK though another US No. 1, this was shown, in part, on 'Juke Box Jury' on 11-02-67, it was broadcast in the UK in full on 'As You Like It' on 11-02-67, and on 'Top Of The Pops' on 16-02-67 and 23-02-67, while in the USA, it was shown on 'Hollywood Palace' on 25-02-67, 'Clay Cole's Diskotek' on 11-03-67, 'American Bandstand' on 11-03-67 and 'Where The Action Is' on 14-03-67. The video can be found on 'Anthology' and '1+', with the latter featuring inserted outtake footage.

00-02-67 – **Promo Video**

Strawberry Fields Forever

A strong candidate for one of the finest music videos ever made, this was taped in Sevenoaks' Knole Park on 30-01-67 and 31-01-67. The video was shown on 'Top Of The Pops' on 16-02-67 and 02-03-67, 'Hollywood Palace' on 25-02-67, 'Clay Cole's Diskotek' on 11-03-67, 'American Bandstand' on 11-03-67 and 'Where The Action Is' on 14-03-67. The video is on 'Anthology' with inserted home movie footage, and, in its original form, on '1+'. Incidentally, while in Sevenoaks John Lennon bought an old circus poster, which quickly became the inspiration for the song 'Being For The Benefit Of Mr. Kite!'.

00-06-67 – **Promo Video**

A Day In The Life

Although not released as a single, a video for the penultimate track from 'Sgt. Pepper's Lonely Hearts Club Band' was taped on 10-02-67, during a recording session with the orchestra, primarily for a proposed TV special on the album that failed to materialise. Not broadcast at the time but circulating in unofficial circles for years, it can be seen, in slightly re-edited form, on 'Anthology', and, the way it was originally intentioned, on '1+'.

25-06-67 – **'Our World' (UK)**

All You Need Is Love

'Our World' was the first live, international, satellite TV production, broadcast to an estimated 500 million people in more than 30 countries. There was no better way to publicise a new single, so 'All You Need Is Love' was The Beatles memorable contribution to the show, and was pretty much guaranteed to reach No. 1 on both sides of the Atlantic. Taped in black and white, and subsequently broadcast on 'Top Of The Pops' on 06-07-67, 03-08-67 and 26-12-67, it was

colourised for the 'Anthology' TV series, videos and DVDs, and is also featured in colour on '1+'.

13-07-67 – 'Top Of The Pops' Video (UK)

All You Need Is Love

'Top Of The Pops' only had permission to repeat the 'Our World' footage a limited number of times, so for some editions of the show, a specially commissioned video was shown instead. This was first broadcast on 13-07-67, and repeated on 20-07-67 and 27-07-67.

00-11-67 – **Promo Video #1**

Hello Goodbye

Following the surreal Promo Videos they made for 'Penny Lane', 'Strawberry Fields Forever' and 'A Day In The Life' earlier in the year, The Beatles decided to return to the more straightforward mimed-in-the-studio videos of earlier times. Taped in London's Saville Theatre on 10-11-67, this 1st version features the band in their 'SGT. Pepper' outfits, the only time they wore them on TV, though George would wear his again for solo videos in 1974 and 1988. Another No. 1 in the UK and USA, this was shown in the states on 'The Ed Sullivan Show' on 26-11-67 and 'Hollywood Palace' on 27-11-67. A montage of the 3 videos, though mainly using footage from this 1st one, is on 'Anthology', and it is included in its original form on '1+'.

00-11-67 – **Promo Video #2**

Hello Goodbye

For this one, The Beatles wear standard (1967) clothes, as well as *featuring Ringo playing a proper drum kit rather than the toy one he used in the 1st video. Again it is on '1+'*

00-11-67 – **Promo Video #3**

Hello Goodbye

Often referred to as the 'twisting' video owing to some brief but manic dancing sequences, this video is compiled from outtake footage of the 1st and 2nd videos. As with the other videos, this is on '1+'.

23-11-67 – **'Top Of The Pops' Video #1 (UK)** – *MISSING/LOST*

Hello Goodbye

By 1967, there was a ban on miming on UK TV, even in Promo Videos, so 'Top Of The Pops' refused to broadcast any of the 3 videos that were made on 10-11-67. For the 23-11-67 edition of the show, they used re-dubbed footage of the group in 'A Hard Day's Night' in 1964, much to the annoyance of the group.

00-12-67 – **Promo Video #4**

Hello Goodbye

As 'Top Of The Pops' wouldn't/couldn't show any of the other videos, NEMS supplied them with footage of The Beatles working on 'Magical Mystery Tour' in the film cutting room. Intercut with recent photos, this '4th' video was broadcast on 07-12-67, 14-12-67, 21-12-67, 25-12-67 and 28-12-67, though following this, 'Top Of The Pops' came up with a couple of new videos – see the entries for 11-01-68 and 25-12-68.

26-12-67 – 'Magical Mystery Tour' movie (UK)

Magical Mystery Tour / The Fool On The Hill / Flying / I Am The Walrus / Blue Jay Way / Your Mother Should Know

Although planned before Brian Epstein's death on 27-08-67, the 'Magical Mystery Tour' TV movie was the first project The Beatles did without his guidance. Long dividing critics and fans, both the TV movie and the soundtrack are a bit hit-and-miss, though few can deny the brilliance of performances like 'The Fool On The Hill' and 'I Am the Walrus'. Filmed on location in Hampshire, Devon, Cornwall, Somerset, Kent and London from 11-09-67 to 01-10-67, it was first broadcast in the UK, in black and white, on 26-12-67, and repeated in colour on 05-01-68, though few people in the UK had colour TV sets at the time. 'The Fool On The Hill' was broadcast on 'Top Of The Pops' on 28-12-67, 'Magical Mystery Tour', 'The Fool On The Hill', 'Flying', 'I Am The Walrus' and 'Your Mother Should Know' are all in 'Anthology', and the whole movie is available on DVD.

11-01-68 – 'Top Of The Pops' Video #2 (UK) – *MISSING/LOST*

Hello Goodbye

Despite having a 4th video supplied to them by NEMS, 'Top Of The Pops' used dubbed footage from 'Magical Mystery Tour' for this edition of the show.

00-02-68 – **Promo Video**

Lady Madonna

To get around the UK miming ban for their latest video, filmed on 11-

02-68, The Beatles chose to be filmed randomly working in the studio, where they used the time to record the new song 'Hey Bulldog'. It wouldn't be until 1999 that the footage synced to 'Hey Bulldog' would be issued, but meanwhile two, very similar, edits of the 'Lady Madonna' video was released. A UK No. 1 and a US No. 4, the video was shown on 'Top Of The Pops' on 14-03-68, 28-03-68, 04-04-68 and 25-12-68, 'All Systems Freeman' on 15-03-68, and, in the USA, 'Hollywood Palace' on 30-03-68. A new edit was issued on 'Anthology', while one of the 1968 edits is on '1+'.

00-06-68 – **Studio Rehearsals, EMI Studios, London (UK)**

Helter Skelter / Blackbird

Sometime in mid June (probably around the 11th or 13th of June), The Beatles were briefly captured working on an acoustic 'Helter Skelter' and, for a little longer, Paul solo on 'Blackbird'. These were taped for a 10-minute Promo Film on the newly-formed 'Apple' organisation (also on the film is Mary Hopkin performing 'In The Morning' in Paul's garden, with both Paul and his dog Martha sitting nearby).

17-07-68 – **'Yellow Submarine' movie (UK)**

Yellow Submarine / Eleanor Rigby / All Together Now (version #1) / When I'm 64 / Only A Northern Song / Nowhere Man / Lucy In The Sky With Diamonds / Sgt. Pepper's Lonely Hearts Club Band / With A Little Help From My Friends / All You Need Is Love / Hey Bulldog / It's All Too Much / All Together Now (version #2)

First commissioned in the tail-end of 1966, 'Yellow Submarine' is a truly brilliant animated movie, featuring cartoon caricatures of The

Beatles during their 'Sgt. Pepper' / 'All You Need Is Love' phase. By the summer of 1968 it must've already looked dated, but despite this it has stood the test of time remarkably well, certainly more so than 'Magical Mystery Tour' has done. 'Yellow Submarine' and 'All Together Now' (version #2) are in 'Anthology', while 'Eleanor Rigby' is used as a 'video' on '1+'.

30-07-68 – **Studio Rehearsals, EMI Studios, London (UK)**

Hey Jude

Filmed for a various artists documentary entitled 'Music!', this captures The Beatles working on their next single 'Hey Jude'. Unlike some of the sessions from 1968 and 1969, this captures them in good spirits, though as George wasn't needed at this point he stayed in the control room with George Martin.

00-09-68 – **Promo Video**

Hey Jude

With the UK miming ban still in place, The Beatles chose to make videos with live vocals for both sides of their forthcoming single. Taped over several takes on 04-09-68, 2 versions were issued at the time. One of these (along with a specially filmed intro to make it look like they were actually in the show's studio) was broadcast in the UK on 'Frost On Sunday' on 08-09-68 and 'Top Of The Pops' on 12-09-68, 26-09-68, 10-10-68, 26-12-68 and, to promote a reissue, on 01-04-76. In the US, an alternate video was shown on 'The Smothers Brothers Comedy Hour' on 06-10-68, while a new edit is on 'Anthology', and two versions are on '1+'.

00-09-68 – **Promo Video**

Revolution

Taped the same day as 'Hey Jude' on 04-09-68, this exciting live vocal recording was issued in two, similar, versions. One was shown on 'Top Of The Pops' on 19-09-68, with the other one on 'The Smothers Brothers Comedy Hour' on 13-10-68. Further edits, again similar to the others, are on 'Anthology' and '1+'.

25-12-68 – **'Top Of The Pops' Video #3 (UK)** – *MISSING/LOST*

Hello Goodbye

Along with another broadcast of the 'Lady Madonna' video, 'Top Of The Pops' put together yet another video for 'Hello Goodbye' specially for this edition, though, using dubbed stock footage of a railway, it was the least interesting of them all.

The 'Get Back'/'Let It Be' sessions in January 1969 are, at the same time, the most frustrating, complicated, disappointing and fascinating period of their career. These are divided into two distinct sections: from 02-01-69 to 15-01-69, they were filmed at London's Twickenham Film Studios, then, after a 6-day break, they reconvened at the Apple Studios in Saville Row, London. It should be emphasised that the Twickenham sessions were only for film purposes, and none of the songs practised/jammed/performed here were ever intended to be featured on official singles or albums. Below is a list of all that is known to be circulating, officially and (mostly) unofficially among fans and collectors. This is but a drop in the ocean of what really exists: estimates vary wildly, but a 2018 official figure is around 55 hours. Some of the songs listed below are just brief, off-key, clips, and some other takes were later featured as Promo Videos and/or as part of the 1970 'Let It Be' movie and/or 'Anthology', but below is a full list of all confirmed surviving footage.

02-01-69 – **Twickenham Film Studios, London (UK)**

Don't Let Me Down / I've Got A Feeling / Two Of Us

03-01-69 – **Twickenham Film Studios, London (UK)**

Adios For Strings / Don't Let Me Down / All Things Must Pass / Maxwell's Silver Hammer

'Adios For Strings' and 'Maxwell's Silver Hammer' are featured in the 'Let It Be' movie.

06-01-69 – **Twickenham Film Studios, London (UK)**

Oh! Darling / Don't Let Me Down (2 takes) / Two Of Us

'Oh! Darling' and 'Don't Let Me Down' (take 1) are featured in the 'Let It Be' movie, while 'Don't Let Me Down' is featured in the Promo Video for the song.

07-01-69 – **Twickenham Film Studios, London (UK)**

Get Back / Maxwell's Silver Hammer / Across The Universe / Dig A Pony

'Maxwell's Silver Hammer', 'Across The Universe' and 'Dig A Pony' are featured in the 'Let It Be' movie.

08-01-69 – **Twickenham Film Studios, London (UK)**

I Me Mine (take 1) / Two Of Us / I've Got A Feeling / All Things Must Pass / I Me Mine (take 2)

'I Me Mine' (takes 1 and 2), 'Two Of Us' and 'I've Got A Feeling' are featured in the 'Let It Be' movie, and 'I've Got A Feeling' is in 'Anthology'.

09-01-69 – **Twickenham Film Studios, London (UK)**

Two Of Us / Suzy Parker / I've Got A Feeling / One After 909 / Get Back / Tennessee / House Of The Rising Sun / Commonwealth

'Two Of Us', 'Suzy Parker' and 'One After 909' are featured in the 'Let It Be' movie.

10-01-69 – **Twickenham Film Studios, London (UK)**

Get Back / Jamming [with Yoko Ono]

With tensions between the group escalating, on this day George (temporarily) quit the band, just as Ringo had done during 'The White Album' sessions a few months earlier. Remarkably, the other 3 continued rehearsing without him, not only on this day, but again on the 13th and 14th.

14-01-69 – **Twickenham Film Studios, London (UK)**

Piano Boogie

'Piano Boogie' is featured in the 'Let It Be' movie, though in this context it's impossible to guess The Beatles were still a 3-piece.

21-01-69 – **Apple Studios, London (UK)**

My Baby Left Me / Dig A Pony / Don't Let Me Down

They were now in a new location, and with George back in the band, though the playing often remained scrappy.

22-01-69 – **Apple Studios, London (UK)**

Dig A Pony

From this day until the end of the sessions on 31-01-69, organist Billy Preston would join them, resulting in an improved atmosphere, and, much of the time, improved playing.

23-01-69 – **Apple Studios, London (UK)**

Jamming [with Yoko Ono] / Get Back / I'll Get You / I've Got A Feeling / Help! (take 1) / Please Please Me / Help! (take 2)

24-01-69 – **Apple Studios, London (UK)**

Jamming / Get Back

25-01-69 – **Apple Studios, London (UK)**

Two Of Us / For You Blue (3 takes) / Let It Be

'For You Blue' (take 3) is featured in the 'Let It Be' movie, with the song also in 'Anthology'.

26-01-69 – **Apple Studios, London (UK)**

Octopus's Garden / Let It Be / Dig it / Medley: Shake Rattle and Roll - Miss Ann - Kansas City - Lawdy Miss Clawdy / You Really Got A Hold On Me / Jamming / The Long and Winding Road

'Octopus's Garden', 'Dig It', 'Medley: Shake Rattle and Roll - Miss Ann

- Kansas City - Lawdy Miss Clawdy', 'You Really Got A Hold On Me' and 'The Long and Winding Road' are all featured in the 'Let It Be' movie.

27-01-69 – **Apple Studios, London (UK)**

Dig It / Let It Be / Jamming / Get Back / I've Got A Feeling

'Get Back' is in 'Anthology'.

28-01-69 – **Apple Studios, London (UK)**

Jamming / I've Got A Feeling / I Want You

29-01-69 – **Apple Studios, London (UK)**

All Things Must Pass / Besame Mucho

30-01-69 – **Apple Studios (Rooftop), London (UK)**

Get Back (takes 1 and 2) / Don't Let Me Down (take 1) / I've Got A Feeling (take 1) / One After 909 / I Dig A Pony / God Save The Queen (Instrumental) / I've Got A Feeling (take 2) / Don't Let Me Down (take 2) / Get Back (take 3)

Performing live for the last time, albeit to an audience that mostly can only hear them, this was the highlight of the 'Let It Be' movie. 'Get Back' (an edit of takes 1 and 2), 'Don't Let Me Down' (take 1), 'I've Got A Feeling' (take 1), 'One After 909', 'I Dig A Pony' and 'Get Back' (take 3) are featured in 'Let It Be', and 'Don't Let Me Down' and 'Get Back' are included in the Promo Videos for the songs.

31-01-69 – **Apple Studios, London (UK)**

Two Of Us / The Long and Winding Road / Let It Be

'Two Of Us', 'The Long and Winding Road' and 'Let It Be' are featured in the 'Let It Be' movie, with the latter two songs also in both 'Anthology' and '1+'.

00-04-69 – **Promo Video**

Get Back

Although featuring footage from the 30-01-69 rooftop concert, the actual audio for both the single album versions of 'Get Back' was taped on 28-01-69. Credited to 'The Beatles with Billy Preston', 'Get Back' b/w 'Don't Let Me Down' got to No. 1 in both the UK and US. The video was broadcast on 'Top Of The Pops' on 17-04-69, 24-04-69, 08-05-69, 15-05-69, 22-05-69, 25-12-69, and, promoting a reissue, on 15-04-76, while in the USA, it was shown on 'The Glen Campbell Good Time Hour' on 30-04-69. The video is in 'Anthology' and on '1+'.

00-04-69 – **Promo Video**

Don't Let Me Down

Featuring footage from 06-01-69 and 30-01-69, and audio from 28-01-69, this video was shown on 'The Glen Campbell Good Time Hour' on 30-04-69. Again, it is on both 'Anthology' and '1+'.

01-05-69 – **'Top Of The Pops' (UK)** – THE GO-JO'S – **MISSING/LOST**

Get Back

As well as making low-budget, and often low-quality videos when artists were unable or unwilling to appear on the show, from the late '60s onwards they often used their resident dance troupes. Featured here are the show's first dancers, The Go-Jo's.

29-05-69 – **'Top Of The Pops' (UK)** – *THE GO-JO'S – **MISSING/LOST***

Get Back

This is probably a repeat of the 01-05-69 performance.

00-05-69 – **Promo Video**

The Ballad Of John and Yoko

Although 'The Ballad Of John and Yoko' was a decent enough song, it didn't make that great a Beatles single, as only two of the group (John and Paul) play on it, and of course lyrically it's about John's (and Yoko's) personal lives. Featuring a mixture of footage from the recent movie sessions with clips of John and Yoko, the video is fine, though like the record there's very little of The Beatles in it. A UK No. 1 and US No. 8, it was broadcast in the UK on 'Top Of The Pops' on 05-06-69, 12-06-69, 26-06-69 and 26-12-69, and in the USA on 'The Music Scene' on 22-09-69. It can be seen on both 'Anthology' and '1+'.

19-06-69 – **'Top Of The Pops' (UK)** – *PAN'S PEOPLE – **MISSING/LOST***

The Ballad Of John and Yoko

By now 'Top Of The Pops' featured its most famous dance troupe Pan's People, who did a routine for The Beatles' latest single.

00-10-69 – **Promo Video**

Something

The last promo video to be made while The Beatles were still together as a group, it is also one of their best, featuring every member with their respective spouses, despite the fact that they were all filmed separately. Stalling at No. 4 in the UK but reaching No. 1 in the USA, it was broadcast, as an early edit with alternate footage in place of the later Paul and Linda scenes, on 'Top Of The Pops' on 13-11-69, and can be found in its more common form on both 'Anthology' and '1+'.

00-03-70 – **Promo Video**

Let It Be

Although recorded well over a year earlier, the 'Let It Be' single and album/movie of the same name wasn't issued until the spring of 1970. Filmed at the same 31-01-69 session as the performance in the movie, the promo video features alternate footage. A UK No. 2 and US No. 1, it was broadcast on 'Top Of The Pops' on 05-03-70 and 19-03-70, and on 'The Ed Sullivan Show' on 01-03-70.

13-05-70 – **'Let It Be' movie (UK)**

Adagio For Strings / Don't Let Me Down (version #1) / Maxwell's Silver Hammer / Two Of Us (version #1) / I've Got A Feeling (version #1) / Oh! Darling / One After 909 (version #1) / Piano Boogie / Across The Universe / Dig A Pony (version #1) / Suzy Parker / I Me Mine / For Your Blue / Besame Mucho / Octopus's Garden / You've Really Got A Hold Of Me / The Long and Winding Road (version #1) / Medley: Rip It Up - Shake Rattle And Roll / Medley: Kansas City - Miss Ann - Lawdy Miss Clawdy / Dig It / Two Of Us (version #2) / Let It Be / The Long and Winding Road (version #2) / Get Back (version #1) / Don't Let Me Down (version #2) / I've Got A Feeling (version #2) / One After 909 (version #2) / Dig A Pony (version #2) / Get Back (version #2) / Get Back (version #3, audio only, over credits)

Unlike 'A Hard Day's Night', 'Help!', 'Magical Mystery Tour' and 'Yellow Submarine', there has never been an official DVD release for the 'Let It Be' movie, allegedly held up by the estates of both John Lennon and George Harrison, the two who probably disliked it the most. As at time of writing, rumours abound of an imminent DVD release featuring both the original movie and a new 'Director's cut', but there have been many rumours before. 'The Long and Winding Road' was released as a US single, where it got to No. 1, and the performance from the 'Let It Be' movie is on the '1+' DVD.

25-03-76 – **'Top Of The Pops' (UK)** – *PAN'S PEOPLE*

Yesterday

With a successful reissue / re-promotion campaign for The Beatles singles under way, EMI also took the opportunity to issue 'Yesterday' as a UK single for the first time. Pan's People do a suitably graceful dance to this song for 'Top Of The Pops'.

08-04-76 – **'Top Of The Pops' (UK)** – *PAN'S PEOPLE*

Paperback Writer

One of Pan's People's more literal routines, here they somehow manage the difficult task of doing an energetic dance while 'reading' books.

1976/1968 – **Promo Video #1**

Back In The U.S.S.R.

The first 'new' Beatles single since 1970 was the 8-year-old 'The White Album' track 'Back In The U.S.S.R', released to promote the

'Rock 'n' Roll Music' compilation. 2 different edits of this video were released.

15-07-76 – **'Top Of The Pops' (UK)** – *RUBY FLIPPER*

Back In The U.S.S.R.

By now, Pan's People had been replaced by the male/female dance troupe Ruby Flipper, though, due to their unpopularity, they would be replaced by another all-female group, 'Legs & Co.', by the end of the year. Here they do an unappealing routine while wearing traditional Russian dress.

1982/1964-1969 – **Promo Video**

Movie Medley

In 1982 a medley of hits was released, both to counteract the 'Stars Over 45' medleys charting at this time, and to promote the 'Reel Music' compilation, and it got to No. 10 in the UK and No. 12 in the US charts. Featuring clips from their movies, the video was shown on 'Top Of The Pops' on 24-06-82.

1982/1963 – **Promo Video**

Love Me Do

Throughout the '80s, on the 20th anniversary of their original releases, all of the UK singles were reissued and re-promoted. 'Love Me Do', the most successful of these, had 3 different edits for the promo video, though they were all based on the 'The Mersey Sound' performance, originally broadcast on 09-10-63. The video was broadcast on 'Top Of The Pops' on 14-10-82 and 28-10-82, and is on the '1+' DVD.

1983/1964 – **Promo Video**

Please Please Me

Based on a performance in Washington D.C. on 11-02-64, again, 3 similar edits were made. One of these was shown on 'Top Of The Pops' on 27-01-83.

1984/1964 – **Promo Video**

I Want To Hold Your Hand

This time the 20th anniversary video featured 2 different edits, but, with interest fast waning, this was the last 'new' Beatles video to be released during the '80s.

01-06-87 – **'It Was Twenty Years Ago Today' (UK)**

Sgt. Pepper's Lonely Hearts Club Band

To mark the 20th anniversary of the release of the 'Sgt. Pepper's Lonely Hearts Club Band' album, a 2-hour documentary was broadcast in the UK, though in the US it wasn't shown until 11-11-87. Featuring new interviews with Paul and George, the highlight was a clever animated video featuring the album cover. It can also be seen in 'Anthology'.

1994/1963 – **Promo Video #1**

Baby It's You

To promote the 'Live At The BBC' album, the single 'Baby It's You' was released, and two, completely different, videos were made. This rare 1st version features footage from EMI Studios and 'A Hard Day's

Night' movie, as well as scenes of girls screaming. The single got to No. 7 in the UK, though only struggled to No. 67 in the USA.

1994/1963 – **Promo Video #2**

Baby It's You

This 2nd video, featuring a combination of stills and 8mm colour footage, is the most widely see version, and was featured, in a slightly different edit, on '1+'.

00-11-95 – **Promo Video**

Free As A Bird

At the tail end of 1995, the surviving Beatles (quickly dubbed 'The Threetles' by fans), launched the mammoth 'Anthology' CD series, TV series (with VHS following in 1996 and DVD in 2003), and book (which was not actually published until 2000). What got the most media attention, however, were the two 'new' Beatles recordings. Consisting of late '70s John Lennon solo demos, over-dubbed, none too subtlety, by Paul, George and Ringo, the first of these was 'Free As A Bird'. Getting to No. 2 in the UK and No. 6 in the USA, it is fair to say that this, and the follow-up 'Real Love', got a very mixed reaction. What is almost universally loved though is the promotional video for the song, a strong contender for the greatest music video of all time. Full of clues (some obvious, many cryptic) that reference various Beatles songs, the exact list is open to debate, but may or may not include (in chronological order) the following: Across The Universe / Flying / In My Life / Old Brown Shoe / I'm Only Sleeping / Here Comes The Sun / Rain / Come Together / Some Other Guy / Strawberry Fields Forever /

Maxwell's Silver Hammer / Lady Madonna / I Am The Walrus / A Hard Day's Night / Taxman / Ob-La-Di, Ob-La-Da / Penny Lane / Polythene Pam / Do You Want To Know A Secret? / Help! / Why Don't We Do It In The Road? / Birthday / When I'm Sixty-Four / Dr. Robert / A Day In The Life / Don't Pass Me By / Penny Lane / I Am The Walrus / Helter Skelter / Being For The Benefit Of Mr. Kite! / She Came In Through The Bathroom Window / Lucy In The Sky With Diamonds / Piggies / Happiness Is A Warm Gun / Paperback Writer / Eight Days A Week / One After 909 / A Day In The Life / Savoy Truffle / Penny Lane / Her Majesty / Revolution / Fixing A Hole / Yellow Submarine / Hey Bulldog / Lucy In The Sky With Diamonds / She's Leaving Home / Revolution / Yellow Submarine / Mean Mr. Mustard / The Ballad Of John & Yoko / I Me Mine / Let It Be / Magical Mystery Tour / The Continuing Story of Bungalow Bill / Sexy Sadie / Sgt. Pepper's Lonely Hearts Club Band / Let It Be / Eleanor Rigby / Martha My Dear / The Fool On The Hill / Blackbird / She's Leaving Home / The Long And Winding Road / Lovely Rita / A Hard Day's Night / The End. Premiered by special screenings by US TV's ABC on 19-11-95 and the UK's BBC the following night, the video was also shown on 'Top of The Pops' on 23-11-95, 30-11-95 and 14-12-95. It can be found on the 'Anthology' and '1+' DVDs.

00-01-96 – **Promo Video**

Real Love

Not creating quite the same publicity as the previous single, perhaps because John Lennon's original demo had already been released on the 'Imagine: John Lennon' movie soundtrack in 1988, the accompanying video is more straight-forward than the one for 'Free

As A Bird', featuring shots of the mid-'90s 'Threetles' with archive John Lennon footage. There are two slightly different edits for this video, as, upon discovering that there are quite a few shots of Yoko included, they edited in brief clips of the other Beatles' wives too. Getting to No. 4 in the UK and No. 11 in the USA, the video was shown on 'Top Of The Pops' on 14-03-96, and is on both 'Anthology' and '1+'.

1999/1968 – **Promo Video**

Hey Bulldog

To promote the 1999 'Yellow Submarine Songtrack' album, Apple came up with something very special indeed. As mentioned in the 00-02-68 entry, on 11-02-68, when The Beatles made a video to promote 'Lady Madonna', they were actually seen (but not heard) working on 'Hey Bulldog'. Now, a mere 31 years later, fans finally got the chance to see the footage with the correct soundtrack. The video can be found on '1+'.

2000/1963 – **Promo Video**

She Loves You

The first of 3 videos especially made to promote the '1' CD release in 2000, this video simply features footage of girls screaming.

2000/1964 – **Promo Video #3**

I Feel Fine

Also to promote the '1' CD, a couple of animated 'flash' videos were made, though this one was wisely passed over for the 1965 videos when the '1+' DVD was compiled 15 years later.

2000/1969 – **Promo Video**

Come Together

Another 'flash' video from 2000, this didn't look all that great even then, and looked more unimpressive when it was included on the '1+' DVD.

2003/1969 – **Promo Videos #2 and #3**

Get Back

More newly created videos were made in 2003, this time to promote the 'Let It Be… Naked' album. Utilising January 1969 footage from both Twickenham and Apple studios, 2 similar videos were made for 'Get Back', with one of those later released on '1+'.

2003/1969 – **Promo Video #2**

Don't Let Me Down

Another 'new' video, this uses Apple rooftop outtakes, rather than the studio/rooftop mix on the original 1969 video for the song.

2003/1969 – **Promo Video**

Two Of Us

For 'Two Of Us', a different approach was used, as this features the studio performance (as seen in 'Let It Be') converted to black and white, with coloured animated drawings in the background.

2007/1966/1967 – **Promo Video**

Within and Without You/Tomorrow Never Knows

To promote the controversial 'Love' album of remixes, just this one video was made. It uses clips from the Rain', 'Penny Lane', 'Strawberry Fields Forever' and 'Hello Goodbye' videos, 'I Am the Walrus' and 'Blue Jay Way' from 'Magical Mystery Tour', and 'All You Need Is Love' from 'Our World'. All very clever, but the end result is as disorientating as the music on the album. The video can be seen on '1+'.

2013/1963 – **Promo Video**

Words Of Love

To promote the 'On Air – Live At The BBC Vol. 2' collection, a rather good video combining Beatles footage and animation was made. This is on '1+'.

2015/1964 – **Promo Video**

Eight Days A Week

The only ever TV performance of 'Eight Days A Week' is long lost (see the 03-04-65 entry so a new video, featuring a compilation of clips from the 1965 Shea Stadium concert, was made for the '1+' DVD.

2015/1966 – **Promo Video**

Yellow Submarine

Another video that was made especially for the '1+' DVD, this is compiled from clips of the movie of the same name.

2016/1968 – **Promo Video**

While My Guitar Gently Weeps

Created to commemorate the 10th anniversary of Cirque du Soleil's 'Love' theatrical show, this video features footage of a dancer (presumably from the show), combined with animation. It has little to do with The Beatles, but does nicely compliment the acoustic-version-with-strings soundtrack, the highlight of the 'Love' album.

2018/1968 – **Promo Video #2**

Back In The U.S.S.R.

The first of two videos for the late 2018 expanded reissue of 'The White Album', this features brief Beatles footage along with random clips of Russian-themed scenes, all semi-animated and with the lyrics to the song.

2018/1968 – **Promo Video**

Glass Onion

For this video, the free poster that came with 'The White Album' is very cleverly brought to life, and is one of the more worthy 'new' Beatles videos from recent years.

'THE BEATLES' CARTOONS SERIES

Although largely unknown in the UK, from September 1965 until October 1967, a series of 39 (or 78, as each 18-minute episode featured 2 distinct stories) animated cartoons were shown on US TV. Simply called 'The Beatles', there was much to criticise: The Beatles' voices (voiced by actors) were terrible, so much so that Brian Epstein refused to allow it to be broadcast in their homeland; they wore circa 'A Hard Day's Night' era suits and hairstyles throughout, despite the music eventually going into the early psychedelic era; and The Beatles' characters were clichéd and one-dimensional. All of this was despite the cartoons being Produced by Al Brodax and Directed by George Dunning, the same people who were later involved in the far superior 'Yellow Submarine' feature film. Yet, the series proved to be influential, with later cartoon series on groups (real and fictional) such as 'The Archie Show', 'The Jackson 5ive' and 'The Osmonds' owing it a large debt, and where else can 'The Beatles' be seen performing such songs as 'Not A Second Time', 'Any Time At All', 'What You're Doing', 'The Word' and even 'Komm Gib Mir Deine Hand' and 'Tomorrow Never Knows'? Unfortunately, the chances of any official releases are slim; despite John later saying how much he enjoyed re-runs of the show, every episode was bought by Apple in the '90s, and it hasn't been screened anywhere since.

1. A Hard Day's Night / I Want To Hold Your Hand (Sing-A-Longs: Not A Second Time / Devil In Her Heart)

2. Do You Want To Know A Secret / If I Fell (Sing-A-Longs: A Hard Day's Night / I Want To Hold Your Hand)

3. Please Mr. Postman / Devil In Her Heart (Sing-A-Longs: If I Fell / Do You Want To Know A Secret)

4. Not A Second Time / Slow Down (Sing-A-Longs: Baby's In Black / Misery)

5. Baby's In Black / Misery (Sing-A-Longs: I'll Get You / Chains)

6. You've Really Got A Hold On Me / Chains (Sing-A-Longs: Slow Down / Honey Don't)

7. I'll Get You / Honey Don't (Sing-A-Longs: You've Really Got A Hold On Me / Any Time At All)

8. Any Time At All / Twist and Shout (Sing-A-Longs: I'll Be Back / Little Child)

9. Little Child / I'll Be Back (Sing-A-Longs: Long Tall Sally / Twist and Shout)

10. Long Tall Sally / I'll Cry Instead (Sing-A-Longs: I'll Follow The Sun / When I Get Home)

11. I'll Follow the Sun / When I Get Home (Sing-A-Longs: I'll Cry Instead / Everybody's Trying To Be My Baby)

12. Everybody's Trying To Be My Baby / I Should Have Known Better (Sing-A-Longs: I'm A Loser / I Wanna Be Your Man)

13. I'm A Loser / I Wanna Be Your Man (Sing-A-Longs: No Reply / I'm Happy Just To Dance With You)

14. Don't Bother Me / No Reply (Sing-A-Longs: It Won't Be Long / I Should Have Known Better)

15. I'm Happy Just To Dance With You / Mr. Moonlight (Sing-A-Longs: Don't Bother Me / Can't Buy Me Love)

16. Can't Buy Me Love / It Won't Be Long (Sing-A-Longs: Anna (Go to Him) / Mr. Moonlight)

17. Anna (Go To Him) / I Don't Want To Spoil The Party (Sing-A-Longs: Matchbox / Thank You Girl)

18. Matchbox / Thank You Girl (Sing-A-Longs: I Don't Want To Spoil

The Party / Help!)

19. From Me To You / Boys (Sing-A-Longs: Please Mr. Postman / I Saw Her Standing There)

20. Dizzy Miss Lizzy / I Saw Her Standing There (Sing-A-Longs: Ticket To Ride / From Me To You)

21. What You're Doing / Money (Sing-A-Longs: Dizzy Miss Lizzy / All My Loving)

22. Komm Gib Mir Deine Hand / She Loves You (Sing-A-Longs: Bad Boy / Tell Me Why)

23. Bad Boy / Tell Me Why (Sing-A-Longs: Please Please Me / Hold Me Tight)

24. I Feel Fine / Hold Me Tight (Sing-A-Longs: What You're Doing / There's A Place)

25. Please Please Me / There's A Place (Sing-A-Longs: Roll Over Beethoven / Rock And Roll Music)

26. Roll Over Beethoven / Rock and Roll Music (Sing-A-Longs: I Feel Fine / She Loves You)

27. Eight Days A Week / I'm Looking Through You (Sing-A-Longs: Run For Your Life / Girl)

28. Help! / We Can Work It Out (Sing-A-Longs: The Night Before / Day Tripper)

29. I'm Down / Run For Your Life (Sing-A-Longs: Eight Days A Week / Paperback Writer)

30. Drive My Car / Tell Me What You See (Sing-A-Longs: Yesterday / We Can Work It Out)

31. I Call Your Name / The Word (Sing-A-Longs: She's a Woman / Wait)

32. All My Loving / Day Tripper (Sing-A-Longs: I'm Looking Through You / Nowhere Man)

33. Nowhere Man / Paperback Writer (Sing-A-Longs: And I Love Her / Michelle)

34. Penny Lane / Strawberry Fields (Sing-A-Longs: Good Day Sunshine / Rain)

35. And Your Bird Can Sing / Got To Get You Into My Life (Sing-A-Longs: Penny Lane / Eleanor Rigby)

36. Good Day Sunshine / Ticket To Ride (Sing-A-Longs: Strawberry Fields Forever / And Your Bird Can Sing)

37. Taxman / Eleanor Rigby (Sing-A-Longs: Got To Get You Into My Life / Here, There and Everywhere)

38. Tomorrow Never Knows / I've Just Seen a Face (Sing-A-Longs: She Said She Said / Long Tall Sally [repeat from episode #9])

39. Wait / I'm Only Sleeping (Sing-A-Longs: Penny Lane / Eleanor Rigby [both songs are repeats from episode #35])

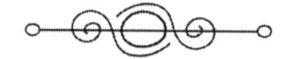

JOHN LENNON

11-12-68 – 'The Rolling Stones' Rock and Roll Circus' (UK)

Yer Blues (2 takes) / Whole Lotta Yoko [Performed by Yoko Ono]

Although John had done solo TV and film projects previously (most notably a couple of appearances in 'Not Only... But Also' and the 'How I Won The War' movie), this was the first time he'd sung and played for TV with a band other than The Beatles. Backed by a one-off supergroup featuring Eric Clapton on guitar, Keith Richards on bass and Mitch Mitchell on drums, they perform a storming version of The White album's 'Yer Blues', plus, joined by Ivry Gitlis on violin, a far less essential jam that was later dubbed 'Whole Lotta Yoko'. Unfortunately, for a variety of alleged reasons, this TV Special wasn't shown at the time, though it finally got an official VHS release in 1996, later followed by a DVD. The version of 'Yer Blues' in the finished film is actually the first of 3 takes. The 2nd take only circulates on audio, but the 3rd is available on the DVD as a bonus track. Other acts on this TV special, as well as hosts The Rolling Stones, are The Who (whom probably out-performed everyone), Marianne Faithfull, Jethro Tull, Taj Mahal and Julius Katchen, though the latter isn't in the finished version, only appearing on the DVD as a bonus track.

00-03-69 – 'Rape (Film No. 6)' Movie (UK)

Everybody Had A Hard Year

During 1968 – 1971, John and Yoko made a series of experimental films. Most of these are tedious in the extreme, but one of the more interesting is 1969's 'Rape (Film No. 6)', not least for this short cameo of John and Yoko after the closing credits. Filmed in the garden in

Weybridge the day after 'The Rolling Stones' Rock and Roll Circus' was taped, 'Everybody Had a Hard Year' was later incorporated into Paul's 'I've Got A Feeling', making a far more interesting song. This clip is also on the 'Lennon Legend' DVD.

00-07-69 – **Promo Video**

Give Peace A Chance

John and Yoko, in addition to making arty films, did a series of peace events during 1969 – 1972, with their May-June 1969 'Bed-In' event in Montreal being the most famous. It was during this that John both wrote and recorded (in bed) 'Give Peace A Chance'. Released under the name 'The Plastic Ono Band', like many of John and Yoko's records in this period, the single got to No. 2 in the UK and No. 14 in the USA. Initially released in two slightly different edits, the video was shown on 'Top Of The Pops' on 10-07-69 and 24-07-69, and later issued on the 1992 'The John Lennon Video Collection' VHS release. For 2003's 'Lennon Legend – The Very Best of John Lennon' DVD, additional war and protest scenes were added to the promo video, including 1980 footage of the crowd in New York's Central Park following John's death, with a similar but slightly different version of the 2003 video being repeated on 2010's 'Power To The People' DVD.

13-09-69 – **'Toronto Rock 'n' Roll Revival', Varsity Stadium (Canada)**

Blue Suede Shoes / Money / Dizzy Miss Lizzy / Yer Blues / Cold Turkey / Give Peace A Chance / Don't Worry, Kyoko (Mummy's Only Looking For Her Hand In The Snow) [Performed by Yoko Ono] / John, John (Let's Hope For Peace) [Performed by Yoko Ono]

With a line-up featuring Eric Clapton (guitar), Klaus Voormann (bass) and Alan White (drums), and on a bill that included Little Richard, Chuck Berry, Jerry Lee Lewis, Bo Diddley, Gene Vincent, The Doors and The Alice Cooper Band, John Lennon/The Plastic Ono Band made their live debut. Although not quite vocally on top form, they performed solid versions of 3 rock 'n' roll classics, a reprise of the Beatles song he'd performed the previous December, the forthcoming single 'Cold Turkey' (here in a very different arrangement to the studio cut), and a loose but fun version of 'Give Peace a Chance'. Despite his obvious nerves and rustiness, John did more than fine, but unfortunately, this was then followed by two lengthy, screechy, Yoko Ono songs, resulting in them leaving the stage to a mixture of cheers and boos. Released as the album 'Live Peace In Toronto', this was a No. 10 hit in the USA, though the full video performance wasn't available publicly (at least officially) until a '80s VHS release, and later a DVD. 'Blue Suede Shoes' circulates unofficially as an alternate 'rough' edit.

00-10-69 – **Promo Video #1**

Cold Turkey

Again featuring Eric Clapton on lead guitar, 'Cold Turkey', John's song about coming off heroin, was a UK No. 12 and US No. 30 hit. The video features speeded-up and quickly-edited footage (only some of it featuring John and Yoko), and was shown on 'Top Of The Pops' on 06-11-69, as well as on 'The John Lennon Video Collection' video. A new video was made for 2003's 'Lennon Legend – The Very Best of John Lennon', see the 2003/1969 entry for details.

15-12-69 – UNICEF Gala, Lyceum Ballroom, London (UK)

Cold Turkey / Don't Worry, Kyoko (Mummy's Only Looking For Her Hand In The Snow) [Performed by Yoko Ono]

For this charity concert, John assembled the greatest line-up of his solo career, with Eric Clapton, Klaus Voormann and Alan White playing their usual instruments, along with George Harrison (guitar), Keith Moon (drums), Billy Preston (keyboards), Bobby Keys (saxophone), Jim Gordon (drums), Delaney Bramlett (guitar) and Bonnie Bramlett (backing vocals). Despite this, and the eventful appearance of two Beatles sharing a stage for the first time since 1966, the end result is rather cacophonous. Only incomplete clips of both songs survive, but they appeared, complete, on the 1972 'Sometime In New York City' album, albeit with Billy Preston's organ replaced by a Nicky Hopkins electric piano overdub.

00-01-70 – **Promo Video**

Instant Karma

Although The Beatles were still together, at least officially, this was John's 3rd hit single in 6 months, getting to No. 5 in the UK and No. 3 in the USA. The video, of which 2 different edits were made, features a hot air balloon ride combined with various clips from 1968-1970. It was shown on 'Top Of The Pops' on 05-02-70.

12-02-70 – **'Top Of The Pops' (UK)**

Instant Karma

Appearing in the 'Top Of The Pops' studio for the first time in nearly 4 years, on 11-02-70 John taped two performances for future broadcast, with both versions featuring live vocals. For this first one both John and Yoko wear denim jackets, with Yoko blindfolded with a sanitary towel while holding placards. This performance was issued on 'The John Lennon Video Collection' video.

19-02-70 – 'Top Of The Pops' (UK)

Instant Karma

For this 2nd performance, John and Yoko wear black polo-necked jumpers, while Yoko, again blindfolded with a sanitary towel, does knitting. This performance was issued on the 'Lennon Legend – The Very Best of John Lennon' DVD, though unfortunately with the live vocal replaced by the studio recording. The original live version circulates unofficially.

05-03-70 – 'Top Of The Pops' (UK)

Instant Karma

This is a repeated of the 12-02-70 appearance.

18-03-71 – 'Top Of The Pops' Video (UK) – *MISSING/LOST*

Power To The People

A No. 6 UK hit and No. 11 US hit, this promo video for the raucous 'Power To The People' was made especially for 'Top Of The Pops', and was broadcast on 18-03-71 on 25-03-71, though it no longer survives. No official (non-'Top Of The Pops') video was made for the song until 1992.

21/22-05-71 – **Tittenhurst, Ascot (UK)**

Imagine / Jealous Guy / Gimme Some Truth / Oh My Love / How Do You Sleep? [with George Harrison] / How? / Oh Yoko!

The highlights of the 1988 'Imagine: John Lennon' documentary movie were several excerpts from the recordings sessions for the 'Imagine' album, and in 2000 a further documentary, entitled 'Gimme Some Truth', was released on DVD, with much additional footage from these sessions. It was reissued as part of the 'Imagine' movie DVD in 2018, a release that also sees incredible split-screen edits of John recording 'Jealous Guy', 'How?' and 'Gimme Some Truth'. Lengthy outtake footage of both 'Oh My Love' and 'How Do You Sleep?' circulate unofficially, the latter featuring George Harrison on slide guitar.

06-06-71 – **Fillmore East, New York (USA)**

Well (Baby Please Don't Go) / Jamrag / Scumbag / Au [all songs are with Frank Zappa and band]

Appearing as special guest of Frank Zappa, John's version of 'Well (Baby Please Don't Go)' would be quite a good performance if Yoko Ono hadn't ruined it with her inappropriate howling, while the other songs are almost unlistenable jams. Circulating unofficially on surprisingly good multi-angle colour footage, the audio of these songs, with a bass overdub by Klaus Voormann, appeared on 'Sometime In New York City'.

00-09-71 – **'Imagine' movie (USA)**

Imagine / Crippled Inside / Jealous Guy / Don't Count The Waves [Yoko Ono] / It's So Hard / Mrs. Lennon [Yoko Ono] / I Don't Wanna Be A Soldier / Mind Train [Yoko Ono] / Power To The People (incomplete) / Gimme Some Truth / Midsummer New York [Yoko Ono] / Oh My Love / How Do You Sleep? / How? / Oh Yoko!

The 1971 'Imagine' movie (not to be confused with the 'Imagine: John Lennon' documentary movie from 1988), is a ground-breaking collection of Promo Videos, taped over several months, made to promote John's 'Imagine' and Yoko's 'Fly' albums. Although it wasn't widely seen at the time, no-one else was doing this in 1971 (Blondie's 'Eat To The Beat' from 1979 is generally regarded as the first video album). The movie was issued, in edited form, as a VHS tape in 1985, and then finally issued on DVD in 2018. Additionally, outtake footage of the 'Imagine' promo video circulates unofficially. The 'Imagine' single was a No. 3 US single in 1971, though, surprisingly, it wasn't issued as a single in the UK until 1975, when it got to No. 6, and, following John's death, was a No. 1 in 1981. The 'Imagine' album was No. 1 in both the UK and the USA. The Promo Video for 'Imagine' was broadcast on 'Top Of The Pops' on 08-01-81, 15-01-81, 22-01-81, 29-01-81, 31-12-81 and 07-01-00, and, as well as in the full 1972 movie, can be found on the 'Lennon Legend – The Very Best of John Lennon' DVD.

12-11-71 – **Bank Street, New York (USA)**

Luck Of The Irish [with Yoko Ono]

Circulating unofficially is almost 20 minutes of black and white footage, featuring John and Yoko rehearsing a song that later appeared on the 'Sometime In New York City' album.

00-12-71 – 'Top Of The Pops' Video (UK)

Happy Christmas (War Is Over)

Unlike in the '60s, the early '70s produced a number of classic Christmas records, and John and Yoko's 1971 seasonal offering is up there with and predates the hits by Slade, Mud, Wizzard, Elton John and all the other glam-era greats. Only making it to No. 42 in the US, in the UK it wasn't released until December the following year, when it made No. 2. This video, featuring footage in and outside a church, intercut with stills of John and Yoko recording with the Harlem Gospel Choir, was made especially for 'Top Of The Pops' and broadcast on 14-12-72.

10-12-71 – 'Ten For Two', Crisler Arena, Ann Arbour (USA)

Attica State / The Luck Of The Irish [with Yoko Ono] / Sisters O Sisters [Performed by Yoko Ono] / John Sinclair

'Ten For Two' was a benefit concert for John Sinclair, a left-wing US activist who was given a 10 year prison sentence for possession of marijuana, for which John and Yoko played acoustically, and performed all new, politically-leaning, songs. All of these songs were later issued on 1972's 'Sometime In New York City', which got to No. 11 in the UK charts, but in the USA, where it was savaged by the critics, it only scraped to No. 48. This, perhaps not incidentally, would be the only time prior to 1980's 'Double Fantasy' where John and Yoko would share songs on the same studio album. The backing band

here are Apple recording artists David Peel and The Lower East Side, who would perform with them at all December 1971 live and TV performances.

17-12-71 – **The Apollo Theatre, New York (USA)**

Attica State / Sisters O Sisters [Performed by Yoko Ono] / Imagine

Another benefit concert, this time for the families who became victims of the riots at Attica State Prison, and another fine acoustic performance, though the inevitable highlight is 'Imagine'.

13-01-72 – **'The David Frost Show' (USA)**

The Ballad Of New York City [Performed by David Peel] / Attica State / The Luck Of The Irish (short version) [with Yoko Ono] / Sisters O Sisters [Performed by Yoko Ono] / John Sinclair / Attica State (Reprise) / The Hippie From New York City [Performed by David Peel]

Taped on 16-12-71, John and Yoko reprise the 4 songs they performed in Ann Arbour, as well as back David Peel on a couple of his own rather ramshackle songs. John and Yoko also partake in an audience Q & A, though John gets annoyed at their response, refusing to be interviewed by David Frost later, where Yoko does the interview solo.

14-02-72 – **'The Mike Douglas Show' (USA)**

It's So Hard

One of US TV's most popular and enduring chat shows, John and Yoko were happy to be invited to co-host 5 shows in a row, where they chatted, showed film clips, and performed several songs while backed by The Elephant's Memory Band, who would join them for live

performances and recording sessions throughout the year. Taped on 14-01-72, this is a solid version of one of the tougher tracks from the 'Imagine' album.

15-02-72 – 'The Mike Douglas Show' (USA)

Midsummer New York [Performed by Yoko Ono]

Taped on 18-01-72, the only song performed today was this bluesy Yoko Ono song.

16-02-72 – 'The Mike Douglas Show' (USA)

Sisters O Sisters [Performed by Yoko Ono] / Memphis, Tennessee [with Chuck Berry] / Johnny B. Goode [with Chuck Berry]

Following an acoustic 'Sisters O Sisters', John is joined by his early rock 'n' roll hero Chuck Berry, and while the end result is better seen than heard (if only Yoko would shut up), it was still undoubtedly a thrill for all involved. Taped on 20-01-72, John's introduction to Chuck Berry was later used for the latter's own 1988 'Hail, Hail, Rock 'n' Roll' movie.

17-02-72 – 'The Mike Douglas Show' (USA)

Imagine

Taped on 27-01-72, here John performs a slightly hesitant version of his classic while playing an electric piano.

18-02-72 –'The Mike Douglas Show' (USA)

The Luck Of The Irish [with Yoko Ono] / Sakura [Performed by Yoko Ono]

Generally, John and Yoko kept away from their more controversial recent songs for their appearances on 'The Mike Douglas Show', but for this last show taped on 28-01-72, they performed a relaxed version of 'The Luck Of The Irish', as well as a traditional Japanese song.

11-03-72 – **'Aquarius' (UK)**

Medley: Bring On The Lucie (Freda Peeple) - Attica State

Taped in the USA in early December 1971, John plays, solo, a snippet of a song that would later appear on the 'Mind Games' album, followed by another version of 'Attica State'.

22-04-72 – **National Peace Rally, New York (USA)**

Give Peace A Chance

Not really a performance in the true sense, John and Yoko attend a peace rally, where they and the crowd sing a chorus of 'Give Peace A Chance'.

11-05-72 – **'The Dick Cavett Show' (USA)**

Woman Is The Nigger Of The World / We're All Water [Performed by Yoko Ono]

A song with a title that would be even more controversial today, back then few radio stations would play a song called 'Woman Is The Nigger Of The World'. Despite this, the song is excellent, and this live version, taped on 03-05-72, is one of John's greatest performances. Yoko Ono can only be an anti-climax afterwards, though this is still a strong version of one of her better songs. 'Woman Is The Nigger Of

The World' was, incredibly, released as a US single, where it did well to get as high as No. 57.

12-08-72 – 'Eye Witness News', St. Regis Hotel, New York (USA)

Medley: Rock Island Line – Maybe Baby – Peggy Sue / Woman Is The Nigger Of The World / Fools Like Me / Caribbean

Taped on 05-08-72, these are loose but fun performances featuring John playing solo electric guitar in a hotel room, though it is clear that Yoko wasn't familiar with most of the oldies, particularly Jerry Lee Lewis' 'Fools Like Me'.

30-08-72 – 'One To One', Madison Square Garden, New York – Afternoon Show (USA)

Power To The People (Intro) / New York City / It's So Hard / Woman Is The Nigger Of The World / Sisters O Sisters [Performed by Yoko Ono] / Well, Well, Well / Instant Karma / Mother / Born In A Prison [with Yoko Ono] / Come Together / Imagine / Cold Turkey / Hound Dog / Give Peace A Chance

Performing two benefit concerts for the Willowbrook School for Children, John, with Yoko and The Elephant's Memory Band, performed on this day the only 2 full-length shows of his post-Beatles career. Although inevitably a little under-rehearsed, John sounds far more inspired than he did in Toronto 3 years earlier. The above songs were issued on VHS as 'Live In New York City' in 1986, though not all songs from the show were included, and fans are still waiting for an official, perhaps expanded, DVD release. The full set-list for the afternoon show is: Power To The People (Intro) / New York City / It's

So Hard / Move On Fast [Performed by Yoko Ono] / Woman Is The Nigger Of The World / Sisters O Sisters [Performed by Yoko Ono] / Well, Well, Well / Instant Karma / Mother / We're All Water [Performed by Yoko Ono] / Born In A Prison [with Yoko Ono] / Come Together / Imagine / Open Your Box [Performed by Yoko Ono] / Cold Turkey / Don't Worry, Kyoko (Mummy's Only Looking For Her Hand In The Snow) [Performed by Yoko Ono] / Hound Dog / Give Peace A Chance

30-08-72 – 'One To One', Madison Square Garden, New York – Afternoon Show (USA)

Move On Fast [Performed by Yoko Ono]

Not included on the 1986 VHS release, this song was broadcast in the UK on 'The Old Grey Whistle Test' on 30-01-73.

30-08-72 – 'One To One', Madison Square Garden, New York – Evening Show (USA)

Come Together / Instant Karma / Sisters O Sisters [Performed by Yoko Ono] / Cold Turkey / Hound Dog / Give Peace A Chance [with Stevie Wonder] / Imagine (audio only, over closing credits)

This was considered by those who were there as the superior of the two shows, despite it being shorter, but only the above songs were broadcast, on US TV, on 14-12-72. The full set-list for the evening show is: Power To The People (Intro) / New York City / It's So Hard / Woman Is The Nigger Of The World / Sisters O Sisters [Performed by Yoko Ono] / Well, Well, Well / Instant Karma / Mother / We're All Water [Performed by Yoko Ono] / Come Together / Imagine / Cold

Turkey / Hound Dog / Give Peace A Chance [with Stevie Wonder]

06-09-72 – **'Jerry Lewis Labor Day Telethon' (USA)**

Imagine / Now Or Never [Performed by Yoko Ono] / Give Peace A Chance

Though John looks a little dishevelled, this is another fine performance, with 'Give Peace A Chance' a jammed, reggae-influenced version. Sadly, this was John's last performance with The Elephant's Memory Band.

30-06-73 – **'Flipside' (USA)**

Winter Song [Performed by Yoko Ono]

Taped on 12-05-73, this features a now long-haired John being interviewed, and Yoko Ono (without John) is seen recording this rather good song. Soon after this, John and Yoko would split for around 18 months, while John went on what he'd later call his 'lost weekend'. Although in retrospect John, and later Yoko, dismissed this period as a time of non-stop partying and very little productivity, John recorded the Mind Games', 'Walls and Bridges' and 'Rock 'n' Roll' albums, participated on No. 1 hits by both David Bowie and Elton John, recorded with Harry Nilsson, Ringo Starr and Keith Moon, and even jammed in a recording studio with Paul McCartney. He hadn't been this productive since The Beatles' touring years, and he would never be this productive again.

In late 1973, the 'Mind Games' single got to No. 26 in the UK and No. 18 in the USA, while the parent album of the same name reached Nos.

13 and 9 respectively. Unfortunately, in direct contrast to the previous few years, there were no Promo Videos or TV performances for this song, though there were later videos in 1992 and 2003 – see the entries for those years.

00-10-74 – **Promo Video #1**

Whatever Gets You Thru The Night

A duet with an (un-credited) Elton John, when this was recorded Elton bet John that this would get to No. 1, and when John was sceptical, he promised Elton that he'd perform the song onstage with him. Although strangely stalling at No. 36 in the UK, it did indeed top the charts in the USA, and John kept his word. The parent album, 'Walls and Bridges', got to No. 6 in the UK, and again topped the charts in the USA. As for the video, taped on 17-10-74, it features a good-humoured John strolling around New York while wearing an all-black outfit that includes a feathered hat. It was to be John's only proper, custom-filmed post-1972 Promo Video, so why it was substituted for a new one on 'The John Lennon Video Collection' and all subsequent DVDs makes no sense whatsoever. Outtake footage for this Promo Video also circulates.

On 28-11-74, John Lennon joined Elton John on stage to play 3 songs, 'Whatever Gets You Through the Night', 'Lucy In The Sky With Diamonds' and 'I Saw Her Standing There'. Backstage afterwards, he was reconciled with Yoko. The 'lost weekend' was over. John would never set foot on a live concert stage again.

00-02-75 – **'Top Of The Pops' Video (UK)** – *MISSING/LOST*

#9 Dream

This was made especially for 'Top Of The Pops', broadcast on 27-02-75. The single, again from 'Walls and Bridges', was a UK No. 23 and, appropriately, a US No. 9.

18-04-75 – 'The Old Grey Whistle Test' (UK)

Stand By Me / Slippin' and Slidin'

Taped in New York's Hit Factory Studios on 17-03-75, both songs are superb live-in-the-studio performances. They were featured, with original live audio, on 'The John Lennon Video Collection', while 'Stand By Me' appeared, with dubbed studio audio and inserted additional scenes, on 'Lennon Legend – The Very Best of John Lennon', as was, in its original live form, 'Slippin' and Slidin''. John's last single prior to retiring from public view for 5 years, 'Stand By Me' got to No. 30 in the UK and No. 20 in the USA, while the album 'Rock 'n' Roll' reached No. 6 on both sides of the Atlantic.

13-06-75 – 'Salute To Sir Lew' (USA)

Slippin' and Slidin' / Imagine

Performing live in New York's Hilton Hotel on 18-04-75, and backed by the band Etcetera, this was John's last ever TV performance. It was broadcast in the USA on 13-06-75, and in the UK 7 days later, but both broadcasts omitted a 3rd song, 'Stand By Me', which ended up on the cutting room floor. 'Imagine' is on 'Lennon Legend – The Very Best of John Lennon', and was also broadcast on 'Top Of The Pops' on 11-12-80.

28-06-75 – 'Un Jour Futur' (France)

Lady Marmalade

During an interview taped on 04-04-75 at The Dakota in New York, John surprised the French host by singing and playing a snatch of Labelle's current disco hit.

06-11-75 – 'Top Of The Pops' (UK) – PAN'S PEOPLE – MISSING/LOST

Imagine

To promote the reissue of the single, 'Top Of The Pops'' current troupe did a routine for the song. It was repeated on 27-11-75.

11-04-80 – Cold Spring Harbour, New York (USA)

Dear Yoko (2 takes)

Although rather poorly lit, this footage of John running through 2 takes of a future 'Double Fantasy' song on his acoustic guitar is priceless. It's interesting to note that he still had long hair and a beard at this point.

1980 – Promo Video #1 – NOT COMPLETED

I'm Losing You

On 19-08-80, footage of John at work in the Hit Factory studios was made, probably for proposed future use in promo videos for '(Just Like) Starting Over' and 'I'm Losing You'. Unfortunately, when John saw the results, he was horrified by his gaunt appearance, and ordered the footage to be destroyed. However, recently, incomplete footage of John recording 'I'm Losing You' has somehow surfaced.

John Lennon was shot dead on 08-12-80.

18-12-80 – **'Top Of The Pops' (UK)** – *LEGS & Co.*

(Just Like) Starting Over

Following John's death, both '(Just Like) Starting Over' and the album 'Double Fantasy' reached No. 1 in the UK, the USA and pretty much everywhere else. However, there was no Promo Video for the song, and no-one had hastily assembled one either. So, the best 'Top Of the Pops' could come up with was to get their current troupe, 'Legs & Co.', to do an inappropriately light-hearted dance around a Christmas tree while wearing skimpy Santa-like outfits (this author is a fan of all the 'Top Of The Pops' dance troupes and doesn't blame the dancers, but it's a shame the show couldn't have come up with something a little better). Fortunately, a couple of proper videos for the song were compiled later; see the 1992 and 2000 entries for details.

00-01-81/1980 – **Promo Video**

Woman

On 26-11-80, footage of John and Yoko walking in Central Park, and then getting undressed on a bed at home, was made for future use, very likely a Promo Video for 'Just Like (Starting Over)', but instead it was used for the follow-up single, 'Woman'. A UK No. 1 and a US No. 2, the video was broadcast on 'Top Of The Pops' on 29-01-81, and can also be found on 'Lennon Legend – The Very Best of John Lennon'.

00-02-81/1980 – **'Top Of The Pops' Video (UK)**

Woman

Despite having already broadcast, on 29-01-81, the official video for 'Woman', for reasons unknown they used their own specially made one for subsequent broadcasts. Featuring footage mostly from 1969, though with a few 1980 stills, it was broadcast on 05-02-81, 12-02-81 and, in part, on 31-12-81.

00-02-81 – **Promo Video** – YOKO ONO

Walking On Thin Ice

Getting positive music reviews for the first time in her life, something several critics commentated on is how Yoko's songs on 'Double Fantasy' sounded more contemporary than John's, and her new single, 'Walking On Thin Ice', isn't a million miles away from what The B-52's and Lene Lovich were doing at the time. A UK No. 35 and US No. 58 hit, the song is taken from her 'Seasons Of Glass' album. The Promo video features some of the same Central Park/bed footage as the 'Woman' video, with additional new solo footage of Yoko and older home movie clips.

00-08-81 – **Promo Video** – YOKO ONO

Goodbye Sadness

Although lacking the impact of 'Walking On Thin Ice', 'Goodbye Sadness' is genuinely touching, both as a song and a video.

1984/1980 – **Promo Video #1**

Nobody Told Me

In 1984, a 'new' John and Yoko album, compiled from unreleased 1980 recordings, was released. Entitled 'Milk and Honey', it got to No. 3 in the UK and No. 11 in the USA, with 'Nobody Told Me', at Nos. 6 and 5 respectively, the first and biggest hit from the album. Shown on 'Top Of The Pops' on 19-01-84, this video, compiled from a number of mostly familiar sources, was also on 'The John Lennon Video Collection'.

1984/1980 – **Promo Video #1**

Borrowed Time

Like most of the 1984 videos, this features footage from a wide variety of eras. A No. 32 UK and No. 108 US hit, it was shown on 'Top Of The Pops' on 29-03-84, and was later on 'The John Lennon Video Collection' videotape.

1984/1980 – **Promo Video**

I'm Stepping Out

Available on 'Lennon Legend – The Very Best of John Lennon', this features a great variety of footage from 1969 to 1980, though the most amusing/touching bit is when John, Yoko and Sean go skinny-dipping at the end.

1984/1980 – **Promo Video**

Grow Old With Me

Compiled from a variety of sources, this video is on 'Lennon Legend –

The Very Best of John Lennon'. 'Grow Old With Me' very nearly became a new Beatles single along with 'Free As A Bird' and 'Real Love' in the mid-'90s, and certainly has the same ghostly, demo-like, quality as the un-dubbed other songs.

1984/1980 – **Promo Video**

Every Man Has A Woman

One of the lesser-known John Lennon videos, this features a storyline of a man meeting a woman in a restaurant, but contains no John Lennon/Yoko Ono footage.

1988/1971 – **Promo Video #2**

Imagine

Used to promote the 1988 'Imagine: John Lennon' documentary movie, this is an interesting conceptual video that features a boy/man walking through a series of doors, and gradually getting older. It's far better than it sounds.

1988/1971 – **Promo Video #2**

Jealous Guy

Again released as promotion for 'Imagine: John Lennon', this features John recording the song, intercut with both Beatles and solo footage.

1992/1971 – **Promo Video #1**

Power To The People

Featuring footage of John and Yoko on a 1971 protest march in London intercut with various clips of conflicts, this was made for the

'The John Lennon Video Collection' VHS release. It is also on both the 'Lennon Legend – The Very Best of John Lennon' DVD and the 'Power To The People' DVD, though all 3 releases feature some slightly differing edits from each other.

1992/1971 – **Promo Video #1**

Happy Christmas (War Is Over)

The first official video for the song, this features footage of the 1992 version of the Harlem Gospel Choir, along with stills of John and Yoko's peace campaigns. It was on 'The John Lennon Video Collection'.

1992/1973 – **Promo Video #1**

Mind Games

Made especially for 'The John Lennon Video Collection., this features clips from the 1974 'Whatever Gets You Through The Night' video, intercut with various other archive clips.

1992/1974 – **Promo Video #1**

#9 Dream

Again made for 'The John Lennon Video Collection' video, this features footage from the usual sources, and isn't especially interesting.

1992/1974 – **Promo Video #2**

Whatever Gets You Thru The Night

Featuring animated footage from John's drawings, this was made for 'The John Lennon Video Collection', and also appears, with minor differences, on 'Lennon Legend – The Very Best of John Lennon'.

1992/1980 – **Promo Video #1**

(Just Like) Starting Over

This video utilises the 1980 Central Park and bed footage that first appeared in the 'Woman' video, though it was allegedly originally filmed with this song in mind. The video can be found on 'The John Lennon Video Collection'.

1998/1970 – **Promo Video #1**

Working Class Hero

Issued to promote 1998's 'Anthology', this mix of well-known clips includes the 'Well, Well, Well' ending, as heard on the box-set.

1998/1974 – **Promo Video**

Only You

When John Lennon supervised Ringo Starr's version of 'Only You', he laid down his own guide vocal, and it is this that was released on 1998's 'Anthology'. The video is compiled from the usual over-familiar sources.

1998/1980 – **Promo Video**

I'm Losing You

Some of the 'Double Fantasy' songs were originally recorded, as elaborate demos, by John Lennon backed by Cheap Trick, and for this video to promote 'Anthology', actual members of Cheap Trick (in their 1998 guise) appear alongside old footage of John. Essential, both as viewing and listening.

2000/1970 – **Promo Video #2**

Working Class Hero

Issued as a sort of 'video history' to commemorate the 20th anniversary of John's death, this compilation of Beatles and solo clips again uses the 'Anthology' version, albeit without the 'Well, Well, Well' ending, and is interrupted throughout by comments from John. There were 2 versions of this video, one which leaves the 'F'-word intact, and the other with it censored.

2000/1980 – **Promo Video #2**

(Just Like) Starting Over

Released on the 20th anniversary of John's death on 08-12-00, this concept video of memorabilia and drawings is reminiscent of the video for 'Free As A Bird'. It is on 'Lennon Legend – The Very Best of John Lennon'.

2003/1969 – **Promo Video #2**

Cold Turkey

Instead of the 1969 promo video, for 'Lennon Legend – The Very Best of John Lennon' a new one was made. It features footage from the 1972 'One To One' concert, intercut with clips of John and Yoko leaving court in 1968.

2003/1970 – **Promo Video**

Mother

Comprised of still photos, this surprisingly effective video was made 'Lennon Legend – The Very Best of John Lennon'.

2003/1970 – **Promo Video**

Love

Although the 1970 recording was issued as a UK single in 1982, when it reached No. 41 in the charts, this video, from the usual sources, was compiled especially for 'Lennon Legend – The Very Best of John Lennon' in 2003.

2003/1970 – **Promo Video #3**

Working Class Hero

Another conceptual video, this features a young boy playing John Lennon as a child, amidst all sorts of special effects, stills, clips and drawings. It is on 'Lennon Legend – The Very Best of John Lennon'.

2003/1971 – **Promo Video #2**

Happy Christmas (War Is Over)

For 'Lennon Legend – The Very Best of John Lennon', a new video was made, featuring footage and stills from various wars around the world. While it fits the song, as there's no footage of John (and Yoko), it is a video that many fans probably skip.

2003/1971 – **Promo Video #3**

Jealous Guy

Probably the best of the 3 videos for the song, this features John in the recording studio, with outtake footage from the taping of the

1972 'Imagine' movie. It is on 'Lennon Legend – The Very Best of John Lennon'.

2003/1973 – **Promo Video #2**

Mind Games

In 2003, Yoko bought around 40 minutes of silent footage from the 'Whatever Gets You Thru the Night' video shoot on 17-10-74, and it's from this footage, in stunning quality, that this new video was compiled.

2003/1974 – **Promo Video #2**

#9 Dream

A slight step-up from the 1992 video, this features clips from the experimental 'Smile' film from 1968 (featuring close-up, slow-motion, film of John's face), intercut with other archive clips. It is on 'Lennon Legend – The Very Best of John Lennon'.

2003/1980 – **Promo Video**

Watching The Wheels

Especially made for 'Lennon Legend – The Very Best of John Lennon', this features some excellent home movie footage. When released as a 1981 single, the song got to No. 30 in the UK and No. 10 in the USA.

2003/1980 – **Promo Video**

Beautiful Boy

From 'Lennon Legend – The Very Best of John Lennon', the video for 'Beautiful Boy' is entirely made up of vacation footage from Cold

Spring Harbour on 13-04-80.

2003/1980 – **Promo Video #2**

Nobody Told Me

This newly created video is mostly compiled from 1971 'Imagine' movie footage plus outtakes, and can be found on 'Lennon Legend – The Very Best of John Lennon'.

2003/1980 – **Promo Video #2**

Borrowed Time

Again compiled for 'Lennon Legend – The Very Best of John Lennon', this conceptual video sees John as a young child, and then going through the years from 1969 to 1980.

2006/1971 – **Promo Video #2**

Power To The People

Completely different from the 1992 video and all subsequent edits, this video was made especially to promote 'The U.S. vs. John Lennon' documentary movie, and includes filmed quotes from John himself.

Cynthia Lennon, John's first wife, died on 01-04-15.

PAUL McCARTNEY

00-12-66 – **'The Family Way' Movie (UK)**

The first non-Beatles project to prominently feature Paul McCartney's name on it was the soundtrack album to this 1966 movie starring Hayley Mills and Hywel Bennett. With music by Paul, and played by The George Martin Orchestra, the album was released in the UK in January 1967 and in the USA in June 1967. It didn't chart.

00-03-68 – **Promo Video** – CILLA BLACK

Step Inside Love

Taped in January 1968, the promo video features studio scenes of Paul with Cilla, recording the No. 8 UK hit that he composed for her TV series 'Cilla!'.

00-03-69 – **Promo Video** – MARY HOPKIN

Goodbye

Taped on 01-03-69, this video features Paul with Mary in a recording studio. The Follow-up to 'Those Were The Days', Paul's composition 'Goodbye' reached No. 2 in the UK and No. 13 in the USA.

00-04-70 – **Promo Video #1**

Maybe I'm Amazed

When Paul released his first proper solo album, 'McCartney', no singles were extracted from it. However, the song that stood out is 'Maybe I'm Amazed', so much so that a Video was made to help promote the album. Consisting of stills featuring Paul and Linda, the video was given its own spot on the UK's 'LWT' ITV channel on 19-04-

69, and it was also shown on 'The Ed Sullivan Show' on the same day. This video is on the 2007 'The McCartney Years' 3-disc DVD set, though, as with nearly all the videos on it, this has been cropped to 16:9 format. The 'McCartney' album reached No. 2 in the UK, and topped the charts in the USA.

00-03-71 – **'Top Of The Pops' Video (UK)** – *MISSING/LOST*

Another Day

Perhaps surprisingly, there was no official video or TV appearances to promote Paul McCartney's 1st solo single, credited to Paul and Linda McCartney, though the UK did at least have a video that was taped especially for the 04-03-71 edition of 'Top Of The Pops'. The song reached No. 17 in the UK charts, and topped the charts in the USA.

11-03-71 – **'Top Of The Pops' (UK)** – *PAN'S PEOPLE* – *MISSING/LOST*

Another Day

With Paul unavailable, this time 'Top Of The Pops' used their resident dance troupe, uncharacteristically dressed in office clothing and spending much of the time seated.

00-06-71 – **High Park, Campbeltown, Scotland (UK)**

Bip Bop / Hey Diddle

As well as shooting footage for 2 promo videos, on 05/06-06-71 Paul and Linda were filmed outdoors performing the above songs to Paul's guitar accompaniment.

00-06-71 – **Promo Video**

3 Legs

Taped in Campbeltown, Scotland, on 05/06-06-71, this is one of two videos made to promote 'Ram'. It was broadcast on 'Top Of The Pops' on 24-06-71, but isn't on any official DVD release. 'Ram' got to No. 1 in the UK and No. 2 in the USA. Extracted from the album in the USA was the chart-topping single 'Uncle Albert/Admiral Halsey', though the UK had the far less commercial 'The Back Seat Of My Car' instead, which stalled at No. 39.

00-06-71 – **Promo Video**

Heart Of The Country

Taped on the same dates and at the same location as '3 Legs', this was also broadcast on 'Top Of The Pops' on 24-06-71, and can be found on 'The McCartney Years'.

00-02-72 – **The I.C.A., London (UK)**

The Mess / Wildlife / Bip Bop / Blue Moon Of Kentucky / Seaside Woman / Give Ireland Back To The Irish / My Love / Lucille

In the summer of 1971, Paul and Linda recruited Denny Laine on guitar and Denny Sewell on drums, to form the band Wings, and record the album 'Wildlife'. Much decried by critics, the album did ok chart-wise, peaking at No. 11 in the UK and one place higher at No. 10 in the USA. Next, Paul wanted to take the band out on the road, so to bolster the line-up added ex-The Grease Band guitarist Henry McCullough. The above songs are from their first, filmed, rehearsals, though not all the listed songs currently circulate. Included is their controversial new single, 'Give Ireland Back To The Irish', which, despite being banned by the BBC, got to No. 16 in the UK, and No. 21 in the USA. Coincidentally, or perhaps not, John and Yoko wrote and recorded their similarly-themed 'The Luck Of The Irish' around the same time. Note, from now until the end of the '70s, Paul's record releases, TV performances and concerts would be credited 'Wings', 'Paul McCartney and Wings' or similar.

25-05-72 – 'Top Of The Pops' (UK) – *MISSING/LOST*

Mary Had A Little Lamb

From the sublime to the ridiculous, following the BBC ban of 'Give Ireland Back To The Irish', Paul came up with something that no-one could find offensive, with the possible exception of those who thought he was capable of so much better. Despite this, 'Mary Had A Little Lamb', got to No. 9 in the UK and No. 28 in the USA, and he even appeared on 'Top Of The Pops' for the first time since 1966, though sadly the footage is lost.

01-06-72 – 'Top Of The Pops' (UK) – *MISSING/LOST*

Mary Had A Little Lamb

This is a repeat of the 25-05-72 performance.

00-06-72 – **Promo Video #1**

Mary Had A Little Lamb

No less than 4 different videos were made for 'Mary Had A Little Lamb', all taped at London's BBC TV centre on 06-06-72. This first one features a farmyard set (complete with live chickens), as well as a live vocal, and was broadcast on 'Top Of The Pops' on 29-06-72. None of the videos are on 'The McCartney Years' DVD, probably because Paul quickly came to the conclusion that the record was an embarrassment, though perhaps not as quickly as most listeners.

00-06-72 – **Promo Video #2**

Mary Had A Little Lamb

This 2nd video features what can best be described as a 'psychedelic' background, and was broadcast in the USA on 'The Flip Wilson Show' on 12-10-72.

00-06-72 – **Promo Video #3**

Mary Had A Little Lamb

Now on an 'outdoors' studio set, this video also features animated scenes, and was broadcast in the UK on 'The Basil Brush Show' on 24-06-72.

00-06-72 – **Promo Video #4**

Mary Had A Little Lamb

For this 4th video, Paul plays piano while wearing a pointed wizard's hat and a red clown's nose. Only currently circulating in part, it is probable that it was never broadcast.

00-08-72 – **'The Bruce McMouse Show' (UK)**

Big Barn Bed / Eat At Home / Bip Bop / The Mess / Wild Life / Mary Had A Little Lamb / Blue Moon Of Kentucky / I Am Your Singer /

Seaside Woman / My Love / Maybe I'm Amazed / Hi, Hi, Hi / Long Tall Sally

Following a UK university tour from 09-02-72 to 23-02-72, from 09-07-72 until 24-08-72 Wings toured Europe. Some shows were filmed, for use in a short film called 'The Bruce McMouse Show', which mixed live footage with animation. Semi-forgotten for decades, in 2018 it was finally issued on DVD, as part of a deluxe (and expensive) 'Red Rose Speedway' reissue. While the animation is a little silly, the live footage is a revelation, with several surprises, including Linda singing 'Seaside Woman' years before it was released and an early, rather different, arrangement of 'My Love'.

00-12-72 – **Promo Video #1 (UK)**

Hi, Hi, Hi

Finally releasing a single that proved he could still rock, 'Hi, Hi, Hi' b/w the reggae-like 'C Moon' got to No. 5 in the UK and No. 10 in the USA. The video, taped on 25-11-72, features a live vocal, but this was replaced by the studio version for 'The McCartney Years'.

00-12-72 – **Promo Video (UK)**

C Moon

Taped on the same day as the A-side, 'C Moon' was broadcast with a live vocal on 'Top Of The Pops' on 04-01-73, and is, with the studio soundtrack, on 'The McCartney Years'.

00-03-73 – **Promo Video (UK)**

My Love

A simple studio performance with live vocals, this video is available in several slightly different edits, of which one of them, dubbed with the studio version, appears on 'The McCartney Years'. One of Paul's finest ballads, it got to No. 9 in the UK, but was a much deserved No. 1 in the USA. The album it is from, Red Rose Speedway', also did better in the USA, reaching No. 1 against the UK's No. 5.

05-04-73 – 'Top Of The Pops' (UK) – *MISSING/LOST*

My Love

This is another 'Top Of The Pops' performance that is missing in action.

16-04-73 – 'James Paul McCartney' (USA)

Big Barn Bed / Medley: Blackbird – Bluebird – Michelle – Heart Of The Country / Mary Had A Little Lamb / Medley: Little Woman Love – C Moon / My Love / Uncle Albert / Pub Sing-along Medley [Paul, Family and Friends] / Gotta Sing, Gotta Dance / Live and Let Die / Beatles Medley [sung by members of public] / The Mess / Maybe I'm Amazed / Long Tall Sally / Yesterday

Taped, sporadically, mostly at Elstree Studios from 19-02-73 to 01-04-73, this one-off TV special has much to commend it: The medley, featuring 'Blackbird' with 3 other songs, is performed solo by Paul, while Linda, at her most beautiful, photographs him; 'Mary Had A Little Lamb' is performed outdoors in the countryside, unlike the earlier promo videos that just pretend to be outside; 'My Love' and 'Live and Let Die' feature Wings backed by a full orchestra; 'Gotta Sing, Gotta Dance' is an extravagant Busby Berkeley-type number;

'Uncle Albert', though without the 'Admiral Halsey' part, features Paul as a boss in an office with Linda as his secretary, and would've made a great promo video; 'The Mess', 'Maybe I'm Amazed' and 'Long Tall Sally' (the latter replaced by 'Hi, Hi, Hi' for the 10-05-73 UK broadcast) is a fully live performance with an enthusiastic audience; and 'Yesterday', apparently a request from Denny Sewell, is performed over the closing credits. Some of Paul's critics may have sniped that this was all-round family entertainment, but it does show off his many abilities, and what's more he was no longer completely unwilling to perform Beatles songs again.

11-05-73 – **'Top Of The Pops' (UK)** – *MISSING/LOST*

My Love

This is a repeat of the 05-04-73 broadcast.

00-06-73 – **Promo Video**

Live and Let Die

The theme to the latest James Bond movie, 'Live and Let Die' got to No. 9 in the UK and No. 2 in the USA. This video is simply the opening of the movie but minus the credits, and was broadcast on 'Top Of The Pops' on 22-06-73.

Shortly after this, in August, both Henry McCullough and Denny Sewell quit, so, with a new album to record, Paul, Linda and Denny went to a primitive studio in Lagos, Nigeria, to record as a trio. Out of this adversity came Wings' and probably Paul's most acclaimed album.

00-11-73 – **Promo Video #1**

Helen Wheels

As well as being a fun song, the accompanying video is amongst one of Paul's most entertaining. Featuring the trio of Paul, Linda and Denny, and filmed indoors and outdoors with Paul playing both bass and drums, this was on 'Top Of The Pops' on 15-11-73, and is on 'The McCartney Years'. The single got to No. 12 in the UK and No. 10 in the USA.

08-11-73 – **'Top Of The Pops' (UK)** – *PAN'S PEOPLE* – **MISSING/LOST**

Helen Wheels

Instead of the promo video, Pan's People do another dance to represent the single.

19-12-73 – **'Lift Off With Ayshea' (UK)** – *MISSING/LOST*

Helen Wheels

A very popular show at the time, this was Paul's only appearance, but unfortunately it is lost.

00-12-73 – **Promo Video #1**

Band On The Run

Not only surviving but blossoming from band members departures, 'Band On The Run' is one of Paul's most impressive and enduring songs, and got to No. 3 in the UK and No. 1 in the USA. The partly animated video, little seen at the time, is on 'The McCartney Years'.

00-12-73 – **Promo Video**

Band On The Run Album Medley

This video features excerpts, with accompanying animation and scenes from the cover's photo-shoot, for 'Band On The Run', 'Nineteen Hundred and Eighty-Five', 'Mrs. Vandebilt', 'Bluebird' and a reprise of 'Band On The Run', and can be seen on 'The McCartney Years'. The album got to No. 1 in both the UK and USA.

00-03-74 – **Promo Video**

Jet

Unlike the excellent song, which got to No. 7 in both the UK and USA, this video is one of Paul's less interesting. It features photo stills with lyrics, all with a horrible blue tinge.

00-07-74 – **Promo Video**

Mamunia

As with 'Band On The Run', this is an animated video, and can be found on 'The McCartney Years'.

24-08-74 – **'The Backyard Tape' (UK)**

Blackpool / Peggy Sue / I'm Gonna Love You Too

Taped behind Abbey Road Studios, a longer audio circulates featuring the following: Blackbird (Takes 1-3) / Blackpool / Blackbird (Take 4) / Country Dreamer / Twenty Flight Rock / Peggy Sue / I'm Gonna Love You Too / Great Day (excerpt) / Sweet Little Sixteen / Loving You / We're Gonna Move (2 takes). It is probable that these songs were filmed too.

00-08-74 – **'One Hand Clapping' (UK)**

One Hand Clapping / Jet / Soily / Medley: C Moon - Little Woman Love / Billy Don't Be A Hero (part) / Maybe I'm Amazed / Drum Improvisation / My Love / Bluebird / Suicide / Medley: Let's Love – Sitting At The Piano / I'll Give You A Ring / Band On The Run / Live and Let Die / Nineteen Hundred and Eighty-Five / Baby Face

Taped in Abbey Road Studios, London, on 27/28/30-08-74 for a possible live-in-the-studio album and/or a TV special, 'One Hand Clapping' ended up being neither, and went unseen for decades. Featuring a new line-up of Wings comprised of Paul, Linda, Denny, guitarist Jimmy McCulloch, and drummer Geoff Britton, this is still worthwhile, despite the somewhat murky quality on even official releases. Perhaps the biggest surprise is 'I'll Give You A Ring', a song that didn't show up officially until the B-side of 'Take It Away' in 1982.

00-10-74 – **Promo Video**

Junior's Farm

With a video that was taped at Abbey Road Studios on 28-08-74 during the 'One Hand Clapping' filming, 'Junior's Farm' got to No. 16 in the UK and No. 3 in the USA.

21-11-74 – **'Top Of The Pops' (UK)**

Junior's Farm / Gonna Make You A Star [with David Essex]

Taped on 20-11-74, this excellent performance of 'Junior's Farm' not only survives, but is readily available on 'The McCartney Years'. Following their own performance, the band stick around long enough

to make a brief but amusing cameo on a performance with David Essex, who sings his No. 1 UK hit.

12-02-75 – **Sea Saint Studios, New Orleans (USA)**

My Carnival

From 16-01-75 to 24-02-75, Wings went to New Orleans to record their next album, 'Venus and Mars', though this did result in yet another line-up change when drummer Geoff Britton quit after recording just 2 songs, to be replaced by American Joe English. A film crew captured them recording 'My Carnival', though it would be 10 years before it was released, as a B-side for 'Spies Like Us' in 1985.

25-04-75 – **'The Midnight Special' (USA)** – ROD STEWART and THE FACES

Mine For Me

This was taped in the UK for US TV in The Odeon Theatre, Lewisham, on 27-11-74, and features Paul and Linda as special guests of Rod Stewart and his band. Written by Paul, 'Mine For Me' was issued as a US single by Rod Stewart (without The Faces), where it reached No. 91.

12-06-75 – **'Top Of The Pops' (UK)** – PAN'S PEOPLE

Listen To What The Man Said

With the band unavailable and no video, Pan's People dance to Wings' UK No. 6 and US No. 1 hit.

00-09-75 – **Promo Video**

Letting Go

'Letting Go', despite the quality of the song, is one of Paul's lesser hits, reaching No. 41 in the UK and No. 39 in the USA. The video was taped in Southampton's Gaumont Theatre on 09-09-75, the first night of a world tour that would last until 21-10-76, and would include the UK, Australia, Denmark, Germany, The Netherlands, France, the USA, Austria, Yugoslavia, Italy and then back to Germany and the UK.

12-09-75 – **Free Trade Hall, Manchester (UK)**

Letting Go

00-11-75 – **Promo Video**

Venus and Mars / Rockshow

Released as a US single, 'Venus and Mars'/'Rockshow' got to No. 12, while the 'Venus and Mars' album topped the charts in both the UK and USA. This video was taped during Wings' September 1975 UK dates.

10-11-75 – **The Festival Hall, Brisbane (Australia)**

Soily

13-11-75 – **Sydney Myer Music Bowl, Melbourne (Australia)**

Medley: Venus And Mars - Rockshow / Jet / Let Me Roll It / Spirits Of Ancient Egypt / Medley: Little Woman Love - C Moon / Maybe I'm Amazed / Lady Madonna / The Long and Winding Road / Live and Let Die / Picasso's Last Words (Drink To Me) / Richard Cory / Bluebird / I've Just Seen A Face / Blackbird / Yesterday / You Gave Me The

Answer / Magneto and Titanium Man / Go Now / Call Me Back Again / My Love / Listen To What The Man Said / Letting Go / Medicine Jar / Junior's Farm / Band On The Run / Hi, Hi, Hi / Soily

This is the only known surviving full length filmed performance from the 1975-1976 world tour (1976's 'Rockshow' is actually from several shows), and captures the band on fine form. The 'Little Woman Love' - 'C Moon' medley and 'Junior's Farm' would be dropped from the set-list in favour of some newer songs for the 1976 shows.

30-11-75 – **The Entertainment Centre, Perth** – *Sound-check* **(Australia)**

Yesterday (#1) / Blackbird / Yesterday (#2) / Magneto and Titanium Man

01-12-75 – **The Entertainment Centre, Perth** – *Sound-check* **(Australia)**

Yesterday

01-12-75 – **The Entertainment Centre, Perth (Australia)**

Hi, Hi, Hi

00-04-76 – **Promo Video**

Silly Love Songs

Featuring footage from Wings' 1975-1976 world tour, this is on 'The McCartney Years'. The single got to No. 2 in the UK and No. 1 in the USA, as did, coincidentally, the album the song is from, 'Wings At The Speed Of Sound'.

20-05-76 – **'Top Of The Pops' (UK)** – *RUBY FLIPPER*

Silly Love Songs

Instead of using the promo video, the short-lived and mixed gender 'Ruby Flipper' promotes the song for 'Top Of The Pops'.

01-06-76 – **Chicago (USA)**

Rockshow / Let Me Roll It

May/June 1976 – **'Rockshow' Movie (USA)**

Venus And Mars - Rock Show / Jet / Let Me Roll It / Spirits Of Ancient Egypt / Medicine Jar / Maybe I'm Amazed / Call Me Back Again / Lady Madonna / The Long and Winding Road / Live and Let Die / Picasso's Last Words (Drink To Me) / Richard Cory / Bluebird / I've Just Seen A Face / Blackbird / Yesterday / You Gave Me The Answer / Magneto and Titanium Man / Go Now / My Love / Listen To What The Man Said / Let 'Em In / Time To Hide / Silly Love Songs / Beware My Love / Letting Go / Band On The Run / Hi, Hi, Hi / Soily

Although not released until November 1980, this was taped in 1976, at 4 different US concerts: New York, 25-05-76, Seattle, 10-06-76, Los Angeles, 22-06-76, and Los Angeles, 23-06-76. The original 1980 movie and 1981 VHS release had 6 songs missing, with the full version finally released on DVD in 2013. Several incomplete clips from this plus other concerts were also shown in 'Wings Over The World', a 1975-1976 world tour documentary that was first shown in 1979. 'Band On The Run', 'Jet', 'Let 'Em In' and 'Listen To What The Man Said' from this have all been used as promo videos in later years, and

'Venus and Mars - Rockshow', 'Jet', 'Maybe I'm Amazed', 'Lady Madonna', 'Listen To What The Man Said' and 'Bluebird' are all on 'The McCartney Years' DVD set.

19-08-76 – **'Top Of The Pops' (UK)** – RUBY FLIPPER

Let 'Em In

With no video and no band, again 'Top Of The Pops' latest troupe dance to Paul McCartney and Wings' latest hit. 'Let 'Em In' got to No. 2 in the UK and No. 3 in the USA.

00-09-76 – **'Top Of The Pops' Video (UK)** – ***MISSING/LOST***

Let 'Em In

This was made especially for 'Top Of The Pops', broadcast on 02-09-76.

25-09-76 – **Piazza San Marco, Venice (Italy)**

Rockshow / Jet / Band On The Run

26-12-76 – **'Top Of The Pops' (UK)** – LEGS & Co.

Let 'Em In

Another performance by a dance troupe, though by this time Ruby Flipper had been replaced by Legs & Co...

00-02-77 – **Promo Video**

Maybe I'm Amazed

Compiled from still images, this video of one of Paul's greatest songs was released to promote the live single. It got to No. 28 in the UK and

No. 10 in the USA, while the triple-album it is taken from, 'Wings Over America', reached No. 8 in the UK and No. 1 in the USA. Unfortunately, later in the year, both Jimmy McCulloch and Joe English would quit, leaving the band as a trio once again.

00-04-77 – **Promo Video** – DENNY LAINE

Moondreams

Although the video doesn't feature Paul, he both played on the song and filmed the video.

00-11-77 – **Promo Video #1**

Mull Of Kintyre

'Mull Of Kintyre' topped the UK charts for an unprecedented 9 consecutive weeks, much to the bemusement of US fans, where the single's flipside, the up-tempo 'Girls' School', got the most airplay, and the single stalled at No. 33. There were 2 completely different videos, with this 1st one taped near Paul's Scottish farmhouse in Campbletown on 13-10-77. It was broadcast on 'Top Of The Pops' on 24-11-77, 01-12-77, 08-12-77, 15-12-77, 22-12-77, 05-01-78, and 26-01-78, shown in the USA on 'The Midnight Special' on 09-12-77, and is on 'The McCartney Years'

00-11-77 – **Promo Video #2**

Mull Of Kintyre

Often referred to as the 'misty' video, this was taped in Elstree Studios on 09-12-77. It was broadcast on 'Top Of The Pops' on 25-12-77, 19-01-78 and 25-12-78, and is also on 'The McCartney Years' (note, there was no 'Top Of The Pops' edition on 12-01-78 due to industrial action). Incidentally, this 2nd video almost became the 3rd, as Paul, Linda and Denny filmed another one on 02-12-77 while sitting around a garden patio table, but that version was scrapped.

25-12-77 – 'The Mike Yarwood Christmas Show' (UK)

Mull Of Kintyre

By late 1977, performances on TV were becoming much rarer, so Mike Yarwood got quite a scoop by getting them on his Christmas special while performing the biggest UK hit of all time. Paul, Linda and Denny mime while seated, and are eventually accompanied by the inevitable bagpipers.

14-01-78 – 'The South Bank Show' (UK)

Lucille (incomplete) / Mull Of Kintyre

Taped at Abbey Road Studios on 03/04-10-77, Paul can be seen, while playing drums, performing a short snippet of 'Lucille', before a lengthier clip of him laying down his vocal for 'Mull Of Kintyre'. The footage is from the very first edition of the long-running arts programme 'The South Bank Show'.

00-03-78 – **Promo Video**

With A Little Luck

Taped on 21-03-78, this features Paul, Linda, Denny and new drummer Steve Holly, miming in a studio while surrounded by a dancing crowd. The single reached No. 5 in the UK and No. 1 in the USA, while the video was shown on 'Top Of The Pops' on 06-04-78 and 20-04-78, and is also on 'The McCartney Years'. The parent album, 'London Town', got to No. 4 in the UK and No. 2 in the USA.

00-06-78 – **Promo Video**

I've Had Enough

Only a moderate hit at No. 42 in the UK and No. 25 in the USA, the video is available in two different edits, with the rarer one featuring some 4-way split-screen effects. Featuring the full, final, Wings line-up of Paul, Linda, Denny, Steve and new guitarist Laurence Juber, the video is on 'The McCartney Years'.

00-08-78 – **Promo Video**

London Town

Taped on 21-03-78 and featuring just the core trio of Paul, Linda and Denny, this simple but delightful video also includes a cameo by Victor Spinetti of A Hard Day's Night/Help!/Magical Mystery Tour fame. Only reaching No. 60 in the UK and No. 39 in the USA, the video can be seen on 'The McCartney Years', and in full un-cropped form too.

03-10-78 – **Abbey Road Studios, London (UK)**

Rockestra Theme / So Glad To See You Here

For 2 songs on the forthcoming 'Back To The Egg' album, Paul recruited a huge, all-star, band, whom he dubbed 'Rockestra'. Among the luminaries are Hank Marvin, Pete Townshend, Dave Gilmour, John Bonham, John Paul Jones, Ronnie Lane, Kenney Jones, Tony Ashton and Ray Cooper. Long unreleased, in 2001 the raw footage was compiled into a video for the song 'Rockestra' to coincide with the release of the 'Wingspan' album and DVD, while footage of the storming rocker 'So Glad To See You Here' circulates unofficially.

00-00-78 – **Promo Video** – LINDA McCARTNEY

The Oriental Nightfish

Although the somewhat scary and sexual animated video was made in 1978, the accompanying song wasn't issued until 1998's posthumous 'Wide Prairie' album. The video was featured, along with the 1980 'Seaside Woman' animation, as bonus features on an eighties VHS release of 'Rupert and The Frog Chorus', causing kids everywhere to have nightmares.

00-04-79 – **Promo Video**

Goodnight Tonight

Taped on 03-04-79, and featuring the band in both '20s and '70s clothing, this video is available in at least 4, similar, edits, with one of those broadcast on 'Top Of The Pops' on 19-04-79, as well as on 'The McCartney Years'. A No. 5 hit both sides of the ocean, this video and the next 7 listed ('Getting Closer', 'Baby's Request', 'Old Siam Sir', 'Winter Rose – Love Awake', 'Spin It On', 'Again and Again and Again' and 'Arrow Through Me') were also on a TV special entitled 'Back To The Egg', despite this particular song not being on the album. Oddly though, this TV special wasn't broadcast, in the UK, until 10-06-81, when Wings no longer even existed. 'Back To The Egg' (the album) got to No. 6 in the UK and No. 8 in the USA.

00-06-79 – **Promo Video**

Getting Closer

All of the 'Back To The Egg' TV special songs (with the exception of 'Goodnight Tonight') were taped in Kent and Sussex, from 28-05-79 to 06-06-79, with this one featuring the band in a van at night and in an aircraft hangar. 'Getting Closer' was released as a single, getting to No. 60 in the UK and No. 22 in the USA.

00-06-79 – **Promo Video**

Baby's Request

Miming on Camber Sands beach while dressed in WW2 military outfits, this is one of the best videos from the 'Back To The Egg' shoot. Paul must think so too, as, after long admitting he wasn't a fan of the album, he included this as the only 'Back To The Egg' video on 'The McCartney Years'. The video is also available with a sepia effect instead of the usual full colour, while Paul, unusually, re-cut the song for his 2012 'Kisses On The Bottom' project.

00-06-79 – **Promo Video**

Old Siam Sir

Filmed here inside Lympne Castle in Kent, 'Old Siam Sir' was a No. 35 hit single, though it deserved better.

00-06-79 – **Promo Video**

Winter Rose – Love Awake

The kind of gentle ballads that Paul can write in his sleep, these are filmed both in and outside Lympne Castle, including, for the 'Winter Rose' section, some rather convincing fake snow.

00-06-79 – **Promo Video**

Spin It On

Back in the aircraft hanger, the frantic new wave-influenced 'Spin It On' was a highlight of Paul's 1979 UK tour, where it was performed at an even frenetic pace.

00-06-79 – **Promo Video**

Again and Again and Again

Miming in a field full of yellow flowers, this song features Denny Laine singing lead vocals on what was one of the best songs on the album.

00-06-79 – **Promo Video**

Arrow Through Me

Another very modern sounding song for the time, 'Arrow Through Me' was a minor US hit at No. 29, and was also heard in the 1980 Chevy Chase comedy movie, 'Oh! Heavenly Dog'.

14-09-79 – **'The Buddy Holly Tribute Concert', Hammersmith Odeon (UK)**

Raining In My Heart [Performed by Denny Laine] / It's So Easy / Bo Diddley [with The Crickets, Don Everly and Albert Lee]

Paul McCartney had always been a big Buddy Holly fan of course, and that is never more evident than here, performing with his heroes.

Following this, from 23-11-79 to 17-12-79, Wings would tour the UK; it would turn out to be their final tour (though they'd add one special charity show on the 29-12-79), and Paul wouldn't tour again for another decade.

00-11-79 – **Promo Video**

Wonderful Christmas Time

Taped on 16-11-79, this video features all of the 1979 Wings line-up, despite the song actually being recorded by Paul solo. A No. 6 UK hit that stalled at No. 47 in the USA, the video was shown on 'Top Of The Pops' on 13-12-79, 03-01-80 and, 18 years later, on 25-12-07, and is also featured on 'The McCartney Years'

29-12-79 – **'The Concert For The People Of Kampuchea', Hammersmith Odeon (UK)**

Got To Get You Into My Life / Getting Closer (incomplete) / Every Night / Old Siam Sir (incomplete) / Hot As Sun / Arrow Through Me (incomplete) / Coming Up / Lucille / Let It Be / Rockestra Theme [The last 3 songs feature Pete Townshend, Gary Brooker, Robert Plant, John Paul Jones, John Bonham, Ronnie Lane, Kenney Jones, Dave Edmunds and others]

For this special charity concert, Wings, with arguably the best line-up they ever had, hit the stage for the last time. 'Got To Get You Into My Life', 'Every Night', 'Coming Up', 'Lucille', 'Let It Be' and 'Rockestra Theme' were broadcast on TV on UK TV on 04-01-81 (as well as released on the various artists charity album), while the other listed songs have escaped on various official and unofficial releases, but the full uncut show is many people's (including this author's) wish. If ever it is released, expect the following set-list: Got To Get You Into My Life / Getting Closer / Every Night / Again and Again and Again / I've Had Enough / No Words / Cook Of The House / Old Siam Sir / Maybe I'm Amazed / The Fool On The Hill / Hot As Sun / Spin It On / Twenty Flight Rock / Go Now / Arrow Through Me / Coming Up / Goodnight Tonight / Yesterday / Mull Of Kintyre / Band On The Run / Lucille / Let It Be / Rockestra Theme

Early 01-80 – **Japan Tour Rehearsals (UK)**

Eleanor Rigby / Got To Get You Into My Life (take 1) / With A Little Luck / Coming Up / Got To Get You Into My Life (take 2) / Got To Get You Into My Life (take 3)

Rehearsing in Paul's home at Lower Gate Farm, Peasmarsh, the band prepares for a scheduled tour of Japan, due to run from 21-01-80 to 02-02-80. The tour didn't happen, as, on arriving in the country on 16-01-80, customs found a large stash of marijuana in the McCartney's luggage. It could have led to a long time in prison, but, after spending 10 days in a cell, he was promptly deported without charge.

Following this incident, and the death of John Lennon later the same year, Paul lost interest in both touring and Wings, though Denny Laine would last long enough to feature on some of the early sessions for what would become the 'Tug Of War' album.

00-04-80 – **Promo Video**

Coming Up

Premiered on the 1979 Wings tour, when issued as a single it would be as a Paul McCartney solo recording (though a live Wings version was on the B-side), and would get to No. 2 in the UK and No. 1 in the USA, while the 'McCartney II' parent album would top the charts in the UK and get to No. 3 in the USA. However, it's the video that is most impressive. Taped in London's Ewart Studios on 26/27-03-80, Paul is filmed multiple times as different characters (while Linda also appears twice), which, through the marvels of technology, all share the stage together. Amongst the most memorable characters Paul plays are Hank Marvin from The Shadows (and not Buddy Holly, as many people assume), Ron Mael from Sparks, and, most convincingly of all, Paul McCartney from The Beatles, complete with Hofner violin and collarless jacket. The video was shown on 'Top Of The Pops' on 24-04-80 and 25-12-80, and is on 'The McCartney Years'.

00-06-80 – **Promo Video**

Waterfalls

This is another very clever video, featuring as it does Paul leaving his writing desk for a quick stroll around the garden, where he encounters fireworks, a fairground carousel and a polar bear, before returning to his desk... and all seemingly done in 1 take. The song too is excellent, one of his best ballads, which deservedly got to No. 9 in the UK, though it failed dismally at No. 106 in the USA. The video was shown on 'Top Of The Pops' on 09-07-80, and is on 'The McCartney Years'. The next single, the weird and wonderful 'Temporary Secretary', didn't have a video and nor was it a hit, though that didn't stop Paul from surprising everyone by performing it live, for the first time, at London's O2 Arena in 2015.

00-07-80 – **Promo Video #1** – LINDA McCARTNEY (as SUZY and THE RED STRIPES)

Seaside Woman

Although this animated video wasn't released until 1980, the song had been released as a single in 1977. It was a minor US hit too, peaking at No. 59.

00-02-82 – **'The Cooler' (UK)** – RINGO STARR

See the RINGO STARR section for more details!

00-03-82 – **Promo Video**

Ebony and Ivory [with Stevie Wonder]

Now flying without Wings, Paul was free to use whatever musicians he wanted, as well as giving himself more opportunities to record with famous friends (old and new) such as Carl Perkins, Michael Jackson, and Stevie Wonder, whom he duets with here. After such off the wall songs as 'Temporary Secretary' and 'Old Siam Sir', it was at first strange to hear Paul McCartney seemingly playing it safe with polished pop, but, that said, his early '80s period produced some of the classiest music of the era. 'Ebony and Ivory' is one such song, and it effortlessly topped the charts both sides of the Atlantic, as did the album 'Tug Of War'. The video, memorably featuring Paul and Stevie walking on a giant keyboard, was shown on 'Top Of The Pops' on 08-

04-82, 22-04-82, 29-04-82, 06-05-82 and 25-12-82, and is also on 'The McCartney Years'

00-03-82 – **Promo Video**

Ebony and Ivory [solo version]

This is basically the duet version with Paul doing all the vocals, and was used as a bonus track on the 12" single. The video features Paul playing piano in a darkened studio, occasionally joined by a black prisoner who is listening to the song on his Walkman. Not surprisingly, this was not on 'The McCartney Years'.

00-07-82 – **Promo Video**

Take It Away [with Ringo Starr]

A better video than 'Ebony and Ivory', this shows Paul with a band, both rehearsing and on stage, a band that includes Ringo Starr, George Martin and 10cc's Eric Stewart. Taped on 18/19/21/22/23-06-82, it was shown on 'Top Of The Pops' on 15-07-82 and 29-07-82, and is on 'The McCartney Years'. The single got to No. 15 in the UK and No. 10 in the USA.

00-10-82 – **Promo Video #1**

Tug Of War

One of Paul's most stunning ballads, this video, taped on 23/24-09-82 sees Paul and Linda singing in a plain photographic studio, interspersed with other scenes, and was used as the opening song of disc 1 on 'The McCartney Years'. Released as a single, it stalled at just

No. 53 in both the UK and the USA, probably because most people interested would've bought the album by now.

00-10-82 – **Promo Video #2**

Tug Of War

Not released at the time, this features Paul working in a recording studio.

00-10-82 – **Promo Video**

Here Today

One of the highlights not only of 'Tug Of War', but of Paul's whole career, is the song 'Here Today'. A sort of sadder follow-up to 'Yesterday', it was Paul's feelings about John put into words. Many years later, he regularly performed the song in concert, when it gained even more poignancy following the deaths of Linda and George. Taped on 23/24-09-82, the video features Paul in the recording studio, similar to the 2nd 'Tug Of War' video. Apparently this is an official MPL promo video, but if so, it is nothing special at all, and certainly doesn't do the song justice. Also circulating is a video comprised of still images of John, and while it's better than the above, it is unofficial, and was probably compiled by a TV station at the time.

11-11-82 – **'Top Of The Pops' (UK)** – ZOO

The Girl Is Mine [with Michael Jackson]

From the album 'Thriller', no video was made for this mediocre duet with Michael Jackson, so 'Top Of The Pops' latest (and final) troupe danced to it. The song got to No. 8 in the UK and No. 2 in the USA.

00-10-83 – **Promo Video** – *TRACEY ULLMAN*

They Don't Know

Paul makes a brief cameo in the video for Tracey Ullman's big hit, probably as a favour to her for appearing in the forthcoming 'Give My Regards To Broad Street' movie. The song got to No. 2 in the UK and No. 8 in the USA.

00-10-83 – **Promo Video**

Say Say Say [with Michael Jackson]

Taped on 04/05/06-10-83 in California, this elaborate video cost a whopping $500,000, and it shows. Getting to No. 2 in the UK and No. 1 in the USA, the video was debuted on 'The Late Late Breakfast Show' on 29-10-83, shown on 'Top Of The Pops' on 03-11-83 and 17-11-83, and is on 'The McCartney Years'. The album the song is taken from, 'Pipes Of Peace', was generally considered inferior to 'Tug Of War', reaching No. 4 in the UK but just No. 15 in the USA.

00-12-83 – **Promo Video**

Pipes Of Peace

One of Paul's best-loved videos, this was taped on Chobham Common in Surrey in early December, and recreates a famous Christmas Day 2014 truce between English and German soldiers. The video was shown on 'Top Of The Pops' on 22-12-83, 12-01-84 and 19-01-84, and is also on 'The McCartney Years'. Musically too, this was considered by most to be superior to the previous single, though, despite being a UK No. 1, it stalled at No. 23 in the USA.

00-12-83 – **Promo Video**

So Bad

A simple studio video, featuring Paul and Linda accompanied by Ringo Starr and Eric Stewart, it can be found, in original un-cropped form, on 'The McCartney Years'.

00-04-84 – **Promo Video** – BOB MARLEY

One Love

Paul makes a brief cameo in this video for Bob Marley's posthumous UK No. 5 hit.

09-06-84 – **'Aspel and Company' (UK)**

That'll Be The Day [with Tracey Ullman and Michael Aspel]

Taped on 07-06-84, the song is just a loose jam, performed following an interview.

00-09-84 – **Promo Video**

No More Lonely Nights [ballad version]

Largely taped on 10-04-84, and featuring scenes from the 'Give My Regards To Broad Street' movie, this fine ballad got to No. 2 in the UK and No. 6 in the USA. Premiered on MTV on 02-10-84, and shown on 'Top Of The Pops' on 04-10-84 and 18-10-84, the video is on 'The McCartney Years'.

00-09-84 – **Promo Video**

No More Lonely Nights [Playout Version]

During the closing credits for 'Give My Regards To Broad Street', a very different version of 'No More Lonely Nights' can be heard. The rarely screened video features Paul, Linda and Shalamar's Jeffrey Daniel, combined with archive footage of various dance scenes, including rare colour film from 'Ready, Steady, Go!'.

14-10-84 – 'The South Bank Show' (UK)

For No One

A documentary on the making of 'Give My Regards To Broad Street', the highlight was this acoustic run-through, which was taped in London's AIR Studios in December 1983.

25-10-84 – 'Give My Regards To Broad Street' movie (UK)

Yesterday / Here, There and Everywhere / Wanderlust / Ballroom Dancing / Silly Love Songs / Not Such A Bad Boy / So Bad / No Values / For No One / Eleanor Rigby / The Long and Winding Road / No More Lonely Nights / Yesterday (busking version)

Taped, sporadically, from November 1982 to July 1984, 'Give My Regards To Broad Street' is highly entertaining (this author prefers it to 'Magical Mystery Tour' and 'Let It Be'), despite the criticism at the time. Co-starring Ringo and Barbara, along with a host of other big names, it was also the first time that Paul had totally embraced his Beatle past, recording new versions of several songs, though at the time it was Ringo who was more reluctant, refusing to drum on any of the Beatles songs. The 'Give My Regards To Broad Street' sound-track album topped the charts in the UK, but only reached No. 21 in the USA.

00-11-84 – 'Rupert and The Frog Song' (UK)

We All Stand Together

Made throughout 1981 – 1983, 'Rupert and The Frog Song' is an animated short film, released to cinemas as a support feature to 'Give My Regards To Broad Street'. The song featured in this, 'We All Stand Together', is a children's song very much in the Disney tradition, though, as so often in the past ('Maxwell's Silver Hammer', 'Mary Had A Little Lamb', 'Mull Of Kintyre', etc), it did little for Paul's street-credibility.

00-11-84 – **Promo Video**

We All Stand Together

A different performance in both audio and video to the one in 'Rupert and The Frog Song', this animated video was shown on 'Top Of The Pops' on 06-12-84, 20-12-84 and 03-01-85. It got to No. 3 in the UK charts, but wasn't issued in the USA.

13-07-85 – 'Live Aid', Wembley Stadium, London (UK)

Let It Be [with David Bowie, Pete Townshend, Bob Geldof, Alison Moyet and others] / Do They Know It's Christmas {Finale, with entire all-star cast]

There had been big charity events before, and there have been plenty of more since, but none had quite the impact, financially and culturally, that 'Live Aid' did. Following storming performances by Queen, Status Quo, U2, David Bowie, The Who and others, Paul bravely took to the stage solo without a band. Unfortunately, his microphone failed, so no-one could hear his vocals, and, towards the end of the song, David Bowie, Pete Townshend, Alison Moyet and Bob Geldof joined the stage to give him some moral support (Paul later went into the studio to re-record his vocal, which is why it is audible on all subsequent broadcasts and official releases). As well as on the mammoth Live Aid box-set, Paul's performance can be seen on 'The McCartney Years'.

12-09-85 – **'Arena: Buddy Holly' (UK)**

Words Of Love

Later screened in the USA and released on VHS as 'The Real Buddy Holly Story', Paul can be seen strumming 'Words Of Love' in a barn, though the real highlight of this documentary was a partial airing of The Quarrymen's 'That'll Be The Day' demo, the first time this had been heard in public.

00-11-85 – **Promo Video**

Spies Like Us

Taped on 09/10-10-85, and with a song from the movie of the same name, the video was shown on 'Top Of The Pops' on 06-01-86. A UK No. 13 and US No. 7 hit, there are actually 2 different edits for the video: in the US version, actresses Vanessa Angel and Donna Dixon can briefly be seen miming to the backing vocals, but due to the still-antiquated UK miming rules, those scenes were edited from the UK version. It is this latter edit that is on 'The McCartney Years'.

19-06-86 – **Wembley Arena – *Rehearsals* (UK)**

I Saw Her Standing There / Long Tall Sally / Get Back (several takes of each song) [with Eric Clapton, Elton John, Tina Turner, Mark Knopfler, Phil Collins and others]

These rehearsals circulate unofficially.

20-06-86 – 'The Princes Trust Concert', Wembley Arena, London (UK)

I Saw Her Standing There / Long Tall Sally / Get Back [with Eric Clapton, Elton John, Tina Turner, Mark Knopfler, Phil Collins, Bryan Adams and others]

Spurred on by Live Aid (despite the microphone failure), Paul was gradually coming round to the idea of performing live again throughout the latter half of the '80s. Performing, for the first time since The Beatles, 'I Saw Her Standing There' and 'Get Back', as well as 'Long Tall Sally', Paul does a fine job, even though he strums an acoustic guitar instead of playing bass. This was broadcast on 28-06-86.

00-07-86 – **Promo Video**

Press

Taped on 16-06-86, the video sees Paul miming on the tube (London underground train), much to the obvious bemusement of many of the passengers, and was later included on 'The McCartney Years'. As with all the singles from the 'Press To Play' album, 'Press' was only moderately successful, reaching No. 25 in the UK and No. 21 in the USA, while the album got to No. 8 in the UK and No. 30 in the USA.

18-07-86 – **Abbey Road Studios (UK)**

Press

This was broadcast on 'Wogan' on 01-08-86, and, as an alternate edit, on 'McCartney' on 29-08-86.

00-11-86 – **Promo Video**

Pretty Little Head

Starting with a snippet of 'She's Leaving Home', and then showing a girl running away from home while Paul sings via a giant billboard, it's a case of 'nice video, shame about the song', and it isn't surprising that this only got to No. 76 in the UK charts. Taped on 18-10-86, the video is on 'The McCartney Years'.

00-11-86 – **Promo Video**

Stranglehold

Instead of 'Pretty Little Head', the USA had 'Stranglehold' as a single, not that it helped as this did even worse than the UK single at No. 81. Taped on 04-11-86, the so-so video features Paul with a band miming in a club.

29-11-86 – **'The Royal Variety Command Performance' (UK)**

Only Love Remains

Taped on 24-11-86, Paul performs, with a band, a nice version of his new single, not that it helped sales.

00-12-86 – **Promo Video**

Only Love Remains

Taped on 19-11-86, this features Paul with both band and orchestra in a simple studio set-up. The song is one of Paul's better songs from this period, and peaked at No. 34 in the UK charts.

12-12-86 – 'The Tube' (UK)

Only Love Remains / Whole Lotta Shakin' Goin' On (excerpt)

For this performance, taped on 11-12-86, Paul is joined by just Linda and Vicki Brown on backing vocals plus a saxophone player.

1986/1980 – **Promo Video #2** – LINDA McCARTNEY (as SUZY and THE RED STRIPES)

Seaside Woman

An updated remix of the earlier version, this features Linda singing and super-imposed over the original cartoon.

00-05-87 – **Promo Video** – FERRY AID

Let It Be

A charity record to aid the Zeebrugge ferry disaster fund, this remake of The Beatles' classic features Paul with Kate Bush, Boy George, Gary Moore, Mark Knopfler, Edwin Starr and a host of others. While not the greatest version you'll ever hear, the cause was good, and it topped the UK charts.

00-11-87 – **Promo Video**

Once Upon A Long Ago

A stand-alone single that wasn't made for any specific album (though it is on 'All The Best!'), this got to No. 10 in the UK charts, Paul's biggest hit in 3 years. Taped on 16/17-10-87 outdoors in Plymouth and combined with brief animation, the video, available in 2 similar edits, was shown on 'Top Of The Pops' on 03-12-87, and is on 'The McCartney Years'.

18-11-87 – 'Yoru No Hit Studio Deluxe' (Japan)

Once Upon A Long Ago

Taped in the UK for Japanese TV broadcast, this is the first of several TV appearances around the world to promote the new single, something that, after years of doing very little TV, would become far more common practice from now.

20-11-87 – 'Wogan' (UK)

Jet / Listen To What The Man Said

Taped the previous day, Paul and band perform, with live vocals, 2 Wings classics to promote the 'All The Best!' compilation.

24-11-87 – 'The Roxy' (UK)

Once Upon A Long Ago

This performance, set on a school pantomime stage, could be mistaken for an alternate promo video, and in some ways it suits the song better. It was taped on 17-11-87.

27-11-87 – 'The Last Resort' (UK)

Don't Get Around Much Anymore / I Saw Her Standing There / Lawdy

Miss Clawdy

Reportedly suffering writers block, Paul cut an album of rock 'n' roll classics in 1987, initially as an exclusive album for the Russian market. Eventually released world-wide as 'CHOBA B CCCP', it got to No. 63 in the UK and No. 109 in the USA. Here, playing electric guitar and ably backed by the show's house band Steve Nieve and The Playboys, Paul performs live versions of 2 songs from the album plus a Beatles classic.

02-12-87 – **'Countdown' (The Netherlands)**

Once Upon A Long Ago

This was taped on 30-11-87.

03-12-87 – **'Top Of The Pops' (UK)**

Once Upon A Long Ago

Taped on 02-12-87, this was Paul's first 'Top Of The Pops' performance since 1974.

05-12-87 – **'Le Telethon' (France)**

Once Upon A Long Ago

This was taped on 04-12-87.

12-12-87 – **'Going Live' (UK)**

Once Upon A Long Ago

20-12-87 – **'Wetten Dass' (Germany)**

Once Upon A Long Ago

23-12-87 – **'Sacrée Soirée' (France)**

Once Upon A Long Ago

This was taped on 04-12-87.

1987/1975/1976 – **Promo Video**

Live and Let Die

A re-issue promo video, made to help promote 'All The Best!' this features footage from 1975 and 1976 concerts.

27-02-88 – **'San Remo '88' (Italy)**

Once Upon A Long Ago / Listen To What The Man Said

00-09-88 – **Promo Video** – *THE CRICKETS*

T-Shirt

Paul produced, sang and played piano on this song, and also appears in the video.

00-02-89 – **Promo Video** – *ELVIS COSTELLO*

Veronica

Paul doesn't appear in this video, but he did co-write and play on the song. Getting to No. 31 in the UK, it reached No. 19 in the USA, where it was Elvis's biggest hit.

00-05-89 – **Promo Video**

My Brave Face

For 1989's 'Flowers In The Dirt' album, Paul made a dramatic return to form, also embracing his Beatles past more than ever, particularly on the jangly, harmony-led, 'My Brave Face'. Taped on 10/11-04-89, the video too harks back to the past, featuring a vague storyline about a fanatical Japanese Beatles fan, and including Beatles footage. A No. 18 UK and No. 25 US hit, the video was shown on 'Top Of The Pops' on 18-05-89, and is also on 'The McCartney Years'. The 'Flowers In The Dirt' album did well, at least in the UK where it topped the charts, though it only reached a disappointing No. 21 in the USA.

18-05-89 – 'Mensch Meier' (Germany)

Put It There

This is the first of many TV appearances to promote the new album, with this particular song eventually becoming a single. Featured here are Paul's new touring band, which, as well as Linda, features Hamish Stuart (guitars and bass), Robbie McIntosh (guitar), Paul 'Wix' Wickens (keyboards) and Chris Whitten (drums). This line-up would last until late 1990, and, with just one change, until the end of 1993.

19-05-89 – 'Wogan with Sue Lawley' (UK)

Figure Of Eight / My Brave Face

24-05-89 – 'Countdown' (The Netherlands)

My Brave Face

Taped on 22-05-89, an un-broadcast rehearsal of 'How Many People' also circulates.

31-05-89 – 'Sacrée Soirée' (France)

My Brave Face

This was taped on 24-05-89.

07-06-89 – 'Yoru No Hit Studio Deluxe' (Japan)

This One / My Brave Face

This was taped in Twickenham Film Studios, London, for Japanese TV.

09-06-89 – 'Fuera De Serie' (Spain)

My Brave Face

This was taped on 07-05-89 in Twickenham Film Studios, London, for Spanish TV.

10-06-89 – 'Put It There' (UK)

C Moon / My Brave Face / Rough Ride / Figure Of Eight / Things We Said Today / I Saw Her Standing There / The Long And Winding Road / How Many People / That Day Is Done / This One / Put It There / Hello Goodbye / Twenty Flight Rock / Just Because / Summertime / Lucille / Ain't That A Shame / Distractions / Party Party / Let It Be

Taped from February to April 1989, this shows the band performing and rehearsing in the studio, though some songs listed above are incomplete. It was broadcast in the USA on 11-11-89, and a longer edit was released on VHS, and, eventually, DVD.

13-06-89 – 'La Luna' (Spain)

My Brave Face / We Got Married / This One

Taped on 08-06-89, also circulating is an un-broadcast performance

of 'Distractions'.

16-06-89 – 'Avis de Recherché' (France)

My Brave Face

This was taped on 24-05-89.

16-06-89 – 'St. Vincent Estate' (Italy)

This One / My Brave Face

This was taped on 15-06-89.

27-06-89 – The Playhouse Theatre, London (UK)

Coming Up / This One

Paul and the band did 2 London warm up gigs for 'The Paul McCartney World Tour' on 26/27-06-89 and another one in New York on 24-08-89, then, from 26-09-89 to 29-07-90, they performed in Norway, Sweden, Germany, France, Italy, Switzerland, The Netherlands, the USA, Canada, the UK, Japan and Brazil.

00-07-89 – Promo Video #1

This One

This is one of the few instances when 2, entirely different, videos were made to promote a new single. This 1st version was taped on 23/24-06-89, and features Paul and the band sitting cross-legged in very '60s clothing and with painted eyes on their eyelids. All very effective, but Paul wasn't entirely happy with it, and made a 2nd video... which makes this version's appearance (only) on 'The McCartney Years' all *the more odd. The single got to No. 18 in the UK, but stalled at a disastrous No.94 in the USA.*

00-07-89 – **Promo Video #2**

This One

Taped in early July 1989, this 2nd video sees Paul and band wearing bowler hats and filmed in a jerky stop-motion fashion. Impressive enough, but most people would prefer the 1st version.

03-08-89 – **'Top Of The Pops' (UK)**

This One

This was taped on 25-07-89.

24-08-89 – **The Lyceum Theatre, New York (USA)**

Medley: Blue Suede Shoes - Matchbox / Figure Of Eight / This One / Coming Up

These songs are from the pre-show press conference, not the warm-up gig later this evening.

26-09-89 – **Drammenshallen, Drammen (Norway)**

Figure Of Eight

03-10-89 – **Sporthalle, Hamburg (Germany)**

Figure Of Eight

00-11-89 – **Promo Video #1**

Figure Of Eight

A No. 42 UK hit and a No. 92 US hit, the video was taped in the Hallenstadion, Zurich, on 29/30-10-89, and is on 'The McCartney Years'.

00-11-89 – **Promo Video**

Ou Est Le Soleil?

An awful song, the video, taped on 14-07-89 and featuring Paul and Linda super-imposed over simple videogame graphics, isn't much better.

00-11-89 – **Promo Video**

Party Party

This is another lesser song, with a video featuring messy and fast-moving animation.

05-11-89 – **Hall Tony Garnier, Lyon (France)**

Figure Of Eight

10-11-89 – **The Ahoy, Rotterdam (The Netherlands)**

Figure Of Eight

00-02-90 – **Promo Video #1**

Put It There

A rather good acoustic song that was a No. 32 UK hit, this video, taped on 22-01-90, features Paul alone singing and playing, interspersed with scenes of a father and son. It is on 'The McCartney Years'.

00-02-90 – **Promo Video #2**

Put It There

This video is similar to the 1st video, though features just footage of Paul, with no father and sons scenes.

07-03-90 – **The Dome, Tokyo (Japan)**

Figure Of Eight / Jet / Got To Get You Into My Life / Rough Ride / Band On The Run / We Got Married / Let 'Em In / The Long and Winding Road / The Fool On The Hill / Sgt. Pepper's Lonely Hearts Club Band / Good Day Sunshine / Can't Buy Me Love / Put It There / Things We Said Today / Eleanor Rigby / This One / My Brave Face / Back In The U.S.S.R. / I Saw Her Standing There / Coming Up / Let It Be / Ain't That A Shame / Live and Let Die / Hey Jude / Yesterday / Get Back / Medley: Golden Slumbers - Carry That Weight - The End

Following the disappointment of the cancelled 1980 tour, the 6 gigs Paul performed in Japan were particularly welcomed. From these shows onwards, 'Let 'Em In' was added, replacing 'Maybe I'm Amazed' from the earlier gigs.

20-04-90 – **Maracana Stadium, Rio De Janeiro (Brazil)**

Figure Of Eight / Jet / Got To Get You Into My Life / Rough Ride / Band On The Run / We Got Married / Let 'Em In / The Long and Winding Road / The Fool On The Hill / Sgt. Pepper's Lonely Hearts Club Band / Can't Buy Me Love / Put It There / Things We Said Today / Eleanor Rigby / This One / My Brave Face / Back In The U.S.S.R. / I Saw Her Standing There / Coming Up / Let It Be / Ain't That A Shame /

Live and Let Die / Hey Jude / Yesterday / P.S. Love Me Do / Get Back / Medley: Golden Slumbers - Carry That Weight - The End

21-04-90 – **Maracana Stadium, Rio De Janeiro –** *Sound-check* **(Brazil)**

Jam / Matchbox / C Moon / Leaning On A Lamp Post

Paul often did (and still does) unusual songs during sound-checks and a few of these later appeared on the 'Tripping the Live Fantastic' album.

21-04-90 – **Maracana Stadium, Rio De Janeiro (Brazil)**

Figure Of Eight / Jet / Got To Get You Into My Life / Rough Ride / Band On The Run / We Got Married / Let 'Em In / The Long and Winding Road / The Fool On The Hill / Sgt. Pepper's Lonely Hearts Club Band / Good Day Sunshine / Can't Buy Me Love / Put It There / Things We Said Today / Eleanor Rigby / This One / My Brave Face / Back In The U.S.S.R. / I Saw Her Standing There / Coming Up / Let It Be / Ain't That A Shame / Live and Let Die / Hey Jude / Yesterday / P.S. Love Me Do / Get Back / Medley: Golden Slumbers - Carry That Weight - The End

'P.S. Love Me Do', an ill-advised modernised update of 'Love Me Do' and 'P.S. I Love You', was broadcast in 'Lennon: A Tribute', on 05-05-90.

23-06-90 – **The SECC Arena, Glasgow (UK)**

Mull Of Kintyre (incomplete)

This is the only time the song was performed on the tour, and was featured in the 'From Rio To Liverpool' documentary, broadcast in the

UK on 17-12-90.

28-06-90 – **The King's Dock, Liverpool (UK)**

Medley: Strawberry Fields Forever – Help! – Give Peace A Chance

For Paul's first Liverpool show in 11 years, he did something very special indeed! Again, this was in the 'From Rio To Liverpool' documentary, broadcast in the UK on 17-12-90. Also circulating is around 20 minutes of 'raw' footage from this show.

30-06-90 – **The Silver Clef Award Winners Charity Concert, Knebworth Park (UK)**

Coming Up / Birthday / Hey Jude / Can't Buy Me Love

This was broadcast in the USA on 14-07-90 and in the UK on 06-08-90, while this version of 'Birthday' was later released as a single.

29-07-90 – **Soldier Field, Chicago (USA)**

Got To Get You Into My Life

1989 – 1990 – **'Get Back' (various locations)**

Band On The Run / Got To Get You Into My Life / Rough Ride / The Long and Winding Road / The Fool On The Hill / Sgt. Pepper's Lonely Hearts Club Band / Good Day Sunshine / I Saw Her Standing There / Put It There / Eleanor Rigby / Back In The U.S.S.R. / This One / Can't Buy Me Love / Coming Up / Let It Be / Live and Let Die / Hey Jude / Yesterday / Get Back / Golden Slumbers - Carry That Weight - The End / Birthday (The last song features audio only, over closing credits)

This tour movie, released in October 1991, was directed by none other than Dick Lester, the director of 'A Hard Day's Night' and 'Help!'.

04-09-90 – 'Buddy Holly Week', The Lone Star Cafe, New York (USA)

Rave On / Lucille / Oh Boy [with The Crickets, Dion DiMucci and Dave Edmunds]

00-10-90 – Promo Video #1

Birthday

To promote the 'Tripping The Live Fantastic' album, a series of live videos were issued (all the songs below up to and including 'Get Back'), every one of them different from the performances that are in the 'Get Back' movie. Also released was this live remake of The Beatles' classic. A UK No. 29 hit, this first video features intercut scenes of a birthday party, and was shown on 'Top Of The Pops' on 25-10-90, as well as included on 'The McCartney Years'. 'Tripping The Live Fantastic' got to No. 17 in the UK and No. 26 in the USA.

00-10-90 – Promo Video #2

Birthday

This video features no birthday party scenes but is otherwise similar to the 1st version.

00-11-89 – Promo Video #2

Figure Of Eight

00-11-90 – Promo Video

We Got Married

This video was taped on stage in Inglewood, USA, on 27-11-89.

00-11-90 – **Promo Video**

The Long and Winding Road

This video was taped in Rio De Janeiro, Brazil, on 21-04-90.

00-11-90 – **Promo Video**

I Saw Her Standing There

00-11-90 – **Promo Video**

Sgt. Pepper's Lonely Hearts Club Band

00-11-90 – **Promo Video**

Band On The Run

00-11-90 – **Promo Video**

Get Back

00-12-90 – **Promo Video #1**

All My Trials

A rather dreary version of the old standard, 'All My Trials' was a non-US single which reached No. 35 in the UK charts. This video consists of scenes of poverty, and features no footage of Paul and the band. It can be found on 'The McCartney Years' DVD.

00-12-90 – **Promo Video #2**

All My Trials

This 2nd version features the poverty scenes intercut with footage of the band miming the song, taped at Thames Water Pumping Station, London, on 16-11-90.

14-12-90 – **'Wogan' (UK)**

All My Trials

By this time, drummer Chris Whitten had left to join Dire Straits, with Blair Cunningham replacing him. The line-up of Hamish, Robbie, Wix and Blair would remain with Paul and Linda until the end of 1993.

20-12-90 – **'Countdown' (The Netherlands)**

All My Trials / The Long and Winding Road / Let It Be

This was taped in Limehouse Studios, London, on 13-12-90.

22-12-90 – **'Fantastico' (Italy)**

The Long and Winding Road / Let It Be

This was taped in Limehouse Studios, London, on 13-12-90.

24-12-90 – **'Rock O Pop' (Spain)**

All My Trials / Let It Be

This was taped in Limehouse Studios, London, on 13-12-90.

30-01-91 – **'Beat UK' (Japan)**

All My Trials

This was taped in Limehouse Studios, London, on 13-12-90.

03-04-91 – **'MTV Unplugged' (UK)**

Be-Bop-A-Lula / I Lost My Little Girl / Here, There and Everywhere / Blue Moon Of Kentucky / We Can Work It Out / I've Just Seen A Face / Every Night / She's A Woman / And I Love Her / That Would Be Something / Blackbird / Good Rockin' Tonight / Singing The Blues / Singalong Junk

In the '90s, there was a bit of a craze for rock acts to perform intimate, stripped-back, acoustic concerts, a format that suited Paul more than most. Taped on 25-01-91 he took the opportunity to dig out songs from throughout his career, including one of the first songs he ever wrote, 'I Lost My Little Girl', and a couple of songs from 'McCartney'. Also performed, but not broadcast were 'Mean Woman Blues', 'Matchbox', 'The Midnight Special, 'San Francisco Bay Blues', 'The Fool', 'Things We Said Today', 'Hi-Heel Sneakers' and 'Ain't No Sunshine', with the complete uncut show circulating unofficially. The soundtrack was issued as the album 'Unplugged (The Official Bootleg)', a No. 7 UK and No. 14 USA hit, while 'I Lost My Little Girl', 'Every Night', 'And I Love Her' and 'That Would Be Something' are all on 'The McCartney Years'.

28-06-91 – 'Paul McCartney's Liverpool Oratorio', The Anglican Cathedral, Liverpool (UK)

I War / II School / III Crypt / IV Father / V Wedding / VI Work / VII Crises / VIII Peace

Paul's first, of several, dabbles with classical music, 'Paul McCartney's Liverpool Oratorio' didn't chart in the UK, and peaked at just No. 177 in the USA.

07-06-91 – **Cornwall Coliseum, St. Austell (UK)**

We Can Work It Out

To promote the 'Unplugged (The Official Bootleg)' album, Paul and band did a series of 6 'secret' shows in the UK (3 shows), Spain, Italy and Denmark. There was supposed to also be a gig in France, but this was cancelled due to the death of Linda's father.

00-12-92 – **Promo Video**

Hope Of Deliverance

Taped at night in Ashdown Forest, Sussex, on 24-11-92 (with additional filming in London's Black Island Studios on 26-11-92) and available in 2 differing edits, the video for this No. 18 UK and No. 83 USA hit is on 'The McCartney Years'. The album it is from, 'Off The Ground', is full of tour-friendly songs, and got to No. 5 in the UK and No. 17 in the USA.

00-01-93 – **Promo Video**

Deliverance

A manic, almost instrumental, remix of 'Hope Of Deliverance', the frantic and fast-moving video doesn't feature Paul.

01-01-93 – **'A Carlton New Year' (UK)**

Hope Of Deliverance / Michelle / Biker Like An Icon

This was taped in The Mean Fiddler, London, on 20-11-92.

07-01-93 – **'Top Of The Pops' (UK)**

Hope Of Deliverance

23-01-93 – 'Wetten Dass' (Germany)

Hope Of Deliverance

This was taped on 21-01-93.

03-02-93 – 'Up Close' (USA)

Twenty Flight Rock / Get Out Of My Way / Fixing A Hole / Looking For Changes / Penny Lane / Biker Like An Icon / Michelle / Hope Of Deliverance / I Wanna Be Your Man / Off The Ground / Sgt. Pepper's Lonely Hearts Club Band / My Love / Lady Madonna

This great performance was taped over 2 nights in The Ed Sullivan Theatre, New York, on 10-12-92 and 11-12-92. Also performed on 10-12-93 but not broadcast were 'I Owe It All To You', 'Big Boys Bickering', 'Can't Buy Me Love', 'Peace In The Neighbourhood', 'C Moon', 'C'mon People', and 'Live and Let Die'. The complete uncut 10-12-92 show circulates unofficially. Shortly after this, Paul would begin 'The New World Tour', which lasted from 18-02-93 to 16-12-93, and featured shows in Italy, Germany, Australia, New Zealand, the USA, Canada, Austria, the UK, Sweden, Norway, The Netherlands, France, Belgium, Spain, Japan, Mexico, Brazil, Argentina and Chile.

00-02-93 – Promo Video

Big Boys Bickering

This is taken from 'Up Close', with added footage of people and animals suffering.

00-02-93 – **Promo Video**

C'mon People

Taped on 16/18-11-92, the video for this No. 41 UK hit cleverly features everyone else speeded up, while Paul performs the song at normal speed on piano, and is on 'The McCartney Years'.

11-02-93 – **'Saturday Night Live' Rehearsals (USA)**

Jam #1 / Blue Suede Shoes / Jam #2 / Twenty Flight Rock / Get Out Of My Way (take 1) / Get Out Of My Way (take 2) / Biker Like An Icon (take 1) / Linda Lu / Biker Like An Icon (take 2)

13-02-93 – **'Saturday Night Live' (USA)**

Biker Like An Icon / Get Out Of My Way / Hey Jude

18-02-93 – **'Top Of The Pops' (UK)**

C'mon People

This was taped on 17-02-93.

13-03-93 – **The Oval, Adelaide (Australia)**

Drive My Car / Coming Up

00-04-93 – **Promo Video**

Get Out Of My Way

This was taped on 12-01-93, and is a straight performance video.

00-04-93 – **Promo Video #1**

Biker Like An Icon

Confusingly, there are at least 4, quite different, videos for this excellent song. Version #1 features a storyline of a girl running away to join her biker boyfriend, and features no actual footage of Paul. This is the one selected for 'The McCartney Years'.

00-04-93 – **Promo Video #2**

Biker Like An Icon

Version #2 is (mostly) a straight studio mimed performance, and was taped on 12-01-93, at the same session as the 'Get Out Of My Way' video.

00-04-93 – **Promo Video #3**

Biker Like An Icon

Version #3 features the storyline video, but with Paul's performance from 12-01-93 super-imposed on the right of the screen (even more confusingly, this particular video is available with both the studio recording as a soundtrack, and with the 'Paul Is Live' concert audio).

00-04-93 – **Promo Video #4**

Biker Like An Icon

Version #4 has a 3-way split screen, with the girl running away storyline in the middle, Paul on the right, and other band members on the left.

00-04-93 – **Promo Video**

Off The Ground

Taped in early December 1992, amusingly, this features Paul literally 'off the ground', flying through the air, while Linda and the rest of the band look out of a window at him, eventually all coming off the ground too. The video is on 'The McCartney Years'.

16-04-93 – **The Earth Day Concert, The Hollywood Bowl, Hollywood (USA)**

Hope Of Deliverance [with k.d. lang] / Hey Jude (incomplete) [includes Ringo Starr]

A special concert to enhance environmental awareness, with a couple of rather special guests.

27-04-93 – **Backstage, The Liberty Bowl Memorial Stadium, Memphis (USA)**

My Old Friend / Maybelline / Lend Me Your Comb / Matchbox / Blue Suede Shoes / The World Is Waiting For The Sunrise [all songs are with Carl Perkins]

Prior to his Memphis concert, Paul took the time to jam and reminisce with Carl Perkins, a performer that every one of The Beatles loved.

21-05-93 – **Winnipeg Stadium, Winnipeg (Canada)**

All My Loving / Mull Of Kintyre

02-06-93 – **Milwaukee County Stadium, Milwaukee (USA)**

Drive My Car

15-06-93 – **The Blockbuster Pavilion, Charlotte, North Carolina**

(USA)

Drive My Car / Looking For Changes / Another Day / All My Loving / Let Me Roll It / Peace In The Neighbourhood / Off The Ground / Can't Buy Me Love / Robbie's Bit (Thanks Chet) / Good Rockin' Tonight / We Can Work It Out / Every Night / Hope Of Deliverance / Michelle / Biker Like An Icon / Yesterday / My Love / Lady Madonna / Live and Let Die / Let It Be / Magical Mystery Tour / C'mon People / The Long and Winding Road / Paperback Writer / Penny Lane / Sgt. Pepper's Lonely Hearts Club Band / Band On The Run / I Saw Her Standing There / Hey Jude

This was broadcast live on US TV, though several songs weren't shown due to commercial breaks. It was later broadcast, in more complete form, in the UK on 13-11-93.

14-11-93 – **The Dome, Tokyo –** *Sound-check* **(Japan)**

Just Because / Bring It On Home To Me / Every Night / C Moon / The Long and Winding Road

14-11-93 – **The Dome, Tokyo (Japan)**

Let Me Roll It

15-11-93 – **The Dome, Tokyo –** *Sound-check* **(Japan)**

Matchbox / No Other Baby / Good Rockin' Tonight / Be Bop A Lula / The Midnight Special / Don't Let The Sun Catch You Crying / Ain't That A Shame / Get Out Of My Way / Linda Lou / Twenty Flight Rock

The biggest surprise of this sound-check is 'No Other Baby', a song Paul was to issue as a single 6 years later.

15-11-93 – **The Dome, Tokyo (Japan)**

Drive My Car / Coming Up / All My Loving / Let Me Roll It / Off The Ground / Can't Buy Me Love / Good Rockin' Tonight / We Can Work It Out / Hope Of Deliverance / Biker Like An Icon / Yesterday / Lady Madonna / Magical Mystery Tour / Let It Be / Live and Let Die / Paperback Writer / Back In The U.S.S.R. / Sgt. Pepper's Lonely Hearts Club Band / Band On The Run / I Saw Her Standing There / Hey Jude

25-11-93 – **Foro Sol, Mexico City (Mexico)**

Drive My Car / Looking For Changes

03-12-93 –**Morumbi Stadium, Sao Paulo (Brazil)**

Peace In The Neighbourhood / Off The Ground

11-12-93 – **River Plate Stadium, Buenos Aires (Argentina)**

C'mon People

16-12-93 – **Nacional Stadium, Santiago (Chile)**

Drive My Car / C'mon People / Live and Let Die (incomplete)

1993 – **'Paul Is Live In Concert On The New World Tour' (various locations)**

Drive My Car / Let Me Roll It / Looking For Changes / Peace In The Neighbourhood / All My Loving / Good Rocking Tonight / We Can Work It Out / Hope Of Deliverance / Michelle / Biker Like An Icon / Here, There and Everywhere / Magical Mystery Tour / C'Mon People / Lady Madonna / Paperback Writer / Penny Lane

/ Live and Let Die / Kansas City / Let It Be / Yesterday / Hey Jude

Released in March 1994, a highlight is 'Kansas City', performed as a one-off in the place of the same name on 31-05-93 (The Beatles did exactly the same thing when they played in Kansas City 29 years earlier!). The album from this tour, 'Paul Is Live', got to a disappointing No. 34 in the UK and No. 78 in the USA.

00-02-94 – **Promo Video** – *R.A.A.D.D.*

Drive My Car [with Ringo Starr]

Standing for 'Recording Artists Against Drink-Driving', this awareness video includes Ringo Starr, Julian Lennon, David Crosby, Graham Nash, Phil Collins and many others, and was first broadcast on 'The American Music Awards' on 07-02-94.

23-06-94 – **Friar Park, Henley-on-Thames (UK)** – *THE THREETLES*

Raunchy / Thinking Of Linking / Blue Moon Of Kentucky / I Will / Dehra Dun / Ain't She Sweet [with George Harrison and Ringo Starr]

For the 1995 'Anthology' project, Paul, George and Ringo got together at George's home (both indoors and out in the garden) to jam on a few numbers. Not all of the day's filming has been released, but what little has been seen is magical indeed.

16-10-95 – **The Royal Albert Hall, London (UK)**

Ballad Of The Skeletons [with Allen Ginsburg]

Paul played guitar on this performance, just as he did on the studio version.

00-12-95 – **Promo Video** – *THE SMOKIN' MOJO FILTERS*

Come Together

Taped in Abbey Road Studios, London, on 04-09-95, this No. 19 charity record for 'War Child' features a one-off super-group that also includes Paul Weller, Noel Gallagher and Steve Craddock.

00-10-96 – **Promo Video** – *ALLEN GINSBURG*

Ballad Of The Skeletons

Although Paul doesn't appear in the actual video, he does play several instruments on the song.

00-04-97 – **Promo Video #1**

Young Boy

Paul deliberately avoided any major solo releases during The Beatles 'Anthology' period, so 1997's 'Flaming Pie' was his first album in 4 years. 'Young Boy', the first single from the album in the UK, peaked at No. 19, but the album did far better, just missing the top of the charts at No. 2 in both the UK and USA. This first video sees Paul recording the song and driving around outside.

00-04-97 – **Promo Video #2**

Young Boy

This 2nd video features Paul performing the song while playing acoustic guitar, superimposed over footage of a surfer.

00-05-97 – **Promo Video #1**

The World Tonight

A No. 23 UK hit and No. 64 US hit, this 1ˢᵗ video features Paul walking around at night with a ghetto blaster on his shoulder.

00-05-97 – **Promo Video #2**

The World Tonight

Version #2 features Paul with a huge yellow umbrella.

00-05-97 – **Promo Video #3**

The World Tonight

Version #3 features scenes from the movie 'Father's Day', starring Billy Crystal and Robin Williams, along with footage from the other Paul videos plus outtakes.

16-05-97 – **'In The World Tonight' (UK)**

Somedays / Flaming Pie / The World Tonight / Heaven On Sunday / Little Willow / Young Boy / The World Tonight / Calico Skies / Great Day / Beautiful Night

This documentary on the making of the 'Flaming Pie' album includes footage of Paul performing/recording some of the songs, which are generally different from the various promo videos. A highlight is a lengthy sequence featuring Ringo drumming and singing with Paul on 'Beautiful Night', complete with George Martin assisting and Linda singing, poignantly, knowing what wasn't far away, looking healthy and happy. This was broadcast in the USA by VH-1 on 16-05-97 and in the UK 2 days later. When it was later issued on VHS (and eventually on DVD), 'Bishopsgate' was added, see the entry below.

17-05-97 – 'Paul McCartney's Town Hall Meeting', Bishopsgate Memorial Hall, London (UK)

Bishopsgate

During a lengthy interview, Paul improvised this new song, and it can be found on the 'In The World Tonight' DVD.

27-06-97 – 'T.F.I. Friday' (UK)

Flaming Pie / Young Boy

One of only 2 TV performances to promote 'Flaming Pie', for this live performance, Paul is backed, rather cleverly, by several other pre-taped Paul McCartney's, where he/they play a variety of instruments via TV monitors.

15-09-97 – 'Music For Montserrat' (UK)

Yesterday / Medley: Golden Slumbers – Carry That Weight – The End / Hey Jude / Kansas City [with Carl Perkins, Eric Clapton, Mark Knopfler, Elton John, Phil Collins, Sting, Jools Holland and others]

Introduced by George Martin, for this charity performance, Paul is backed, extremely well, by an all-star band. Broadcast on 16-09-97, and later released on DVD, this turned out to be one of Carl Perkins' last major performances.

14-10-97 – 'Standing Stone', The Royal Albert Hall, London (UK)

Movement I – After Heavy Light Years: "Fire/Rain" Allegro energico – "Cell Growth" Semplice – "'Human' Theme" Maestoso / Movement II

– He Awoke Startled: "Meditation" Contemplativo – "Crystal Ship" Con moto scherzando – "Sea Voyage" Pulsating, with cool jazz feel – "Lost at Sea" Sognando – "Release" Allegro con spirito / Movement III – Subtle Colours Merged Soft Contours: "Safe Haven/Standing Stone" Pastorale con moto – "Peaceful Moment" Andante tranquillo – "Messenger" Energico – "Lament" Lamentoso – "Trance" Misterioso – "Eclipse" Eroico / Movement IV – Strings Pluck, Horns Blow, Drums Beat: "Glory Tales" Trionfale – "Fugal Celebration" L'istesso tempo Fresco – "Rustic Dance" Rustico – "Love Duet" Andante intimo – "Celebration" Andante – 6:15

'Standing Stone' was another classical album, and another chart flop.

24-11-97 – 'Oprah' (USA)

Young Boy / Flaming Pie

Impressed by playing via TV monitors on 'T.F.I. Friday', Paul repeated the trick on 'Oprah'. Taped on 20-11-97, this was his only US TV appearance to, belatedly, promote 'Flaming Pie'.

00-12-97 – **Promo Video**

Little Willow

The 'Flaming Pie' videos up until now had all been a little amateurish-looking (indeed, there were similar 'home made' videos featured in the 'In The World Tonight' documentary), and didn't really do the generally high quality songs justice. The video for this beautiful ballad actually looks like some money has been spent on it, featuring, as well as shots of Paul performing the song, a moving storyline of a young mother who becomes ill and dies. It was inspired by Ringo's ex-wife Maureen Starkey, who died of cancer in 1994, but by this time Paul's own wife Linda was fighting her own battles. The video is on 'The McCartney Years'

00-12-97 – **Promo Video**

Beautiful Night [with Ringo Starr]

Following the kind of classic piano-led ballad that Paul could've written at almost any time in the previous 25 years, the song breaks into an unexpectedly fast coda, and becomes, effectively, a duet between Paul and Ringo, who also appears in the video. The Paul/Ringo studio segments were taped in Hogs Hill Mill, Icklesham, on 13/14-05-96, while the location scenes were taped on 27-10-97. The video for this No. 25 UK hit is on 'The McCartney Years'.

00-00-97 – **'Tropic Island Hum' (UK)**

Tropic Island Hum

A catchy Disney-like song, in the same vein but superior to 'We All Stand Together', and featuring the voices of both Paul and Linda, 'Tropic Island Hum' was released as a cartoon short for cinematic release in 1997, though it wasn't released as a single until 2004, when it got to No. 21 in the UK charts.

01-03-98 – **'Christopher Reeve: A Celebration Of Hope' (USA)**

Calico Skies

Paul was shown on tape playing this acoustic number from 'Flaming Pie', presumably pre-taped at some unknown date in the UK.

Linda McCartney died on 17-04-98.

18-04-98 – **'Happy Birthday Spike' (UK)**

Medley: Yesterday – The Ying Tong Song

This was pre-taped from Paul's home on an earlier, unknown, date.

00-06-98 – **Promo Video** – *RINGO STARR*

La De Da

See the RINGO STARR section for more details!

00-11-98 – **Promo Video** – *LINDA McCARTNEY*

Wide Prairie

Following Linda's death, Paul released the album 'Wide Prairie' by her, and although she wasn't the greatest of singers, her quirky songs and unique style make one wish she'd released more in her lifetime. Seen here in an animated video, 'Wide Prairie' (the single), was recorded as far back as 1973/1974, and got to No. 74 in the UK charts.

00-11-98 – **Promo Video** – *LINDA McCARTNEY*

The Light Comes From Within

'The Light Comes From Within' was recorded by Linda on 18-03-98, just a month before her death, and when released as a No. 56 UK hit single it was accompanied by this animated video.

00-11-98 – **Promo Video** – *LINDA McCARTNEY*

The White Coated Man

A more serious song than most of her recordings, 'A White Coated Man' is about vivisection. The video (featuring a white coated woman), only circulates in incomplete form, as does the next song.

00-11-98 – **Promo Video** – *LINDA McCARTNEY*

Shadow Cycle

Heard in another (incomplete) animated film, this song is an instrumental.

00-11-98 – **Promo Video** – *LINDA McCARTNEY*

Appaloosa Love

Not released until 1998, the song actually dates from 10 years earlier, as does the video of Linda riding horses.

15-03-99 – **'The 14th Annual Rock and Roll Hall of Fame Induction Ceremony' The Waldorf-Astoria, New York (USA)**

Blue Suede Shoes / What'd I Say / Let It Be [with Eric Clapton, Robbie Robertson, Bonnie Raitt, Billy Joel, Dion, Bruce Springsteen, Bono and others]

Paul kept a low profile for almost a year after Linda's death, finally returning to perform for the 'Rock and Roll Hall of Fame' ceremony, where he was also inducted as a solo performer. Unusually not playing any instruments, he is ably backed by an all-star band, and clearly enjoys himself. Incidentally, joining Paul for his induction speech is his daughter Stella, who wears a T-shirt with the slogan 'About fucking time!', though this is censored on all the telecasts and news reports.

18-04-99 – 'Here, There and Everywhere: A Concert for Linda' (UK)

Lonesome Town / All My Loving [with Elvis Costello, The Pretenders, Tom Jones, Neil Finn, George Michael, Sinead O'Connor and others]

Taped on 10-04-99 in London's Royal Albert Hall, this tribute concert for Linda McCartney featured a variety of performers and well-wishers. Naturally closing the show, he first performed a moving version of Ricky Nelson's 'Lonesome Town', then, joined by other performers on the show, played 'All My Loving' and 'Let It Be', though the latter wasn't included in the TV broadcast.

07-09-99 – 'Buddy Holly Week', Roseland Ballroom, New York (USA)

Rave On [with The Crickets]

18-09-99 – 'The P.E.T.A. Concert For Party Animals', Paramount Studios, Los Angeles – Rehearsal (USA)

Honey Hush / Brown-Eyed Handsome Man / No Other Baby / Try Not To Cry / Lonesome Town / Run Devil Run

18-09-99 – 'The P.E.T.A. Concert For Party Animals', Paramount Studios, Los Angeles (USA)

Honey Hush / Brown-Eyed Handsome Man / No Other Baby / Try Not To Cry / Lonesome Town / Run Devil Run

As a preview for the forthcoming 'Run Devil Run' album, Paul played a

storming set at this charity concert for animal welfare, of which a full length rehearsal also circulates. For this concert and the majority of future promotions for the album, Paul is joined by David Gilmour (guitar), Mick Green (guitar), Ian Paice (drums) and Pete Wingfield (keyboards).

16-10-99 – **'Working Classical', The Philharmonic Hall, Liverpool (UK)**

Opening / Junk / A Leaf / Haymakers / Midwife / Spiral / Warm and Beautiful / My Love / Maybe I'm Amazed / Calico Skies / Golden Earth Girl / Somedays / Tuesday / She's My Baby / The Lovely Linda

'Working Classical' was Paul's latest classical music album, though it didn't chart.

00-11-99 – **Promo Video**

No Other Baby

An old song that he had probably learned via The Vipers' 1958 recording, Paul had never sounded more committed and soulful than here. In a video that was taped on 12/13-10-99, he is seen rowing a boat in rough sea, and this can be found on 'The McCartney Years'. A UK No. 42 hit, the parent album of mostly '50s revivals, 'Run Devil Run', reached No. 12 in the UK and No. 27 in the USA.

00-11-99 – **Promo Video**

Brown-Eyed Handsome Man

The B-side to 'No Other Baby', this version of the Chuck Berry/Buddy Holly classic is given a terrific Cajun update. The video, taped on 22/23-10-99, features a diverse group of people line dancing, interspersed with shots of Paul performing the song, and is on 'The McCartney Years'.

06-11-99 – 'Later… With Jools Holland' (UK)

Honey Hush / No Other Baby / Brown-Eyed Handsome Man / Party

This was taped on 02-11-99.

13-11-99 – 'Red Alert With The National Lottery' (UK)

Brown-Eyed Handsome Man / No Other Baby / Party [with Lulu]

One of the UK's greatest singers, Lulu is the perfect duet partner for 'Party'.

20-11-99 – 'The Apocalypse Tube' (UK)

Brown-Eyed Handsome Man / No Other Baby / Honey Hush / Party [with Fran Healy] (2 versions) / Lonesome Town

03-12-99 – 'Parkinson' (UK)

Honey Hush / Twenty Flight Rock / When The Wind Is Blowing (Mary's Song) / Yesterday / The Long and Winding Road / Your Loving Flame / Mist Over Central Park (Cabaret Song) / Suicide / All Shook Up

Taped on 02-11-99, this includes 'Your Loving Flame', a song that wouldn't be released until 2 years later on 'Driving Rain'. Rehearsals for all songs except 'Suicide' also circulate.

11-12-99 – 'Wetten Dass' (Germany)

No Other Baby

14-12-99 – **The Cavern, Liverpool (UK)**

Honey Hush / Blue Jean Bop / Brown Eyed Handsome Man / Fabulous / What It Is / Lonesome Town / Twenty Flight Rock / No Other Baby / Try Not To Cry / Shake A Hand / All Shook Up / I Saw Her Standing There / Party

Performing in The Cavern for the first time since 1963, Paul and his hot band play most of the songs from 'Run Devil Run', as well as 'Twenty Flight Rock' and 'I Saw Her Standing There'. A fun and exciting performance, this was broadcast in slightly edited form in the UK the next day, and later issued, complete, on DVD.

00-12-99 – **Promo Video** – HEATHER MILLS

Vo!ce

Basically featuring Paul singing and playing while Heather, his new girlfriend, talks over an electronic dance track, this was a minor UK hit at No. 87. Paul also appears in the hard-to-find video.

1999/1973 – **Promo Video #2**

Helen Wheels

Otherwise similar to the 1973 video, the 1999 version has added special effects in the background.

1999/1973 – **Promo Video #2**

Band On The Run

A new video to promote the CD re-issue of the 'Band On The Run' album.

00-05-01 – 'Wingspan' (UK)

Medley: Picasso's Last Words (Drink To Me) – Let Me Roll It – Mrs. Vandebilt

Paul performs this medley to his beautiful daughter Heather as part of the 'Wingspan' documentary on the Wings era.

00-10-01 – Promo Video

From A Lover To A Friend

In a video that was taped on 21-09-01, Paul is seen in a recording studio performing his first single from the much-derided 'Driving Rain' album. The single scraped to No. 45 in the UK, and the album reached just No. 46 in the UK and No. 26 in the USA, disastrous for an album of new material. The video is available in 2 different edits, though none are on 'The McCartney Years' DVD set, and neither are any other songs from this album. Many of 'Driving Rain's songs are inspired by his relationship with Heather Mills, so it is probable that Paul would rather just forget them.

20-10-01 – 'The Concert For New York City', Madison Square Garden, New York (USA)

I'm Down / Yesterday / Freedom / Let It Be / Freedom (Reprise) [with Pete Townshend, Roger Daltrey, Eric Clapton, James Taylor, Sheryl Crow, Jon Bon Jovi and others]

Introduced by Jim Carrey, Paul performs a naturally powerful set at this charity concert to honour the victims of the 9/11 terrorist attack, with the new song 'Freedom' being particularly impassioned.

Curiously, 'Yesterday' is performed by Paul without a guitar, while backed by a string section.

21-10-01 – **The Hudson Hotel, New York (USA)**

I Saw Her Standing There [with Dan Ackroyd, Jim Carrey and Sheryl Crow]

Part of a jam session, this song was caught on film.

00-11-01 – **Promo Video**

Freedom

This video features Paul in a recording studio, intercut with clips of him performing the song at 'The Concert For New York'. Memorably dubbed by Ian Hislop on 'Have I Got News For You' as 'Give War A Chance', the song was Paul's reaction to 9/11, though he expressed misgivings over the song later. The video was shown on 'Top Of The Pops' on 23-11-01, but didn't chart in the UK, and only reached No. 97 in the USA.

00-11-01 – **Promo Video**

Driving Rain

Featuring a mixture of live and off-stage footage, this video was only available via a secret website, found when buying the 'Back In The U.S.' DVD, and the audio soundtrack is Paul's demo for the song.

24-11-01 – **'CD: UK' (UK)**

Freedom

This is notable for being the only UK TV performance of 'Freedom'.

29-11-01 – **'Good Rockin' Tonight: The Legacy Of Sun Records' (USA)**

That's All Right Mama

Taped in Sear Sound Studio, New York, on 09-03-00, Paul is backed by Scotty Moore and DJ Fontana, the legendary guitarist and drummer for Elvis Presley.

15-12-01 – **'Wetten Dass' (Germany)**

Freedom

Paul performs an acoustic solo version of his latest single.

16-12-01 – **'The Nobel Peace Prize Concert' (Norway)**

Your Loving Flame / Freedom / Let It Be [with Anastacia, Morten Harket, Wyclef Jean and Natalie Imbruglia]

This was taped in Oslo on 11-12-01.

2001/1970 – **Promo Video #2**

Maybe I'm Amazed

An unnecessary new video, featuring footage similar to the '3 Legs' and 'Heart Of The Country' videos, this was made to promote the 'Wingspan' compilation.

2001/1972/1976 – **Promo Video #2 (UK)**

Hi, Hi, Hi

This new video features a combination of the 1972 video and live footage from 'Rockshow', along with other clips.

2001/1979 – **Promo Video**

Rockestra Theme

Filmed in late 1978 for the 1979 'Back To The Egg' album, a video was finally assembled in 2001. See the 03-10-78 entry for more details.

03-02-02 – **'Super Bowl XXXVI' (USA)**

Freedom

00-03-02 – **Promo Video #1**

Lonely Road (Nu Nu)

One of Paul's more interesting videos from 'Driving Rain', this features Paul driving through a desert in an open-top sports car.

00-03-02 – **Promo Video #2**

Lonely Road (Nu Nu)

Another video filmed in a recording studio.

24-03-02 – **'The 74th Annual Academy Awards' (USA)**

Vanilla Sky

'Vanilla Sky' was featured in the strange movie of the same name, and would be a classic if it wasn't for the fact that it largely repeats the melody and chords of 'Biker Like An Icon'.

00-05-02 – **Promo Video #1**

Your Loving Flame

A weird video, this sees Paul walking backwards through a strange long tunnel, and then floating through the air.

00-05-02 – **Promo Video #2**

Your Loving Flame

This is yet another recording studio video. Incidentally, short clips of 2 other songs in the studio, 'She's Giving Up Talking' and 'Magic', circulate. It is probable that full length versions exist in Paul's vaults, but don't hold your breath waiting for him to release them.

03-05-02 – **'The Tonight Show With Jay Leno' (USA)**

Let It Be

This was taped on 02-05-02.

April-May 2002 – **'Back In The U.S.', 2002 (USA)**

Hello Goodbye / Jet / All My Loving / Live and Let Die / Coming Up / Blackbird / We Can Work It Out / Here, There and Everywhere / Eleanor Rigby / Matchbox / Your Loving Flame / Fool On The Hill / Getting Better / Here Today / Something / Band On The Run / Let Me Roll It / Back In The U.S.S.R. / My Love / Maybe I'm Amazed / Freedom / Let It Be / Hey Jude / Can't Buy Me Love / Lady Madonna / The Long and Winding Road / Yesterday / Medley: Sgt. Pepper's Lonely Hearts Club Band (Reprise) - The End / I Saw Her Standing There / Driving Rain / Every Night / Medley: You Never Give Me Your Money - Carry That Weight / Bring It To Jerome (Sound-check) / The Midnight Special (Sound-check) / San Francisco Bay (Sound-check) (The last 6 songs are DVD bonus tracks)

In the spring of 2002, Paul went back on tour for the first time in 9 years, and with him were Rusty Anderson (guitar), Brian Ray (guitar, bass), Abe Laboriel Jr. (drums), and, returning from the 1989-1993 era, Paul 'Wix' Wickens (keyboards). Although no-one would've guessed it, this same line-up is still backing Paul 17 years later at time of writing (spring of 2019), which is almost as long as The Beatles and Wings together! Entitled 'The Driving Rain Tour', they played in the USA (plus one show in Canada) from 01-04-02 to 18-05-02. Later in the year would come 'The Back In The U.S. Tour' from 21-09-02 to 29-10-02, 'Driving Mexico' from 02-11-02 to 05-11-02, and 'Driving Japan' from 11-11-02 to 18-11-02. From these tours came the above 'Back In The U.S.' DVD, and a US No. 8 hit album, also called 'Back In The U.S.'.

09-05-02 – **Reunion Arena, Dallas (USA)**

Mother Nature's Son

This outtake from the DVD tapings circulates unofficially.

03-06-02 – **'Party At The Palace' (UK)**

Her Majesty / Blackbird / While My Guitar Gently Weeps / Sgt. Pepper's Lonely Hearts Club Band / All You Need Is Love / Hey Jude [the last 2 songs are grand finales, with Eric Clapton, Rod Stewart, Brian Wilson, Elton John, Joe Cocker, Cliff Richard, Tom Jones, Brian May, Roger Taylor and others]

To commemorate 50 years of her majesty Queen Elizabeth II being on the throne, a special star studded concert was broadcast from the grounds of Buckingham Palace in London. Paul's performance featured several surprises, including a song he'd (sort of) written for The Queen 33 years earlier, a tribute to George, and a superb 'All You Need Is Love'.

29-11-02 – 'Concert For George', The Royal Albert Hall, London (UK)

For You Blue / Something / All Things Must Pass / While My Guitar Gently Weeps [lead vocals by Eric Clapton] / My Sweet Lord [lead vocals by Billy Preston] / Wah Wah [lead vocals by Eric Clapton and Jeff Lynne] [all listed songs are with Ringo Starr, Eric Clapton, Dhani Harrison, Billy Preston, Jeff Lynne and others]

Although this was a concert to celebrate the life of George Harrison, who died exactly 1 year previously, it was a surprisingly upbeat affair, just the way George would've liked it. It is still moving to hear Paul play great versions of 'For You Blue', 'Something', and, in particular, 'All Things Must Pass'. Even George, the most cynical Beatle, would've been impressed.

16-12-02 – 'The Secret Website Show' (USA)

You Never Give Me Your Money / Waiting For Your Train / Honey Hush / Foxy Lady / Blackbird / Calico Skies / Honey Don't / Celebration (instrumental) / Welcome (Instrumental Jam) / India / Lady Madonna

Taped at the sound-check in The Arena, New Orleans, on 12-10-02, this performance could be accessed by those who bought the interactive 'Back In The U.S.' DVD. 'India' is a song that Paul wrote in 1968, in (where else?) India.

19-03-03 – **Tour Rehearsals, London Docklands Arena (UK)**

Back In The U.S.S.R. / Hello Goodbye / Birthday / My Love / Let 'Em In / Let It Be / Let Me Roll It

'Back In The U.S.S.R.' was broadcast by MSN on the same day, while the remaining titles were broadcast on the same internet channel on 25-03-03.

24-05-03 – **Red Square, Moscow, 24th May 2003 (Russia)**

Hello Goodbye / Jet / All My Loving / Getting Better / Medley: Let Me Roll It - Foxy Lady / Lonely Road / Your Loving Flame / Blackbird / Every Night / We Can Work It Out / Medley: You Never Give Me Your Money - Carry That Weight / The Fool On The Hill / Here Today / Something / Eleanor Rigby / Here, There and Everywhere / I've Just Seen A Face / Calico Skies / Two Of Us / Michelle / Band On The Run / Back In The U.S.S.R. / Maybe I'm Amazed / Let'Em In / My Love / She's Leaving Home / Can't Buy Me Love / Birthday / Live and Let Die / Let It Be / Hey Jude / The Long and Winding Road / Lady Madonna / I Saw Her Standing There / Yesterday / Back in the U.S.S.R. (Reprise) / Sgt. Pepper's Lonely Hearts Club Band (Reprise) / The End

From 25-03-03 to 01-06-03, Paul and his band did the 'Back In The World' tour, encompassing shows in France, Spain, Belgium, the UK, The Netherlands, Germany, Denmark, Sweden, Italy, Austria, Hungary, Russia and Ireland. The tour was not without problems though, as at some point, owing to Paul's sore throat, he dropped the hard to sing 'Coming Up', 'Driving Rain' and 'Maybe I'm Amazed', replacing them with the vocally gentler 'Things We Said Today', 'I've

Just Seen a Face' and 'Two of Us'. Paul's first time in Russia, the show in Red Square was partially released on DVD, but the full show circulates in unofficial circles. From this tour came the 'Back In The World Live' album, a UK No. 5 hit.

22-10-03 – **Abbey Road Studios, London (UK)**

Whole Life [with Dave Stewart]

This song was recorded for the '46664' AIDS charity, set up in honour of Nelson Mandela.

28-05-04 – **Parque De Bela Vista, Lisbon (Portugal)**

Get Back / She's A Woman / Live and Let Die

This was broadcast on 30-05-04.

30-05-04 –**La Peineta Stadium, Madrid (Spain)**

Jet / Got To Get You Into My Life / Flaming Pie / All My Loving / Medley: Let Me Roll It - Foxy Lady / You Won't See Me / She's A Woman / Maybe I'm Amazed / The Long and Winding Road / In Spite Of All The Danger / Blackbird / We Can Work It Out / Here Today / All Things Must Pass / Yellow Submarine / I'll Follow The Sun / For No One / Calico Skies / I've Just Seen A Face / Eleanor Rigby / Drive My Car / Penny Lane / Get Back / Band On The Run / Back In The U.S.S.R. / Live and Let Die / I've Got A Feeling / Madrid / Lady Madonna / Hey Jude / Yesterday / Let It Be / I Saw Her Standing There / Helter Skelter / Medley: Sgt. Pepper's Lonely Hearts Club Band (Reprise) - The End

From 25-05-04 to 26-06-04, came the '2004 Summer Tour', with shows in Spain, Portugal, Switzerland, Germany, The Czech Republic,

Denmark, Norway, Finland, Russia, France and the UK. This tour is represented on video by at least 3 full uncut shows, of which this is the earliest.

20-06-04 – **Palace Square, St. Petersburg –** *Sound-check* **(Russia)**

Jam / Coming Up (with Peter Gunn Theme) / Honey Don't / Matchbox / Jam / Celebration / Medley: C Moon – Celebration / The Midnight Special / San Francisco Bay Blues / Follow Me / Weather Jam / Lady Madonna / Rain Dance, Sun Dance Jam

20-06-04 – **Palace Square, St. Petersburg (Russia)**

Jet / Got To Get You Into My Life / Flaming Pie / All My Loving / Medley: Let Me Roll It - Foxy Lady / You Won't See Me / She's A Woman / Maybe I'm Amazed / The Long and Winding Road / In Spite Of All The Danger / Blackbird / We Can Work It Out / Here Today / All Things Must Pass / I'll Follow The Sun / For No One / Calico Skies / I've Just Seen A Face / Eleanor Rigby / Drive My Car / Penny Lane / Get Back / Band On The Run / Back In The U.S.S.R. / Live and Let Die / I've Got A Feeling / St. Petersburg / Lady Madonna / Hey Jude / Yesterday / Let It Be / I Saw Her Standing There / Helter Skelter / Medley: Sgt. Pepper's Lonely Hearts Club Band (Reprise) - The End

Highlights of this show, along with parts of the 2004 Red Square show, were issued on DVD, but again the full show circulates unofficially, as does the sound-check.

26-06-04 – **Worthy Farm, Glastonbury (UK)**

Jet / Got To Get You Into My Life / Flaming Pie / All My Loving / Let Me Roll It / She's A Woman / Maybe I'm Amazed / The Long and Winding Road / In Spite Of All The Danger / Blackbird / We Can Work It Out / Here Today / All Things Must Pass / Yellow Submarine / I'll Follow the Sun / Calico Skies / Eleanor Rigby / Drive My Car / Penny Lane / Get Back / Band on the Run / Back In The U.S.S.R. / Live and Let Die / I've Got A Feeling / Lady Madonna / Hey Jude / Yesterday / Follow Me / Let It Be / I Saw Her Standing There / Helter Skelter / Medley: Sgt. Pepper's Lonely Hearts Club Band - The End

Paul's first time at this famous festival, 12 songs were broadcast on TV (of which 11 are on 'The McCartney Years'), and the complete show is available unofficially.

00-12-04 – **Promo Video** – BAND AID 20

Do They Know It's Christmas

Paul never got to sing on the original 1984 Band Aid recording, but he got another chance 20 years later. Taped in Mayfair Studios, London, on 12-11-04, the record topped the UK charts.

06-02-05 – **'Super Bowl XXXIX' (USA)**

Drive My Car / Get Back / Live and Let Die / Hey Jude

This performance, Paul's 2nd for the Super Bowl, is on 'The McCartney Years'.

02-07-05 – **'Live 8', Hyde Park, London (UK)**

Sgt. Pepper's Lonely Hearts Club Band [with U2] / Get Back / Drive My Car [with George Michael] / Helter Skelter / Medley: The Long and

Winding Road - Hey Jude [grand finale, with many others]

A benefit concert to commemorate the 20th anniversary of 'Live Aid', this is a superb performance by Paul, who really did steal the show. 'Sgt Pepper's Lonely Hearts Club Band' is performed at the beginning of the show by U2, with Paul as a special guest, while, uniquely, 'The Long and Winding Road' segues into the 'Na Na Na Na' chorus of 'Hey Jude', for which many other performers join the stage, including George Michael, Annie Lennox, Mariah Carey, Bob Geldof, Midge Ure, Pete Townshend, David Gilmour and UB40. 'Sgt. Pepper's Lonely Hearts Club Band' from this concert was issued as a single, getting to No. 27 in the UK and No. 48 in the USA.

00-08-05 – **Promo Video**

Fine Line

After the poor reception to 'Driving Rain', it almost seemed that Paul had given up recording to concentrate on being a live nostalgia act, but in 2005 he released 'Chaos and Creation In The Backyard', which turned out to be a real return to form. 'Fine Line' features Paul performing the song in a studio, largely with a lined drawing effect. Released as a single, the song got to No. 20 in the UK charts, while the album reached No. 10 in the UK and No. 6 in the USA. The 'Fine Line' video is on 'The McCartney Years' DVD set, the only post-'90s promo video there.

10-09-05 – **'ReAct Now' (USA)**

Fine Line

12-09-05 – 'Chaos At Abbey Road' (UK)

Friends To Go / In Spite Of All The Danger / Twenty Flight Rock / How Kind Of You / Band On The Run / Lady Madonna / English Tea / Heartbreak Hotel / Jenny Wren / I've Got A Feeling / Blackbird

Taped in Abbey Road Studios on 28-07-05, this features several songs performed by Paul solo, without a band. Also available is a documentary, 'Between Chaos and Creation', that includes in-studio excerpts of several songs from the 'Chaos and Creation In The Backyard' album.

27-10-05 – Wells Fargo Arena, Des Moines (USA)

Magical Mystery Tour / Flaming Pie (2nd song is incomplete)

Autumn 2005 – 'The Space Within Us', 2005 (USA)

Magical Mystery Tour / Flaming Pie / Let Me Roll It / Drive My Car / Till There Was You / I'll Get You / Eleanor Rigby / Maybe I'm Amazed / Got To Get You Into My Life / Fine Line / I Will / I'll Follow The Sun / Good Day Sunshine / For No One / Hey Jude / Fixing A Hole / Penny Lane / Medley: Too Many People - She Came in Through the Bathroom Window / Let It Be / English Tea / I've Got A Feeling / Follow Me / Jenny Wren / Helter Skelter / Yesterday / Get Back / Please Please Me / Whole Lotta Shakin' Goin' On (Sound-check) / Friends To Go (Sound-check) / How Kind Of You (Sound-check)

This DVD release, taped from several shows, is from 'The 'US' Tour', which ran from 16-09-05 to 30-11-05, and also included a show in Toronto, Canada. A fine performance indeed, though it's a shame that

a couple of the new songs were only played at sound-checks.

07-11-05 – 'AOL Music Sessions' (USA)

English Tea / Fine Line / Follow Me / Friends To Go / Let It Be / The Long and Winding Road

This was taped during tour rehearsals at The Hit Factory, Miami, on 15-09-05.

14-11-05 – 'The Ellen DeGeneres Show' (USA)

Fine Line / English Tea / Get Back

This was taped on 10-11-05.

15-11-05 – 'The Ellen DeGeneres Show' (USA)

Drive My Car

This was taped on 10-11-05, the same day as the previous show's performance.

21-11-05 – 'Artist Confidential' (USA)

Fine Line

This was taped in the XM Performance Theatre, Washington DC, in early November 2005.

00-11-05 – **Promo Video**

Jenny Wren

An acoustic song with similarities to 'Blackbird', the video for this No. 22 UK hit was taped on 28-07-05, the same day as the live 'Chaos At

Abbey Road' show, though the difference is that this performance is mimed.

08-02-06 – 'The 48th Annual Grammy Awards' (USA)

Fine Line / Helter Skelter / Yesterday [with Jay-Z and Chester Bennington]

'Yesterday' is a truly dreadful hip hop update, and although the late Chester Bennington sings well, Jay Z's spoken lyric seems to just consist of 'Aha', 'Yo' and 'Right'.

00-09-06 – 'Duets: An American Classic' (UK)

The Very Thought Of You [with Tony Bennett]

Taped in Abbey Road Studios, this duet shouldn't work, but it does. For better or worse, Paul would cut a whole album of songs like these a few years later.

03-11-06 – 'Ecce Cor Meum', The Royal Albert Hall, London (UK)

I Spiritus / II Gratia / Interlude (Lament) / III Musica / IV Ecce Cor Meum *(This was broadcast on 11-11-06)*

The 'Ecce Cor Meum' album is another classical excursion, and another commercial flop, though it's still far more fun than duets with Jay Z. The concert was broadcast on 11-11-06.

00-06-07 – **Promo Video**

Dance Tonight

A catchy No. 26 UK hit and No. 69 US hit, the video for 'Dance Tonight' is one of Paul's best, and features him taking delivery of a ukulele, for which magical things start happening when he plays it. The album it is from, 'Memory Almost Full' was a big success, getting to No. 5 in the UK and No. 3 in the USA.

08-06-07 – 'Later... With Jools Holland' (UK)

Dance Tonight / I've Got A Feeling / Only Mama Knows / Lady Madonna

This was taped on 04-06-07.

13-06-07 – The Highline Ballroom, New York (USA)

Dance Tonight / Nod Your Head / I Saw Her Standing There

This was broadcast on 14-06-07.

05-07-07 – 'The iTunes Festival', Institute Of Contemporary Arts, London (UK)

Coming Up / Drive My Car / Only Mama Knows / Dance Tonight / C Moon / The Long and Winding Road / The Midnight Special / Blackbird / Here Today / Back In The U.S.S.R. / Jet / House Of Wax / I've Got A Feeling / Get Back / Hey Jude

This was broadcast on 06-09-07.

00-08-07 – Promo Video

Nod Your Head

A slightly silly rocker and a silly video, though it does feature cameos by Ringo and Barbara. The single got to No. 85 in the UK, and No. 110 in the USA.

00-09-07 – **Promo Video**

Ever Present Past

An amusing video filmed in an art gallery, it is more memorable than the song.

22-10-07 – **'Paul McCartney Live At L'Olympia', Paris (France):**

Blackbird / Dance Tonight / Only Mama Knows / Flaming Pie / Got To Get You Into My Life / C Moon / The Long and Winding Road / I'll Follow The Sun / That Was Me / Here Today / Calico Skies / Eleanor Rigby / Michelle / Band On The Run / Back In The U.S.S.R. / House Of Wax / I've Got A Feeling / Live And Let Die / Hey Jude / Let It Be / Lady Madonna / I Saw Her Standing There / Get Back

Instead of a full tour, to promote 'Memory Almost Full' Paul and his usual great band did a couple of smaller intimate concerts for TV. This one was broadcast on 16-11-07.

25-10-07 – **'BBC Electric Proms '07', The Roundhouse, London (UK)**

Magical Mystery Tour / Flaming Pie / Got To Get You Into My Life / Dance Tonight / Only Mama Knows / C Moon / The Long and Winding Road / I'll Follow The Sun / That Was Me / Here Today / Blackbird / Calico Skies / Eleanor Rigby / Band On The Run / Back In The U.S.S.R. / House Of Wax / I've Got A Feeling / Live and Let Die / Baby Face / Hey Jude / Let It Be / Lady Madonna / I Saw Her Standing There / Get Back

31-12-07 – **'Jools Holland's Annual Hootenanny' (UK)**

Dance Tonight [with Kylie Minogue] / Got To Get You Into My Life

Taped on 13-12-07, 'Dance Tonight' is always a nice little song, but it sounds (and looks) even nicer with the addition of the lovely Kylie.

20-02-08 – **'The Brit Awards 2008' (UK)**

Dance Tonight / Live and Let Die / Hey Jude / Lady Madonna / Get Back

'Lady Madonna' and 'Get Back' were broadcast at a later date.

01-06-08 – **'The Liverpool Sound', Anfield Stadium, Liverpool (UK)**

Hippy Hippy Shake / Jet / Drive My Car / Flaming Pie / Got To Get You Into My Life / Medley: Let Me Roll It - Foxy Lady / My Love / C Moon / The Long and Winding Road / Dance Tonight / Blackbird / Calico Skies / In Liverpool / I'll Follow The Sun / Eleanor Rigby / Something / Penny Lane / Band On The Run [with Dave Grohl] / Back In The U.S.S.R. [with Dave Grohl] / Live and Let Die / Let It Be / Hey Jude / Yesterday / Medley: A Day In The Life - Give Peace A Chance / Lady Madonna / I Saw Her Standing There [with Dave Grohl]

Not wanting to do another full tour, in the summer of 2008 Paul did several one-off gigs, with his voice inevitably in better shape than when he does longer tours. There's a couple of real surprises here too; the storming 'Hippy Hippy Shake' rocks much harder than The Beatles' BBC versions, while 'In Liverpool' is a lovely unreleased song that Paul has had knocking around for years.

14-06-08 – **Independence Square, Kiev (Ukraine)**

Drive My Car / Jet / All My Loving / Only Mama Knows / Flaming Pie / Got To Get You Into My Life / Medley: Let Me Roll It - Foxy Lady / C

Moon / My Love / Let 'Em In / The Long and Winding Road / Dance Tonight / Blackbird / Calico Skies / I'll Follow The Sun / Mrs. Vandebilt / Eleanor Rigby / Something / Good Day Sunshine / Penny Lane / Band On The Run / Birthday / Back In The U.S.S.R. / I've Got A Feeling / Live and Let Die / Let It Be / Hey Jude / Medley: A Day In The Life - Give Peace A Chance / Lady Madonna / Get Back / I Saw Her Standing There / Yesterday / Medley: Sgt. Pepper's Lonely Hearts Club Band (Reprise) - The End

18-07-08 – **Shea Stadium, New York (USA)**

I Saw Her Standing There / Let It Be [both songs are with Billy Joel]

On 16/18-07-08, Billy Joel played the final 2 shows at Shea Stadium before it was demolished, inviting one of the people who made it world famous for the last show.

20-07-08 – **Plaines Of Abraham, Quebec (Canada)**

Jet / Drive My Car / Only Mama Knows / All My Loving / Flaming Pie / Got To Get You Into My Life / Medley: Let Me Roll It - Foxy Lady / C Moon / My Love / Let 'Em In / Fine Line / The Long and Winding Road / Dance Tonight / Blackbird / Calico Skies / I'll Follow The Sun / Michelle / Mrs. Vandebilt / Eleanor Rigby / Something / Medley: A Day In The Life - Give Peace A Chance / Good Day Sunshine / Medley: Too Many People – She Came In Through The Bathroom Window / Penny Lane / Band On The Run / Birthday / Back In The U.S.S.R. / I've Got A Feeling / Live and Let Die / Let It Be / Hey Jude / Lady Madonna / Get Back / I Saw Her Standing There / Yesterday / Medley: Sgt. Pepper's Lonely Hearts Club Band (Reprise) - The End

00-12-08 – **Promo Video**

Sing The Changes

From 'Electric Arguments', a UK No. 79 album released under the name 'The Fireman', the video features Paul superimposed on speeded up, nighttime, footage.

00-01-09 – **Promo Video**

222

Another song from 'Memory Almost Full', the song is an instrumental, and the video mostly consists of flashing fireworks effects.

08-02-09 – **'The 51st Annual Grammy Awards' (USA)**

I Saw Her Standing There [with Dave Grohl]

04-04-09 – **'Change Begins Within: Live At Radio City Music Hall' (USA)**

Drive My Car / Jet / Got To Get You Into My Life / Let It Be / Here Today / Band On The Run / With A Little Help From My Friends [with Ringo Starr] / Cosmically Conscious / I Saw Her Standing There [The last two songs are with Ringo Starr, Sheryl Crow, Donovan, Eddie Vedder, Moby, Ben Harper, Paul Horn, Angelo Badalamenti, Betty LaVette, Jim James, and The TM Choir]

A charity concert for The David Lynch Foundation, this concert remained frustratingly unavailable (apart from shaky audience footage) for years, but was finally released on DVD in 2017. As well as featuring Ringo, the show is notable for including 'Cosmically

Conscious', a wonderful song that Paul wrote in Rishikesh, India, in 1968, though the only full version was later buried on a 1993 B-side.

28-05-09 – **'A Sideman's Journey' (UK)**

I'm In Love Again [with Ringo Starr and Klaus Voorman]

Taped on 19-05-08, Paul and Ringo jam with their old friend at Paul's Hog's Hill Mill studio.

00-07-09 – **Promo Video**

Dance 'Til We're High

From 'Electric Arguments', for this video Paul walks around at night while singing the song.

15-07-09 – **'The Late Show with David Letterman' (USA)**

Get Back / Sing The Changes / Coming Up / Band On The Run / Let Me Roll It / Helter Skelter / Back In The U.S.S.R.

Performed on the roof of The Ed Sullivan Theatre, only 'Get Back' and 'Sing the Changes' were actually broadcast, with the full show being issued as a bonus on the 'Good Evening New York City' DVD instead.

17/21-07-09 – **'Good Evening New York City' (USA)**

Drive My Car / Jet / Only Mama Knows / Flaming Pie / Got To Get You Into My Life / Let Me Roll It / Highway / The Long and Winding Road / My Love / Blackbird / Here Today / Dance Tonight / Calico Skies / Mrs. Vandebilt / Eleanor Rigby / Sing the Changes / Band On The Run / Back In The U.S.S.R. / I'm Down / Something / I've Got A Feeling / Paperback Writer / Medley: A Day In The Life - Give Peace A Chance /

Let It Be / Live and Let Die / Hey Jude / Day Tripper / Lady Madonna / I Saw Her Standing There [with Billy Joel] / Yesterday / Helter Skelter / Get Back / Medley: Sgt. Pepper's Lonely Hearts Club Band (Reprise) - The End

From 17-07-09 to 19-08-09, Paul did the 'Summer Live '09' tour, a series of 9 US concerts, of which highlights from the first 3 concerts in Citi Field, New York were compiled into both a DVD, and a live album that reached No. 28 in the UK and No. 16 in the USA.

19-11-09 – 'Children In Need Rocks The Albert Hall' (UK)

Back In The U.S.S.R. / Get Back / Hey Jude [finale, with Take That, Annie Lennox, Lily Allen, Dizzee Rascal and others]

This was taped in The Royal Albert Hall, London, on 12-11-09.

00-12-09 – Promo Video

(I Want To) Come Home

A beautiful orchestrated ballad, the video, taped in London's AIR Studios on 06-07-09, features Paul recording the song, which is intercut with scenes from the Robert De Nero movie 'Everybody's Fine', which featured this song.

13-12-09 – 'The X Factor UK Live Final' (UK)

Drive My Car / Live and Let Die

This TV appearance was during a night off in the 'Good evening Europe Tour', which ran from 02-12-09 to 22-12-09, with shows in Germany, The Netherlands, France, Ireland and the UK.

19-05-10 – **Hog's Hill Mill (Outdoors), Icklesham (UK)**

Every Night / Molly Malone / We've Been Everywhere (I've Been Everywhere) / I've Just Seen A Face / The Midnight Special / Calico Skies / Jam

Filmed with one camera, these acoustic, outside, tour rehearsals, were posted on Paul McCartney's website.

28-05-10 – **Foro Sol, Mexico City (Mexico)**

Medley: Venus And Mars - Rockshow / Jet / All My Loving / Letting Go / Got To Get You Into My Life / Highway / Medley: Let Me Roll It - Foxy Lady / The Long and Winding Road / Nineteen Hundred and Eighty Five / Let 'Em In / My Love / Shine A Light / I've Just Seen A Face / And I Love Her / Blackbird / Here Today / Dance Tonight / Mrs. Vandebilt / Eleanor Rigby / Something / Sing The Changes / Band On The Run / Ob-La-Di, Ob-La-Da / Back In The U.S.S.R. / I've Got A Feeling / Paperback Writer / Medley: A Day In The Life - Give Peace A Chance / Let It Be / Live and Let Die / Hey Jude / Day Tripper / Lady Madonna / Get Back / Yesterday / Helter Skelter / Medley: Sgt. Pepper's Lonely Hearts Club Band (Reprise) - The End

From 28-03-10 to 10-06-11, Paul did his 'Up and Coming' tour, covering the USA, Puerto Rico, Mexico, Ireland, the UK, Canada, Brazil, Argentina, Peru and Chile.

02-06-10 – **'The Gershwin Prize For Popular Song', The White House, Washington DC (USA)**

Got To Get You Into My Life / Ebony and Ivory [with Stevie Wonder] / Michelle / Eleanor Rigby / Let It Be / Hey Jude

Performing at The White House in the presence of Barack and Michelle Obama (hence the song 'Michelle'), the big surprise here was Paul and Stevie Wonder reuniting to play their big 1982 hit.

13-06-10 – **The Isle Of White Festival (UK)**

Jet / Ob-La-Di, Ob-La-Da / Back In The U.S.S.R. / Live and Let Die / Helter Skelter

27-06-10 – **'Hard Rock Calling 2010', Hyde Park, London (UK)**

Jet / All My Loving / Letting Go / Got to Get You Into My Life / Medley: Let Me Roll It - Foxy Lady / The Long And Winding Road / Let 'Em In / My Love / Looking Though You / Blackbird / Dance Tonight / Mrs. Vandebilt / Eleanor Rigby / Band On The Run / Ob-La-Di, Ob-La-Da / Back In The U.S.S.R. / Live and Let Die / Hey Jude / Tripper

This was broadcast on 10-09-10.

07-07-10 – **Radio City Music Hall, New York (USA)**

Birthday [with Ringo Starr]

Paul was a big surprise guest at Ringo's 70th birthday bash, as witnessed by Yoko's shocked (but happy) expression!

26-10-10 – **'Later Live… With Jools Holland' (UK)**

Jet / Band On The Run

29-10-10 – **'Later… With Jools Holland' (UK)**

Jet / Nineteen Hundred and Eighty-Five / Let Me Roll It

This was taped on 26-10-10, and features a difference version of 'Jet' to the earlier live broadcast.

10-11-10 – **River Plate Stadium, Buenos Aires (Argentina)**

Medley: Venus And Mars - Rockshow / Jet / All My Loving / Letting Go / Got To Get You Into My Life / Highway / Medley: Let Me Roll It - Foxy Lady / The Long and Winding Road / Nineteen Hundred and Eighty Five / Let 'Em In / My Love / I'm Looking Through You / Two Of Us / Blackbird / Here Today / Dance Tonight / Mrs. Vandebilt / Eleanor Rigby / Something / Sing The Changes / Band On The Run / Ob-La-Di, Ob-La-Da / Back In The U.S.S.R. / I've Got A Feeling / Paperback Writer / Medley: A Day In The Life - Give Peace A Chance / Let It Be / Live and Let Die / Hey Jude / Day Tripper / Lady Madonna / Get Back / Yesterday / Helter Skelter / Medley: Sgt. Pepper's Lonely Hearts Club Band (Reprise) - The End

11-11-10 – **River Plate Stadium, Buenos Aires (Argentina)**

Magical Mystery Tour / Jet / All My Loving / Letting Go / Drive My Car / Highway / Medley: Let Me Roll It - Foxy Lady / The Long and Winding Road / Nineteen Hundred and Eighty Five / Let 'Em In / My Love /I've Just Seen A Face / Bluebird / And I Love Her / Blackbird / Here Today / Dance Tonight / Mrs. Vandebilt / Eleanor Rigby / Something / Sing The Changes / Band On The Run / Ob-La-Di, Ob-La-Da / Back In The U.S.S.R. / I've Got A Feeling / Paperback Writer / Medley: A Day In The Life - Give Peace A Chance / Let It Be / Live and Let Die / Hey Jude / Day Tripper / Lady Madonna / Get Back /

Yesterday / Helter Skelter / Medley: Sgt. Pepper's Lonely Hearts Club Band (Reprise) - The End

21-11-10 – **Morumbi Stadium, Sao Paulo (Brazil)**

Medley: Venus and Mars – Rockshow / Jet / All My Loving / My Love / Blackbird / Dance Tonight / Band On The Run / Ob-Li-Di, Ob-La-Da / Let It Be / Live and Let Die / Get Back / Yesterday / Helter Skelter / Medley: Sgt. Pepper's Lonely Hearts Club Band (Reprise) - The End

09-12-10 – **'Late Night with Jimmy Fallon' (USA)**

Scrambled Eggs [with Jimmy Fallon] / Here Today

The first song is just a short version of 'Yesterday' with its original, unpublished, lyrics, but 'Here Today' is a particularly moving version of one of Paul's greatest songs.

11-12-10 – **'Saturday Night Live' (USA)**

Jet / Band On The Run / Medley: A Day In The Life - Give Peace A Chance / Get Back

22-05-11 – **Olimpico Stadium, Rio De Janeiro (Brazil)**

Hello Goodbye / Jet / All My Loving / Letting Go / Drive My Car / Sing The Changes / Let Me Roll It / The Long and Winding Road / Nineteen Hundred and Eighty-Five / Let 'Em In / I've Just Seen A Face / And I Love Her / Blackbird / Here Today / Dance Tonight / Mrs. Vanderbilt / Eleanor Rigby / Something / Band On The Run / Ob-La-Di, Ob-La-Da / Back In The U.S.S.R. / I've Got A Feeling / Paperback Writer / Medley: A Day In The Life - Give Peace A Chance / Let It Be / Live and Let Die /

Hey Jude / Day Tripper / Get Back / Yesterday / Helter Skelter / Medley: Sgt. Pepper's Lonely Hearts Club Band (Reprise) - The End

Although this show is part of the 'Up and Coming' tour, from 15-07-11 to 29-11-12 he'd start a new tour, called 'On The Run', with shows in the USA, Canada, United Arab Emirates, Italy, France, Germany, the UK, Sweden, Finland, Russia, The Netherlands, Switzerland, Belgium, Uruguay, Paraguay, Columbia, Brazil and Mexico.

2011/1980 – **Promo Video**

Blue Sway

Set to ocean footage, 'Blue Sway' is an atmospheric instrumental that was recorded at the 'McCartney II' sessions, but unreleased until 2011.

00-02-12 – **Promo Videos #1, #2, #3, #4, #5 and #6.**

My Valentine

An album of pre-rock era standards (something Ringo had done 42 years earlier), 'Kisses On The Bottom' did surprisingly well, reaching No. 3 in the UK and No. 5 in the USA, though the single 'My Valentine' only got to No. 136 in the UK, and nowhere in the USA. There are 6 different videos for the song, all directed by Paul, but none actually featuring him, instead they all star Johnny Depp and/or Natalie Portman.

09-02-12 – **'Live Kisses', Capital Studios (USA)**

I'm Gonna Sit Right Down And Write Myself A Letter / Home (When Shadows Fall) / It's Only A Paper Moon / More I Cannot Wish You /

The Glory Of Love / We Three (My Echo, My Shadow And Me) / Ac-Cent-Tchu-Ate The Positive / My Valentine / Always / My Very Good Friend The Milkman / Bye Bye Blackbird / Get Yourself Another Fool / My One and Only Love

Released as a live DVD, backed by an orchestra and in black and white, Paul performs songs from his 'Kisses On The Bottom' album.

12-02-12 – 'The 54th Annual Grammy Awards' (USA)

My Valentine / Medley: Golden Slumbers – Carry That Weight – The End [with Bruce Springsteen, Joe Walsh and Dave Grohl]

04-06-12 – 'The Queen's Diamond Jubilee Concert' (UK)

Magical Mystery Tour / All My Loving / Let It Be / Live and Let Die / Ob-La-Di, Ob-La-Da [finale, with Stevie Wonder, Madness, Cliff Richard, Elton John, Annie Lennox, Kylie Minogue, Tom Jones, Shirley Bassey, Robbie Williams and others]

As with the 2002 show, this was broadcast live from the grounds of Buckingham Palace, and is another fine performance.

27-07-12 – 'Games of the XXX Olympiad' (UK)

Hey Jude

This starts off sounding very strange indeed, with two audible Paul McCartney voices. What happened was, the organisers wanted him to mime to avoid technical problems, but Paul insisted on playing live, so they reached a compromise by getting him to record a version earlier, then, if there were problems, he could mime to that. All fine in practice, but, following some loud firework explosions, Paul hesitated slightly before starting, so they pressed the 'play' button on the recording, resulting in the 2 voices. Once this passed, everything was fine, with the crowd loving him as always.

00-12-12 – **Promo Video**

The Christmas Song

A continuation of the 'Kisses On The Bottom' theme, here Paul croons the seasonal standard made famous by Nat 'King' Cole.

12-12-12 – **'Concert For Sandy', Madison Square Garden, New York (USA)**

Helter Skelter / Let Me Roll It / Nineteen Hundred and Eighty-Five / My Valentine [with Diana Krall] / Blackbird / Cut Me Some Slack [with Dave Grohl, Krist Novoselic and Pat Smear] / I've Got A Feeling / Live and Let Die

In complete contrast to 'The Christmas Song', the highlight of this charity concert is 'Give Me Some Slack', a noisy collaboration with the remaining members of Nirvana, for which Paul plays a cheap looking 'cigar box' guitar.

15-12-12 – **'Saturday Night Live' (USA)**

My Valentine [with Joe Walsh] / Cut Me Some Slack [with Dave Grohl, Krist Novoselic and Pat Smear] / Wonderful Christmastime

Featuring another performance of the Nirvana reunion song, also performed but not broadcast was 'Birthday' and 'Get Back'.

00-12-12 – **Promo Video** – *THE JUSTICE COLLECTIVE*

He Ain't Heavy, He's My Brother

A charity record, the recording and video also includes Tony Hicks, Bobby Elliot, Gerry Marsden, Robbie Williams, Holly Johnson, Paloma Faith and many others. The record topped the UK charts.

14-06-13 – **'Bonnaroo', Great Stage Park, Manchester, TN (USA)**

Eight Days A Week / Junior's Farm / All My Loving / Listen To What The Man Said / Medley: Let Me Roll It - Foxy Lady / Paperback Writer / My Valentine / Nineteen Hundred and Eighty-Five / The Long and Winding Road / Maybe I'm Amazed / The Midnight Special / We Can Work It Out / Another Day / And I Love Her

From 13-05-13 to 22-10-15, Paul did another lengthy, off and on, tour, this time entitled the 'Out there' tour, playing in Brazil, the USA, Poland, Italy, Austria, Canada, Japan, Uruguay, Chile, Peru, Ecuador, Costa Rica, South Korea, the UK, France, The Netherlands, Denmark, Norway and Sweden.

00-09-13 – **Promo Video** – THE BLOODY BEETROOTS

Out Of Sight

Proving that he can still rock, Paul recorded this single with Italian electronic group the Bloody Beetroots. Slightly reminiscent of the slow 'Anthology' version of 'Helter Skelter' but far weirder, full marks to Paul for trying something a little different. The video sees him singing with the scary-looking, masked, group.

00-09-13 – **Promo Video #1**

New

A new album and a new single, both of them entitled 'New'! 'New' (the song) is a bit like 'Penny Lane', and is seen here in a video that features on and offstage shots, along with the lyrics to the song. 'New' the single only got to No. 105 in the UK, but 'New' the album reached No. 3 in both the UK and the USA.

00-09-13 – **Promo Video #2**

New

Perhaps not really a promo video, though this was posted on Paul McCartney's official YouTube channel at around the time of the song's release, and features a brilliant, almost acapella, performance of the song, with Paul and all of the band members harmonizing.

23-09-13 – **'Jimmy Kimmel Live' (USA)**

Magical Mystery Tour / Save Us / Junior's Farm / Jet / New / Lady Madonna / Birthday / Another Day / Everybody Out There / Ob-La-Di, Ob-La-Da / Band On The Run / Back In The U.S.S.R. / Day Tripper / Let it Be / Hey Jude

00-10-13 – **Promo Video**

Queenie Eye

This video features Paul performing the song in a recording studio, accompanied by Johnny Depp and a large group of dancers.

16-10-13 – **'BBC Radio 2 In Concert with Jo Whiley', Maida Vale Studios, London (UK)**

Eight Days A Week / Save Us / Jet / My Valentine / Nineteen Hundred and Eighty-Five / Another Day / Everybody Out There / Things We Said Today / New / Queenie Eye / Lady Madonna / Being For The Benefit Of Mr. Kite! / Band On The Run / Back In The U.S.S.R. / Hey Jude

Performing in front of a studio audience, this is basically a live radio show with visuals, as is the show below, performed on the same day.

16-10-13 – **'BBC Radio 6 Music – Lauren Laverne', Maida Vale Studios, London (UK)**

Coming Up / New / Get Back

18-10-13 – **'The Graham Norton Show' (UK)**

New

21-10-13 – **'Late Night With Jimmy Fallon' (USA)**

Eight Days A Week / Jet / Everybody Out There / We Can Work It Out / Ob-La-Di, Ob-La-Da / Birthday / Being for the Benefit of Mr. Kite! / Save Us / New / Lady Madonna

This was taped on 07-10-13.

22-10-13 – **'Later Live… with Jools Holland' (UK)**

New / Get Back

25-10-13 – **'Later… With Jools Holland' (UK)**

Save Us / New / Queenie Eye

21-11-13 – **The Dome, Tokyo (Japan)**

Eight Days a Week / Save Us / All My Loving / Listen To What The

Man Said / Let Me Roll It / Paperback Writer / My Valentine / Nineteen Hundred and Eighty-Five / The Long and Winding Road / Maybe I'm Amazed / I've Just Seen A Face / We Can Work It Out / Another Day / And I Love Her / Blackbird / Here Today / New / Queenie Eye / Lady Madonna / All Together Now / Lovely Rita / Everybody Out There / Eleanor Rigby / Being For The Benefit of Mr. Kite! / Something / Ob-La-Di, Ob-La-Da / Band On The Run / Back In The U.S.S.R. / Let It Be / Live and Let Die / Hey Jude / Day Tripper / Hi, Hi, Hi / Get Back / Yesterday / Helter Skelter / Medley: Golden Slumbers - Carry That Weight - The End

Although the same couldn't be said for every show, this Tokyo concert captures Paul at the very top of the game, with 'Maybe I'm Amazed', a song he has often had to drop in the past, featuring high notes that most can only dream of.

09-02-14 – 'The Night That Changed America: A Grammy Salute To The Beatles' (USA)

Birthday / Get Back / I Say Her Standing There / Sgt. Pepper's Lonely Hearts Club Band / With A Little Help With My Friends [Performed by Ringo Starr] / Hey Jude [grand finale, with Ringo Starr, Jeff Lynne, Dhani Harrison and others]

Taped on 27-01-14 in The Los Angeles Conference Centre, this was broadcast exactly 50 years after The Beatles historic debut on 'The Ed Sullivan Show'. Also performed on the night was 'Magical Mystery Tour', but this wasn't broadcast.

00-03-14 – **Promo Video #1**

Save Us

Despite not featuring Paul, the video for this up-tempo song features photos of fans with the song's lyrics, and is very cleverly done.

00-03-14 – **Promo Video #2**

Save Us

This 2nd video features footage of Paul performing in Japan, along with clips of fans, sumo wrestlers, etc.

00-05-14 – **Promo Video**

Appreciate

While not much of a song, the interesting video sees Paul meeting a guitar-playing robot.

00-07-14 – **Promo Video**

Early Days

A lovely acoustic number, the video only briefly features clips of Paul playing, mainly concentrating on a storyline involving friends in the American deep south.

00-09-14 – **Promo Video**

Meat Free Monday

Not available in the shops, Paul wrote the song and posted the video, made up of photo stills, to promote vegetarianism.

00-12-14 – **Promo Video**

Hope For The Future

Written for the 'Destiny' video game, this sees Paul on a different planet (not for the first time some would say).

16-12-14 – **'The Daily Show With Jon Stewart' (USA)**

Hope For The Future

2014/1973 – **Promo Video #3**

Band On The Run

This is an animated lyric video, made to re-promote this perennial song.

2014/1975 – **Promo Video**

Call Me Back Again

Although not featuring Paul, this animated video for the 1975 'Venus and Mars' track is still impressive, as is the Ray Charles-influenced song.

2014/1979 – **Promo Video**

Rudolph The Red-Nosed Reggae

The instrumental B-side to 'Wonderful Christmas Time', this is nicely compiled from 1979 images of Paul and Wings in Santa outfits.

00-01-15 – **Promo Video**

FourFiveSeconds [with Rihanna and Kanye West]

While looking very cool, Paul doesn't actually do a great deal in this song or video, though it did get to No. 3 in the UK and No. 4 in the USA.

08-02-15 – 'The 57th Annual Grammy Awards' (USA)

FourFiveSeconds [with Rihanna and Kanye West]

This is a live performance of the unlikely trio's big hit.

15-02-15 – 'Saturday Night Live 40th Anniversary Special' (USA)

I've Just Seen A Face [with Paul Simon] / Maybe I'm Amazed

'I've Just seen A Face', unfortunately, is just a brief duo between Paul and Paul.

00-05-15 – **Promo Video**

Food Revolution Day

Paul contributed to this officially unreleased song and released video, which also features Jamie Oliver, Ed Sheeran, Alesha Dixon and Jamie Cullum, amongst others.

19-12-15 – 'Saturday Night Live' (USA)

Santa Claus Is Coming To Town [with Bruce Springsteen]

Paul just joins in to do the occasional backing vocals and dance around while Bruce does all the work, but everyone looks like they're enjoying it.

2015/1982 – **Promo Video**

The Man [with Michael Jackson]

In 2015, Paul released some wonderful home movie footage of Paul, Linda and Michael outdoors in Sussex in 1981, with this song as a soundtrack. This is probably not really a proper promo video, but is still well worth seeking out.

2015/1983 – **Promo Video**

Say Say Say (Remix) [with Michael Jackson]

This is a horrible remix that does nothing to improve the song, and the video features modern footage of street dancers with nothing of Paul and Michael.

20-12-16 – **'The Tonight Show Starring Jimmy Fallon' (USA)**

Wonderful Christmastime [with the cast of 'Sing']

This is a unique but short, almost acapella arrangement of Paul's 1979 hit.

00-06-18 – **Promo Video**

Come On To Me

A good mid-tempo rocker with Paul in fine voice, though the video doesn't feature him, with instead an amusing storyline of bored workers on a nightshift. The song is from 'Egypt Station', which got to No. 3 in the UK and topped the charts in the USA, a remarkable achievement for a guy in his mid '70s who's been having hits for 56 years.

21-06-18 – **'Carpool Karaoke' (USA)**

The Beatles – Tell Me What You See

Drive My Car / I Lost My Little Girl / Penny Lane / Let It Be / When I'm Sixty-Four / Blackbird / Come On To Me / A Hard Day's Night / Ob-La-Di, Ob-La-Da / Love Me Do / Back In The U.S.S.R. / Hey Jude

The first 7 songs are snippets only, all 'performed' in a car with host James Corden, with the exception of 'When I'm Sixty-Four', which is played by Paul on a piano. The last 5 songs were taped at The Philharmonic Dining Rooms, Liverpool, with a full band. All songs were taped on 09-06-18. At the time of writing, this performance has received over 40 million(!) views on YouTube.

00-09-18 – **Promo Video**

Fuh You

A lesser but gimmicky song, again this video features a storyline (of sorts) without Paul.

00-09-18 – **Promo Video**

Back In Brazil

At last, Paul appears in his own video again, though only just. This features a storyline about a Brazilian girl who goes to a Paul McCartney concert and briefly meets him.

06-09-18 – **'The Tonight Show Starring Jimmy Fallon' (USA)**

Drive My Car [with Jimmy Fallon] / Come On To Me

'Drive My Car' is just part of a short but amusing sketch.

07-09-18 – **Grand Central Station, New York (USA)**

A Hard Day's Night / Hi, Hi, Hi / Can't Buy Me Love / Letting Go / I've Got A Feeling / Come On To Me / My Valentine / Nineteen Hundred and Eighty-Five / From Me To You / Love Me Do / FourFiveSeconds / Blackbird / Dance Tonight / Who Cares / I Saw Her Standing There / Fuh You / Back In The U.S.S.R. / Ob-La-Di, Ob-La-Da / Birthday / Lady Madonna / Let It Be / Sgt. Pepper's Lonely Hearts Club Band (Reprise) / Helter Skelter / Medley: Golden Slumbers - Carry That Weight - The End

This is one of a handful of 'secret' gigs that Paul played during the 'Egypt Station' promotions in 2018.

05-10-18 – **Zilker Park, Austin (USA)**

A Hard Day's Night / Hi, Hi, Hi / Can't Buy Me Love / Letting Go / Come On To Me / Let Me Roll It / I've Got A Feeling / My Valentine / Nineteen Hundred and Eighty-Five / Maybe I'm Amazed / I've Just Seen A Face / In Spite of All the Danger / From Me To You / Love Me Do / Blackbird / Here Today / Lady Madonna / Fuh You / Being For The Benefit Of Mr. Kite! / Something / Ob-La-Di, Ob-La-Da / Band On The Run / Back In The U.S.S.R. / Let It Be / Live and Let Die / Hey Jude / Sgt. Pepper's Lonely Hearts Club Band / Helter Skelter / Medley: Golden Slumber - Carry That Weight - The End

From 17-09-18 to 16-12-18, Paul did his latest 'Freshen Up' tour, which encompassed Canada, the USA, Japan, France, Denmark, Poland, Austria and the UK. For the final show of the year, at London's O2 Arena, Paul gave the audience an early Christmas present by bringing out Ringo Starr and Ronnie Wood to play on 'Get Back'. At the time of writing (spring 2019), the tour is being extended throughout South America, and then back to the USA and Canada.

00-12-18 – **Promo Video**

Who Cares

An excellent video to a pretty good song, this features Paul as a psychologist, giving advice to actress Emma Stone (looking like a young Nina Hagen), with a mixture of live action footage and animation.

GEORGE HARRISON

00-05-68 – **'Wonderwall' Movie**

George's first big solo project was the soundtrack to the movie 'Wonderwall'. Taped in London and Bombay between November 1967 and February 1968, and with George adding guitar and keyboard contributions to the mainly Indian musicians' work, 'Wonderwall Music' got to No. 49 in the USA but failed to chart in the UK.

10-12-69 – **Falkoner Teatret, Copenhagen (Denmark)** – *DELANEY and BONNIE and FRIENDS*

Medley: Poor Elijah – Tribute To Robert Johnson / I Don't Know Why / Where There's A Will, There's A Way / Special Life / I Don't Want To Discuss It / That's What My Man Is For / Comin' Home

Hating the limelight but enjoying playing, George, along with his friend Eric Clapton, joined American duo Delaney and Bonnie for a few shows, playing, anonymously, in the background. Broadcast on 27-02-70, this footage is a composite of both the matinee and evening shows.

15-12-69 – **UNICEF Gala, Lyceum Ballroom, London (UK)** – *JOHN LENNON*

See the JOHN LENNON section for more details!

21-01-71 – **'Top Of The Pops' (UK)** – *PAN'S PEOPLE*

My Sweet Lord

'My Sweet Lord' is George's most famous and successful solo recording, topping the charts on both sides of the Atlantic, as did the epic 3-disc album, 'All things Must Pass'. Unfortunately, like all of his

pre-1974 singles, there was no promo video made, though the UK's 'Top Of The Pops' programme did feature a dance to the song by their resident dance troupe (as well as a specially made video, see below), and this performance was repeated on 28-01-71 and 27-12-71. The follow-up single in the USA, 'What Is Life', got to No. 10.

00-02-71 – **'Top Of The Pops' Video (UK)** – *MISSING/LOST*

My Sweet Lord

This video was made especially for 'Top Of The Pops', broadcast on 04-02-71, though it no longer survives.

21/22-05-71 – **Tittenhurst, Ascot (UK)** – *JOHN LENNON*

See the JOHN LENNON section for more details!

01-08-71 – **Madison Square Garden, New York – Sound-check (USA)**

If Not For You [Performed by Bob Dylan with George Harrison on harmony vocals] / Come On In My Kitchen [Performed by Leon Russell]

These songs were featured as bonus material on the 2005 DVD issue of 'The Concert For Bangladesh'.

01-08-71 – **'The Concert For Bangladesh', Afternoon Show, Madison Square Garden, New York (USA)**

Love Minus Zero/No Limit [Performed by Bob Dylan]

Not performed in the evening show, again this was featured as bonus material on the 'The Concert For Bangladesh' DVD reissue.

01-08-71 – **'The Concert For Bangladesh', Evening Show, Madison**

Square Garden, New York (USA)

Wah Wah / My Sweet Lord / Awaiting On You All / That's The Way God Planned It [Performed by Billy Preston] / It Don't Come Easy [Performed by Ringo Starr] / Beware Of Darkness [with Leon Russell] / While My Guitar Gently Weeps / Medley: Jumpin' Jack Flash – Youngblood [Performed by Leon Russell] / Here Comes The Sun / A Hard Rain's A-Gonna Fall [Performed by Bob Dylan] / It Takes A Lot To Laugh, It Takes A Train To Cry [Performed by Bob Dylan] / Blowin' In The Wind [Performed by Bob Dylan] / Just Like A Woman [Performed by Bob Dylan] / Something / Bangla Desh [ALL songs feature both George Harrison and Ringo Starr, amongst many others]

Although 'Live Aid' will always be remembered as the biggest musical charity event of all time, it was 'The Concert For Bangladesh' that pioneered shows of this kind. Accompanied by his old mate Ringo (John was invited, but declined when George told him that he didn't want Yoko to perform), and a few 'heavy' friends like Bob Dylan, Leon Russell, Eric Clapton and Billy Preston, this was not only George's solo debut as a headline artist, but it remained his most famous show. Not featured in the movie is Dylan's 'Mr. Tambourine Man', though it is on the soundtrack album. The album 'The Concert For Bangladesh' got to No. 1 in the UK and No. 2 in the USA, remarkable for an expensive box-set, while George's single 'Bangla Desh' reached No. 10 in the UK and No. 23 in the USA. A video of George performing the song, taken from the movie, was shown on 'Top Of The Pops' on 19-08-71, while 'My Sweet Lord' was on the show over 30 years later on 25-01-02, following the song's reissue.

23-11-71 – **'The Dick Cavett Show' (USA)** – *GARY WRIGHT*

Two Faced Man

George, wearing jeans and with long hair and full beard, joins Gary to play some excellent slide guitar.

03-12-71 – **'The David Frost Show' (USA)**

Sitar Demonstration [with Ravi Shankar]

This was taped on 24-11-71.

00-06-73 – **'Top Of The Pops' Video (UK)** – *MISSING/LOST*

Give Me Love (Give Me Peace On Earth)

George didn't exactly rush-release a follow up to 'All Things Must Pass', with some suggesting that it wasn't a wise move using up all of his songs on a triple album. Eventually he released the 'Living In The Material World' album, which did well at No. 2 in the UK and No. 1 in the USA, as did the single 'Give Me Love (Give Me Peace On Earth)' which got to No. 8 in the UK and No. 1 in the USA. There was no official video, but one was put together for the 15-06-73 edition of 'Top Of The Pops', though unfortunately it is lost.

00-10-74 – **U.S. Tour Rehearsals, A&M Studios, Los Angeles (USA)**

Dark Horse

George was always the most reluctant performer in The Beatles, so it came as a surprise when, from 02-11-74 to 20-12-74, he did a lengthy tour of the USA. Unfortunately there is no known professionally-filmed footage from the tour, though this one solitary (and slightly incomplete) song from the tour's rehearsals does circulate unofficially. Poorly received, both the 'Dark Horse' album and the single of the same name failed to chart in the UK, though, presumably helped by the tour, the album got to No. 4 in the USA, and the single reached No. 15.

00-12-74 – **Promo Video**

Ding Dong, Ding Dong

Unlike his former colleagues, up until now George hadn't really pursued the visual medium to promote his music, but with this video he made up for lost time. Taped on 23-12-74, both in and outside his home, he dresses in a variety of outfits, including his Beatles collarless jacket and his 'Sgt. Pepper' outfit (he also wears nothing but a pair of fur boots at one point, hiding his modestly behind a guitar). The single got to No. 38 in the UK and 2 places higher in the USA, while this great video can be found on 'The Apple Years' DVD.

26-12-75 – **'Christmas With Rutland Weekend Television' (UK)**

The Pirate Song

If there was one criticism of George's solo work to date, it is that he was a little over-serious. This is far from true of George in real life of course, whose dry wit could be the match of John's, and it is very apparent here too, on this anarchic TV show featuring Monty Python's Eric Idle and The Bonzo Dog Doo-Dah Band's Neil Innes. Taped on 13-12-75, George first does a sketch where he dresses as a pirate, and then, as himself, is backed by a band that plays the intro to 'My Sweet Lord', only for George to go into a song about pirates. It was in late 1975 that George released a new album, 'Extra Texture (Read All About It)', which got to No. 16 in the UK and No. 8 in the USA. Also released was a single, 'You', which got to No. 38 in the UK and No. 20 in the USA, while the follow up, 'This Guitar (Can't Keep From Crying)' failed to chart.

00-11-76 – **Promo Video**

This Song

Famously, George was successfully sued over copyright for 'My Sweet Lord', allegedly for its supposed similarity to The Chiffons' 'He's So Fine'. Now, continuing his new lighter approach, he released 'This Song', which spoofs the whole affair, as does this intricate video set in a U.S. court. The single failed to chart in the UK and got to No. 25 in the USA, though the album, 'Thirty Three & 1/3', did better, getting to No. 35 in the UK and No. 11 in the USA. The video can be found on 'The Dark Horse Years 1976 – 1992'.

00-11-76 – **Promo Video**

Crackerbox Palace

A US only single that got to No. 19, the video, largely filmed in the grounds of his home, is another mad-cap Python-esque affair, and is on 'The Dark Horse Years 1976 – 1992'.

00-11-76 – **Promo Video**

True Love

An excellent version of an old standard, and accompanied by another elaborate and humorous video that was filmed outdoors, this failed to chart, a fate that befell its follow up 'It's What You Value'. Disappointingly, this video wasn't included on 'The Dark Horse Years'.

20-11-76 – 'Saturday Night Live' (USA)

Here Comes The Sun / Homeward Bound [both songs are with Paul Simon]

As well as broadcasting the videos for 'This Song' and 'Crackerbox Palace', this edition of the long running US TV show featured George playing live. Taped on 18-11-76, and performing duets with Paul Simon where they trade verses, this remains one of George's most memorable TV appearances.

05-02-77 – 'Disco 77' (Germany)

This Song

Taped on 02-02-77, George mimes to his recent single on this popular German TV show.

00-02-77 – 'Warner Bros. Records Promo' (USA)

Go Your Own Way

This snippet of George performing the Fleetwood Mac song was taped at his home in Friar Park.

07-12-78 – Civic Hall, Guilford (UK) – ERIC CLAPTON

Further On Up The Road

This is included in the officially unreleased documentary, 'Eric Clapton and His Rolling Hotel', and features George on guitar.

00-02-79 – **Promo Video**

Blow Away

In 1979, George released a UK No. 39 and US No. 14 album, simply called 'George Harrison', featuring as its most famous track a new version of 'Not Guilty', the then-unreleased song that he'd recorded for 'The White Album'. Unfortunately that wasn't issued as a single, though 'Blow Away' is a good 2nd best. A UK No. 51 and US No. 16, the simple but amusing studio video is another one that sadly failed to show up on 'The Dark Horse Years 1976 – 1992'. The follow up single, 'Love Comes To Everyone', failed to chart, nor was a video made for the song.

00-07-79 – **Promo Video**

Faster

A non-charting UK single that wasn't released in the USA, the video, featuring George with motor racing legend Jackie Stewart, is on 'The Dark Horse Years 1976 – 1992'.

00-05-81 – **Promo Video**

All Those Years Ago

Although 'Free As A Bird' and 'Real Love' are generally regarded as the first time the surviving Beatles recorded together after John's death, it was this song that holds that distinction. With lyrics about John, it features Ringo on drums, and, overdubbed later, Paul, Linda and Denny on backing vocals. If it had been released under The Beatles' name it would no doubt be more famous, but even so it still got to No. 13 in the UK No. 2 in the USA. The video, compiled from well-known Beatles footage, is another one that should've been but isn't on 'The Dark Horse Years 1976 – 1992'. The parent album 'Somewhere In England' did well too, reaching No. 13 in the UK and No. 11 in the USA, but the follow-up, 'Teardrops', failed to chart. In 1982, George released another album, 'Gone Troppo', and the singles, 'Wake Up My Love' and 'I Really Love You', but, with little promotion, they all failed to chart in the UK, and in the USA the album stalled at No. 108 and 'Wake Up My Love' peaked at No. 53. It would be 5 years before there was another album.

00-01-85 – **'Water' Movie (UK)**

Freedom

After several years of musical silence, George appeared, alongside Ringo, Eric Clapton and Ray Cooper, as part of comedian Billy Connolly's backing band in this comedy movie.

00-06-85 – **Promo Video**

Save The World

Originally a song on the 'Somewhere In England' album, in 1985 George re-recorded the song, with suitably amended lyrics, for a Greenpeace fundraising album. The video doesn't feature any footage or images of George.

19-10-85 – **Limehouse Studios, London (UK)**

Everybody's Trying To Be My Baby / Your True Love

Rehearsals for 'Blue Suede Shoes: A Rockabilly Tribute To Carl Perkins and Friends', taped two days later.

01-01-86 – 'Blue Suede Shoes: A Rockabilly Tribute To Carl Perkins and Friends' (UK)

Everybody's Trying To Be My Baby [with Carl Perkins] / Your True Love [with Carl Perkins and Dave Edmunds] / The World Is Waiting For The Sunrise [with Carl Perkins] / Medley: That's Alright Mama - Blue Moon of Kentucky - Night Train to Memphis - Amen / Glad All Over / Whole Lotta Shakin' Goin' On / Gone, Gone, Gone / Blue Suede Shoes / Blue Suede Shoes (Reprise) [All songs from the medley onwards are with Carl Perkins, Ringo Starr, Eric Clapton, Dave Edmunds and others]

Taped in London's Limehouse Studios on 21-10-85, it's difficult to think of another tribute concert, with the possible exception of George's own, posthumous, 'Concert For George', that is quite so thrilling. With him are Ringo, Eric Clapton and Dave Edmunds, and everyone is clearly having a ball, but it was Carl's night. The concert was broadcast in the UK, in slightly edited form ('Glad All Over' was missing), on 01-01-86, and in the USA, uncut, 4 days later. It has since been issued on DVD.

15-03-86 – 'Heartbeat '86', The N.E.C., Birmingham (UK)

Johnny B. Goode [Robert Plant, Denny Laine and others]

'Heartbeat '86' was a charity show for Birmingham Children's Hospital that featured a cast of mainly Brummy acts, and for the finale, George, along with Robert Plant and Denny Laine, traded verses on 'Money (That's What I Want)' and 'Johnny B. Goode'.

Backed by an all-star band that includes members of ELO and The Moody Blues, this was broadcast on 02-08-86, though unfortunately 'Money (That's What I Want)' was omitted.

07-10-86 – **'Handmade In Hong Kong' (UK)**

Shanghai Surprise [with Vicki Brown] / Someplace Else / The Hottest Gong In Town

In 1986, George agreed to write and record some songs for a forthcoming movie starring Madonna and Sean Penn, then newly married and getting media attention worldwide. It is something he soon showed regret for, but this documentary shows him recording the title track (effectively a duet with Vicki Brown), along with 2 other songs. All 3 were later included on 'The Dark Horse Years 1976 – 1992'.

19-02-87 – **Palomino Club, Hollywood (USA)**

Woke Up With The Blues / Checkin' Up On My Baby / She Caught The Katy / Farther On Down The Road / You're Gonna Need Somebody On Your Bond / Medley: Matchbox - Gone, Gone, Gone / Lucille / Crosscut Saw / Bacon Fat / Knock On Wood / In The Midnight Hour / Honey Don't / Blue Suede Shoes / Watching The River Flow / Proud Mary / Johnny B. Goode / Medley: Willie and The Hand Jive - Hey Bo Diddley / Peggy Sue / Dizzy Miss Lizzy / Medley: Twist And Shout - La Bamba

This concert is a live jam featuring Taj Mahal, John Fogerty, Bob Dylan and Jesse Ed Davis. George sings lead or joint-lead vocals on 'Medley: Matchbox – Gone, Gone, Gone', 'Honey Don't', 'Watching The River

Flow', 'Peggy Sue' and 'Dizzy Miss Lizzy'. While not broadcast quality, it is steady, multi-angle footage, and with good sound.

06-06-87 – 'The Princes Trust Concert', Wembley Arena, London (UK)

Stand By Me [Performed by Ben E. King] / While My Guitar Gently Weeps / Here Comes The Sun / With A Little Help From My Friends [Performed by Ringo Starr]

Almost a year after Paul starred in this annual charity event, George and Ringo did the same. With an all-star band that includes Eric Clapton, Elton John, Jeff Lynne, Phil Collins, Ben E. King, Midge Ure and Mark King, George and Ringo join Ben E. King to assist on his classic (also a hit for John), then, with Ringo on drums, he performs 2 Beatles classics, and finally, Ringo runs to the microphone to perform his song. George sounds wonderful, and Ringo sounds rusty vocally, but everyone seems to enjoy the experience. The show was broadcast on 20-06-87, unfortunately with 'Here Comes The Sun' omitted, but that was rectified when an extended version of the show was released on VHS the following year.

00-10-87 – **Promo Video #1**

Got My Mind Set On You

Thanks largely to the encouragement and production skills of Jeff Lynne, in the late '80s George became more successful than he'd been at any other time since 1971. The album 'Cloud Nine' was a UK No. 10 and US No. 8, while 'Got My Mind Set On You', the first and biggest hit from the album, reached No. 2 in the UK and topped the charts in the USA. Not bad for a man who'd all but quit the music business a few years earlier! 2 completely different videos were made, with this first one featuring a young man and woman in an amusement arcade, and George being seen performing the song on a screen. This is on 'The Dark Horse Years 1976 – 1992', though it also circulates as 'raw' footage, featuring just George and the band.

00-10-87 – **Promo Video #2**

Got My Mind Set On You

Perhaps not entirely happy with the 1st video, a 2nd one was made, featuring George sitting in an armchair, in a room where all sorts of weird and wonderful things go on. Available in 2 different edits, this was shown on 'Top Of The Pops' on 05-11-87 and 26-11-87, and is on 'The Dark Horse Years 1976 – 1992'.

20-01-88 – **'The Rock and Roll Hall Of Fame', The Waldorf-Astoria, New York (USA)**

Twist and Shout / All Along The Watchtower / I Saw Her Standing There / Stand By Me / Stop! In The Name Of Love / Medley: Whole Lotta Shaking Going On - Hound Dog - Hi Ho Silver / Born On The Bayou / Like A Rolling Stone / (I Can't Get No) Satisfaction [Songs feature Ringo Starr, Mick Jagger, The Beach Boys, Ben E. King, John Fogerty and others]

Starting in 1986, 'The Rock and Roll Hall of Fame' became an annual event, where notable musicians from the past are inducted, and usually perform afterwards. This year, The Beatles were inducted, and although Paul declined to attend, George and Ringo were there, along with Yoko, Julian and Sean. Afterwards there was a loose, messy but fun jam, at times featuring George and Ringo, along with the other inductees.

0-02-88 – **Promo Video**

When We Was Fab [with Ringo Starr]

Taped on 18-12-87, this combines the wit of George's best '70s videos with late '80s technology and surreal '60s visuals, making something very memorable and unique. George wears his 'Sgt. Pepper' suit for the 3rd time in a music video (the others being 'Hello Goodbye' and 'Ding Dong, Ding Dong'), while Ringo makes an appearance, as does 'the walrus', playing bass (George later joked that it was indeed Paul in the costume, but Paul insisted that it wasn't). The video is probably better than the song, but it still got to No. 25 in the UK and No. 23 in the USA, and can be found on 'The Dark Horse Years 1976 – 1992'.

00-06-88 – **Promo Video**

This Is Love

Although lacking the zaniness of the other recent videos, this one, filmed outdoors in Hawaii, is still extremely good. A UK No. 55 hit, the video is on 'The Dark Horse Years 1976 – 1992'.

00-10-88 – **Promo Video** – THE TRAVELING WILBURYS

Handle With Care

Instead of following up a big selling album with another one, George's next move was more surprising: the forming of a supergroup. Featuring George along with Bob Dylan, Tom Petty, Jeff Lynne and

Roy Orbison, their 1st and best single was 'Handle With Care'. A UK No. 21 and US No. 2, the album 'Traveling Wilburys Vol. 1' did even better in the UK, reaching No. 1, as well as No. 3 in the USA. The video, of which there a couple of different edits, is on the 2007 'The Traveling Wilburys Collection' DVD, albeit cropped to 16:9 format.

08-01-89 – **'The Movie Life Of George' (UK)**

Honey Don't / That's Alright Mama [with Carl Perkins]

The highlight of this documentary was 2 songs taped at a private party in Shepperton Studios on 01-10-88, featuring Carl Perkins with George and Joe Brown.

00-02-89 – **Promo Video** – *THE TRAVELING WILBURYS*

End Of The Line

Just 4 days before the taping for this video on 10-12-88, Roy Orbison suddenly passed away, so, rather than cancel the shoot, they simply showed his guitar in an empty chair as a tribute. Only getting to No. 52 in the UK but No. 2 in the USA, the video, set in a railway carriage, is on 'The Traveling Wilburys Collection'.

00-04-89 – **Promo Video** – *TOM PETTY*

I Won't Back Down [with Ringo Starr]

Taped on 22/23-03-89, Tom Petty is joined by both George and Ringo on this video. Unfortunately Ringo couldn't make the 2nd day of shooting, so a look-a-like was used for some distant shots, much to George's annoyance. The single reached No. 28 in the UK and No. 12 in the USA.

00-06-90 – **Promo Video** – *THE TRAVELING WILBURYS*

Nobody's Child

Released as a charity single to aid Romanian orphans, this video features cartoons, intercut with footage of the orphans, and no footage of the band themselves. A No. 44 UK hit, this video wasn't included on 'The Traveling Wilburys Collection', unlike all their other singles.

00-06-90 – **Promo Video** – *JEFF LYNNE*

Every Little Thing

With a similar sound to The Traveling Wilburys and Tom Petty singles, George and Tom make the briefest of cameos in this semi-animated video.

00-06-90 – **Promo Video** – *JEFF LYNNE*

Lift Me Up

In a semi-animated video similar to the previous one, George again makes a brief appearance, this time dressed as a devil!

00-11-90 – **Promo Video #1** – *THE TRAVELING WILBURYS*

She's My Baby

Carrying on as a 4-piece rather than replacing Roy, 'She's My Baby' only got to No. 79 in the UK, but just missed the top spot at No. 2 in the USA, while the band's 2nd and last album, jokingly entitled 'Traveling Wilburys Vol. 3', got to No. 14 in the UK and No. 11 in the USA. More or less a straight performance video, there are 2, quite *different, edits for this. One of them is on 'The Traveling Wilburys Collection'.*

00-10-90 – **Promo Video** – *THE TRAVELING WILBURYS*

Inside Out

Another straight performance video, again, a rather different edit of this No. 16 US hit was included on 'The Traveling Wilburys Collection'.

00-03-91 – **Promo Video** – *THE TRAVELING WILBURYS*

Wilbury Twist

Taped on 18-01-91, like all the songs from the 2nd album, this is available in more than 1 edit, this time at least 3 of them. A US No. 46 hit, this is on 'The Traveling Wilburys Collection'.

00-12-91 – **The Tokyo Dome, Tokyo (Japan)**

Taxman / Give Me Love (Give Me Peace On Earth) / Cloud 9 / Cheer Down / Devil's Radio

If forming a supergroup was surprising, George's next move was even more so, a tour of Japan, which lasted from 01-12-91 to 17-12-91. There was a full 'Live In Japan' official album, and it's well worth checking out, but the above are the only professionally filmed songs to so far be shown publicly. Taped at one of the Tokyo shows on either the 14th, 15th or 17th (no-one can quite agree which), 'Taxman', 'Cloud 9', 'Cheer Down' and 'Devil's Radio' were released on 'The Dark Horse Years 1976 – 1992' DVD, and 'Give Me Love (Give Me Peace On Earth)' is on 'The Apple Years' DVD. Fans eagerly await the release of a full show. Apart from this tour and the earlier 1974 USA tour,

George was to play just one more full length show, and that was in London's Royal Albert Hall on 06-04-92. In aid of The Natural Law Party, he performed a set similar to the Japanese shows, and was joined for the encore by Ringo. A historic and unique occasion, but sadly this wasn't professionally filmed.

06-06-92 – **'Mr Roadrunner' (UK)**

Between The Devil and The Deep Blue Sea

Playing a ukulele, and backed by a band that includes Jools Holland and Joe Brown, this is a lovely version of an old jazz standard. It would later be released on the posthumous 'Brainwashed' album.

16-10-92 – **'Columbia Records Celebrates The Music Of Bob Dylan', Madison Square Garden, New York (USA)**

If Not For You / Absolutely Sweet Marie / My Back Pages [with Bob Dylan, Roger McGuinn, Tom Petty, Neil Young and Eric Clapton] / Knocking On Heaven's Door [finale, with Bob Dylan, Roger McGuinn, Tom Petty, Neil Young and Eric Clapton and entire cast]

Backed by Booker T. and The M.G.'s, George was the highlight of this lengthy tribute concert. Looking much the same as he did in 1967, he'd never sounded better, with 'Absolutely Sweet Marie' being particularly impressive. It was the last time he ever played on a concert stage.

A top selling album, a supergroup, a Japanese tour... whatever will he do next, reform The Beatles?

23-06-94 – **Friar Park, Henley-on-Thames (UK)** – *THE THREETLES*

See the PAUL McCARTNEY section for more details!

00-04-95 – **Promo Video** – GARY WRIGHT

Don't Try To Own Me

Just as he'd done on 'The Dick Cavett Show' in 1971, George greatly enhanced a song by Gary Wright. This time though, he sang, almost as a duet, and can be both heard and seen in this video, taped around 3 years earlier circa 1992.

24-07-97 – **'George & Ravi – Yin & Yang' (USA)**

All Things Must Pass / Prahbujee [with Ravi Shankar] / Any Road / If You Belonged To Me

On 14-05-97, George joined his old friend Ravi Shankar and Ravi's wife Sukanya, primarily to promote Ravi's album 'Chants Of India', which George produced. During the interview George played 4 songs, listed above. 'All Things Must Pass' and 'Prahbujee' (from Ravi's album) were broadcast on 24-07-97, but 'Any Road' (later on 'Brainwashed') and The Traveling Wilburys' 'If You Belonged To Me' were not broadcast until after George's death. Incidentally, after the taping, George wrote to the show, requesting that the songs weren't shown. They declined his request.

23-01-98 – **Carl Perkins' Funeral, R.E. Womack Memorial Chapel, Jackson, TN (USA)**

Your True Love

How poignant that George, such a fan of Carl Perkins that he'd briefly called himself 'Carl Harrison' in The Beatles' pre-fame days, should do

his last public performance at his hero's memorial service.

George Harrison died on 29-11-01.

2003/2001 – **Promo Video**

Any Road

The posthumous 'Brainwashed' album, released in November 2002, had been a very long time coming, with George working on it, on and off, from 1988 until his death in 2001, with it then completed by his son Dhani and Jeff Lynne. The oldest song on the album was 'Any Road', and this was released as a single in May 2003, along with a video featuring footage from throughout his whole career. The single didn't chart, but the well-received 'Brainwashed' did get to No. 29 in the UK and No. 18 in the USA.

2006/1973 – **Promo Video**

Living In The Material World

This specially made video is 1 of 3 that was released on the 'Living In The Material World' deluxe CD/DVD, but unlike the other 2, isn't on any other release.

2006/1973 – **Promo Video**

Miss O'Dell

Compiled from still images, this is 'The Apple Years' DVD.

2006/1973 – **Promo Video**

Sue Me Sue You Blues

Made for a previously unreleased demo of the song, this is a mixture of animation and lyrics. Again, it can be found on 'The Apple Years' DVD.

2014/1970 – **Promo Video**

What Is Life

From the 'All Things Must Pass' album, this features a storyline of a boy and girl dancing outdoors before meeting. Not the greatest of videos, despite the undoubted quality of the song.

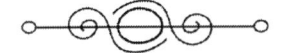

RINGO STARR

06-02-68 – **'Cilla!' (UK)** – *MISSING/LOST*

Nellie Dean / Do You Like Me? [both songs are with Cilla Black]

Of all The Beatles, it is Ringo who has always been the most unthreatening, family-friendly, entertainer, with he being a natural for good old fashioned pre-rock 'n' roll show business. Here Ringo does a couple of entertaining duets with host Cilla Black, performing two songs that date from the early part of the 20th Century. Unfortunately the footage is long lost, but an audio still survives.

24-12-69 – **'With A Little Help From My Friends' (UK)** – *MISSING/LOST*

Octopus's Garden

During 1968 – 1970, the line between The Beatles' group and solo careers often blurred, and that was never more so than here. On 08-12-69, Ringo went into Abbey Road studios to overdub a new lead vocal onto The Beatles' version of 'Octopus's Garden', with anonymous session musicians overdubbing new piano, guitar and bass. The reason for this new Beatles/solo mix was for Ringo to mime on 'With A Little Help From My Friends', a TV special honouring George Martin that was taped on 14-12-69.

00-03-70 – **Promo Video**

Sentimental Journey

Ringo's solo debut, 'Sentimental Journey', was an album of standards, and although no singles were released, an elaborate video was made for the title track. Taped at London's Talk Of The Town on 15-03-70, a short-haired Ringo, wearing a tuxedo and pink bow tie, mimes to a new alternate vocal, while backed by an orchestra and the vocal trio of Marsha Hunt, Madeline Bell and Doris Troy. The video was shown in the UK on 'Frost On Sunday' on 29-03-70 and on 'The Ed Sullivan Show' on 17-05-70, and is also on 'Photograph: The Best of Ringo Starr', the frustratingly short 6-song bonus DVD for the CD of the same name, though with the alternate audio replaced by the studio recording. The 'Sentimental Journey' album sold well, getting to No. 7 in the UK and No. 22 in the USA. He followed this with the fine Nashville-recorded country album 'Beaucoups Of Blues', which got to No. 87 in the USA, with the single of the same name getting to No. 65, though none of them were hits in the UK, and nor were any promo videos made.

13-02-71 – 'Cilla!' (UK) – *MISSING/LOST*

Act Naturally [with Cilla Black]

Taped on 01-10-70 and backed by an orchestra, Ringo and Cilla duet on The Beatles and Buck Owens' classic song.

00-04-71 – **Promo Video #1**

It Don't Come Easy

Ringo's 1st UK solo single and one of his best, 'It Don't Come Easy' got to No. 4 in both the UK and USA. For this song, 2 completely different videos were made. This first one is compiled from Ringo's home movies, from various locations and dates, some of them dating back as far as 1968. Broadcast on 'Top Of The Pops' on 22-04-71, this is also on 'Photograph: The Best of Ringo Starr'.

00-04-71 – **Promo Video #2**

It Don't Come Easy

Taped in Norway on 27-04-71, where Ringo was also taping a TV appearance with Cilla Black, this video features Ringo playing piano in the snow, and was broadcast just 2 days later on 'Top Of The Pops'. 2 different edits survive, but none are on the official DVD.

01-08-71 – **'The Concert For Bangladesh', Madison Square Garden, New York – SOUNDCHECK (USA)**

If Not For You [Performed by Bob Dylan with George Harrison on harmony vocals] / Come On In My Kitchen [Performed by Leon Russell]

These songs were featured as bonus material on the 2005 DVD issue.

01-08-71 – **'The Concert For Bangladesh', Evening Show, Madison Square Garden, New York (USA)**

Wah Wah / My Sweet Lord / Awaiting On You All / That's The Way God Planned It [Performed by Billy Preston] / It Don't Come Easy [Performed by Ringo Starr] / Beware Of Darkness [with Leon Russell] / While My Guitar Gently Weeps / Medley: Jumpin' Jack Flash – Youngblood [Performed by Leon Russell] / Here Comes The Sun / A Hard Rain's A-Gonna Fall [Performed by Bob Dylan] / It Takes A Lot To Laugh, It Takes A Train To Cry [Performed by Bob Dylan] / Blowin' In The Wind [Performed by Bob Dylan] / Just Like A Woman [Performed by Bob Dylan] / Something / Bangla Desh [ALL songs feature both George Harrison and Ringo Starr, amongst many others]

See the GEORGE HARRISON section for more details!

27-11-71 – 'Cilla In Scandinavia' (UK)

It Don't Come Easy / The Snowman Song [with Cilla Black and Basil Brush]

Taped in Norway on 27-04-71, Ringo performs 'It Don't Come Easy' (specially pre-recorded with an orchestra) on a snow-covered mountain, and then, still in the snow, performs the unique 'The Snowman Song' with Cilla Black and fox puppet Basil Brush. Only the latter song currently circulates (thanks to a 'TOTP2' rebroadcast), but the entire show survives in the BBC archives.

00-03-72 – Promo Video

Back Off Boogaloo

'Back Off Boogaloo' is not only Ringo's finest single, but it's also one of the best singles of the Glam Rock era, deservedly getting to No. 2 in the UK and No. 9 in the USA. Taped on 20-03-72 in the grounds of John's home in Tittenhurst Park, Ascot (which Ringo would eventually purchase), the video features Ringo meeting a Frankenstein monster, after which they, rather bizarrely, have a picnic together. 2 similar edits exist for this video, of which one of them is on 'Photograph: The Best of Ringo Starr'. Also surviving are some brief outtakes, featuring Ringo and the monster walking along holding hand while Ringo carries a bunch of daffodils (Ringo actually looks a little like 'Odd Bod Junior' throughout this video, the young monster featured in the cult 1966 comedy movie 'Carry On Screaming').

00-12-72 – **'Born To Boogie' movie (UK)**

Tutti Frutti / Children Of The Revolution [with T. Rex and Elton John]

Taped on 21-03-72, Ringo drums and Elton John plays piano on these songs by T. Rex, as well as directs the movie and appears in other scenes. Also performed was 'The Slider', but this wasn't featured in the movie.

00-11-73 – **'Top Of The Pops' Video (UK)**

Photograph

Some of the videos made for 'Top Of The Pops' were terrible, not even featuring footage of the artists involved, but Ringo is at least in this one, fooling around in Tittenhurst Park. It was broadcast on the show on 01-11-73, with the single making No. 8 in the UK and No. 1 in the USA. Ringo's 1973 album, simply entitled 'Ringo', is the nearest all 4 of The Beatles came to a reunion, with both performer and songwriter contributions from John, Paul and George. It peaked at No. 7 in the UK and No. 2 in the USA, while, also taken from the album, was 'You're Sixteen', which got to No. 4 in the UK and No. 1 in the USA, and the US-only 'Oh My My', which peaked at No. 5.

00-11-74 – **Promo Video**

Only You

Attempting to repeat the success of 'Ringo', the similar 'Goodnight Vienna' album got to No. 30 in the UK and No. 8 in the USA, with 'Only You' getting to No. 28 in the UK and No. 6 in the USA. Filmed on 14-11-74 on top of the Capitol Records Tower in Los Angeles with

Harry Nilsson, the zany video was shown on 'Top Of The Pops' on 19-12-74 and 16-01-75, and is also on 'Photograph: The Best of Ringo Starr'. Also taken from the album was the US No. 3 hit 'No No Song' b/w 'Snookeroo', and the US No. 31 hit '(It's All Down To) Goodnight Vienna'. John Lennon's version of 'Only You', for which he did a guide vocal for Ringo, was released in 1998.

28-04-75 – 'The Smothers Brothers Show' (USA)

No No Song [with The Smothers Brothers]

A lively version of Ringo's recent single, performed with the hosts of the show.

22-05-75 – 'Boogie Woogie Gospel Rock and Roll Show' (USA)

No No Song [with Hoyt Axton]

Another live and loose version, this time performed with the writer of the song, along with Micky Dolenz, Kris Kristofferson, Paul Williams, Buffy Saint-Marie and many more. The song is about giving up drink and drugs, ironic, as everyone here looks drunk or high!

00-09-76 – **Promo Video**

I'll Still Love You

'I'll Still Love You' (also known as 'When Every Song Is Sung') is a George Harrison composition, and one of his very finest too. Taken from the US No. 28 and UK chart flop 'Ringo's Rotogravure' album, the outdoors video, taped in Germany on 08-08-76, features a shaven headed Ringo, as do the other 2 promo videos he made this year. Also released as a single from this album was 'A Dose Of Rock 'n' Roll',

which got to No. 26 in the USA, though no video was made.

00-10-76 – **Promo Video**

You Don't Know Me At All

Taped in late July 1976 in Monte Carlo and in Hamburg, this is Ringo's most notorious 'bald' video, featuring lots of close-ups.

00-11-76 – **Promo Video**

Hey Baby

Taped in Hamburg in early August, this features Ringo and a host of dancers on 2 huge staircases. A US No. 74 hit, interestingly, the soundtrack on the video is both different and longer than the released recording.

00-09-77 – **Promo Video**

Drowning In The Sea Of Love

Taped in Europe, in what looks like a night club and an expensive penthouse apartment, Ringo's surprisingly good version of Joe Simon's soul classic is from the album 'Ringo The 4th'.

00-04-78 – **'The Last Waltz' Movie (USA)**

I Shall Be Released [with Bob Dylan, The Band and Ronnie Wood]

Taped at Winterland Ballroom in San Francisco on 25-11-76, 'The Last Waltz' is the feature length movie of The Band's farewell concert, for which Ringo played on this one song.

26-04-78 – **'Ognir Rrats' (USA)**

I'm The Greatest / Medley: A Dose Of Rock 'n' Roll - Act Naturally / Yellow Submarine / You're Sixteen [with Carrie Fisher] / With A Little Help From My Friends / Heart On My Sleeve / Hard Times / A Man Like Me

A modern update of 'The Prince and The Pauper' (something Tommy Steele did with 'The Duke Wore Jeans' 20 years earlier), this TV special is genuinely funny, and there's much to enjoy musically too, with all songs being new recordings. Amongst the highlights are 'Act Naturally' with the slow part of 'A Dose Of Rock 'n' Roll' used as the intro, a duet with Carrie Fisher (hot at the time due to her recent success in 'Star Wars'), and 'Heart On My Sleeve' and 'Hard Times', live recordings backed by a band that includes Dr. John. 'You're Sixteen' is on 'Photograph: The Best of Ringo Starr', though sadly with the duet soundtrack replaced by the original studio recording, and the entire TV special, re-titled 'Ringo', was shown in the UK on 02-01-83. Additionally, various outtakes circulate from the February-March 1978 taping.

00-07-78 – **Promo Video**

Tonight

Another great video, with Ringo playing an unlikely romantic lead, the song is from the album 'Bad Boy', which again failed in the UK, and got to No. 129 in the USA.

00-06-79 – **Promo Video** – *RON WOOD*

Buried Alive

Taped in April 1979, Ringo plays drums in this video.

03-09-79 – **'The Jerry Lewis Muscular Dystrophy Association Telethon' (USA)**

Money (That's What I Want) / Twist and Shout / Jumpin' Jack Flash [all songs are with Bill Wyman, Todd Rundgren, Doug Kershaw and Kiki Dee]

Ringo jams with another Rolling Stone this time, on a televised charity show. He would work with Todd Rundgren again many times in the future.

00-11-81 – **Promo Video**

Wrack My Brain

Taped on 17/18-09-81, the video sees Ringo in a house of horrors, with various ghouls and monsters, one of them played by his wife Barbara. The song, a No. 38 US hit, is from 'Stop and Smell The Roses', Ringo's 1st album since the death of John. Getting to No. 89 in the US album charts, unfortunately the album and all singles for it failed to chart in the UK.

12-12-81 – **'Parkinson' (UK)**

Singing The Blues [with Barbara Bach, Michael Parkinson, Tim Rice and Jimmy Tarbuck]

This is a loose jam with the other guests on the show.

00-01-82 – **Promo Video**

Stop and Take The Time To Smell The Roses

Taped on 16/17-09-81, this is another amusing video, featuring Ringo both as a posh 'toff' in top hat and tails and as a motorcycle cop. The song is, more or less, the title track of Ringo's latest album.

00-02-82 – **'The Cooler' (UK)**

Private Property / Sure To Fall (In Love With You) / Attention [with Paul and Linda McCartney]

Ringo had long embraced the music video to help promote his music, and this time he, with a little help from Barbara plus Paul and Linda, made a 12 minute film. Taped on 13/14/15/18-01-82, this features a vague storyline about Ringo being thrown into jail, and then falling in love with a beautiful and sexy prison warden, played by Barbara of course. 'Sure To Fall (In Love With You)' is an old Carl Perkins song that The Beatles performed at the BBC, and even, in the Pete Best era, played at their infamous Decca audition. In 1983, Ringo followed this with 'Old Wave', which, although a pretty good album, failed to even get a release in the UK and USA, initially only being available in Germany and Canada. He recorded an aborted album in 1987, but he wouldn't actually release another new studio album until 1992.

00-07-82 – **Promo Video** – *PAUL McCARTNEY*

Take It Away

See the PAUL McCARTNEY section for more details!

08-10-82 – **'Parkinson In Australia' (Australia)**

Medley: Honey Don't – Blue Suede Shoes [with Glenn Shorrock]

Ringo plays drums behind Glenn, but doesn't sing.

00-12-83 – **Promo Video** – *PAUL McCARTNEY*

So Bad [with Ringo Starr]

See the PAUL McCARTNEY section for more details!

04-07-84 – **Washington Monument, Washington D.C. (USA)** – *THE BEACH BOYS*

Back In The U.S.S.R. / Good Vibrations / Fun, Fun, Fun

Ringo plays drums during part of this Beach Boys concert.

25-10-84 – **'Give My Regards To Broad Street' movie (UK)** – *PAUL McCARTNEY*

Wanderlust / Ballroom Dancing / Not Such A Bad Boy / So Bad / No Values

See the PAUL McCARTNEY section for more details!

08-12-84 – **'Saturday Night Live' (USA)**

Medley: With A Little Help From My Friends – What Kind Of Fool Am I? – Act Naturally – I've Gotta Be Me – Octopus's Garden – Photograph – Yellow Submarine – With A Little Help From My Friends (Reprise)

This medley is performed with Billy Crystal, impersonating Sammy Davis Junior.

00-01-85 – **'Water' Movie (UK)**

Freedom [with George Harrison]

See the GEORGE HARRISON section for more details!

00-10-85 – **Promo Video** – ARTISTS UNITED AGAINST APARTHEID

Sun City

Made to highlight apartheid in South Africa, Ringo guests on this song, and is also in the video that includes Bob Dylan, Pete Townshend, Bruce Springsteen, Little Steven, Lou Reed, Peter Gabriel, Bono and many others.

19-10-85 – **Limehouse Studios, London (UK)**

Honey Don't [with Carl Perkins] / Matchbox [with Carl Perkins and Eric Clapton]

Rehearsals for 'Blue Suede Shoes: A Rockabilly Tribute To Carl Perkins and Friends', taped two days later.

00-12-85 – **'Alice In Wonderland' (USA)**

Nonsense

Taped in May 1985, and broadcast on US TV in 2 parts on 09-12-85 and 10-12-85, Ringo plays the mock turtle in this live action musical adaption of the famous fairytale.

01-01-86 – **'Blue Suede Shoes: A Rockabilly Tribute To Carl Perkins and Friends' (UK)**

Honey Don't [with Carl Perkins] / Matchbox [with Carl Perkins and Eric Clapton] / Medley: That's Alright Mama - Blue Moon of Kentucky - Night Train to Memphis - Amen / Glad All Over / Whole Lotta Shakin' Goin' On / Gone, Gone, Gone / Blue Suede Shoes / Blue Suede Shoes (Reprise) [All songs from the medley onwards are with Carl

Perkins, George Harrison, Eric Clapton, Dave Edmunds and others]

See the GEORGE HARRISON section for more details!

06-06-87 – 'The Princes Trust Concert', Wembley Arena, London (UK)

Stand By Me [Performed by Ben E. King] / While My Guitar Gently Weeps [Performed by George Harrison] / Here Comes The Sun [Performed by George Harrison] / With A Little Help From My Friends

See the GEORGE HARRISON section for more details!

26-09-87 – The London Brassiere, Atlanta, G.A. (USA)

Whole Lotta Shakin' Goin' On / Blues At Midnight / Great Balls Of Fire / Mony Mony [with Jerry Lee Lewis and others]

Briefly investing in a restaurant in Atlanta, Jerry Lee Lewis was one of the guests at the grand opening, and Ringo played drums on some of the songs.

20-01-88 – 'The Rock and Roll Hall Of Fame', The Waldorf-Astoria, New York (USA)

Twist and Shout / All Along The Watchtower / I Saw Her Standing There / Stand By Me / Stop! In The Name Of Love / Medley: Whole Lotta Shaking Going On - Hound Dog - Hi Ho Silver / Born On The Bayou / Like A Rolling Stone / (I Can't Get No) Satisfaction [with George Harrison, Mick Jagger, The Beach Boys, Ben E. King, John Fogerty and others]

See the GEORGE HARRISON section for more details!

00-02-88 – **Promo Video** – GEORGE HARRISON

When We Was Fab

See the GEORGE HARRISON section for more details!

00-04-89 – **Promo Video** – TOM PETTY

I Won't Back Down [with George Harrison]

See the GEORGE HARRISON section for more details!

00-06-89 – **Promo Video**

Act Naturally [with Buck Owens]

A duet with the (other) guy who made the song famous, this amusing video, taped on 22-06-89 is on 'Photograph: The Best of Ringo Starr'.

00-06-89 – **Promo Video** – GENTLEMEN WITHOUT WEAPONS

Spirit Of The Forest

Taped on 05-03-89, this song and video were made to highlight the destruction of the rain forests, and features an impressive line-up that includes Brian Wilson, Iggy Pop, Joni Mitchell, Kate Bush, Chris Rea, David Gilmour, Deborah Harry, Belinda Carlisle, Bonnie Rait, Jon Anderson, Kim Wilde, Olivia Newton-John, Richie Havens, Rita Coolidge, Little Steven and more.

Mid. 1989 – **Promo Video** – JAN HAMMER

Too Much To Lose

Taped in March 1989, Ringo guests on this video.

03-09-89 – **The Greek Theatre, Los Angeles (USA)**

It Don't Come Easy / No No Song / Yellow Submarine / Iko Iko [Performed by Dr. John] / The Weight [Performed by Levon Helm, Dr. John and Rick Danko] / Will It Go Round In Circles [Performed by Billy Preston] / Act Naturally / You're A Friend Of Mine [Performed by Clarence Clemons and Billy Preston] / The Shape I'm In [Performed by Rick Danko] / I Wanna Be Your Man / Life In The Last Lane [Performed by Joe Walsh] / Up On Cripple Creek [Performed by Levon Helm and Rick Danko] / Boys / Bein' Angry Is A Full Time Job [Performed by Nils Lofgren] / Right Place, Wrong Time [Performed by Dr. John] / Quarter To Three [Performed by Clarence Clemons] / Rocky Mountain Way [Performed by Joe Walsh] / Photograph / With A Little Help From My Friends

Now teetotal, fit and healthy following a stay in The Betty Ford Clinic the previous year, Ringo finally put into practice an idea he'd been toying with for years, and that is going out on tour with what he'd dub 'The All-Starr Band'. Touring the USA and Japan, it would run from 23-07-89 to 08-11-89, and feature the following guests: Joe Walsh (The Eagles/James Gang), Nils Lofgren (Crazy Horse/The E Street Band), Dr. John, Billy Preson, Rick Danko (The Band), Levon Helm (The Band), Clarence Clemons (The E Street Band) and Jim Keltner, with occasional guests Ringo's son Zak Starkey and Garth Hudson (The Band). Issued on VHS, and later on DVD, Ringo would repeat the idea, with differing line-ups, many times over the coming decades.

05-05-90 – **'Lennon: A Tribute' (UK)**

I Call Your Name

Backed by a band that includes Jeff Lynne and Tom Petty, Ringo taped this in California on 28-03-90, especially for the 'Lennon: A Tribute' event, and he does a very fine job too.

00-10-90 – **Promo Video #3**

It Don't Come Easy

A live version, taped on the 1989 'All Starr Band' tour, this was used to promote Ringo's 1st live album, but unfortunately, like all of Ringo's live albums (there's been 11 so far), it failed to chart.

00-06-91 – **Promo Video** – *NILS LOFGREN*

Valentine

Taped in February 1991, Ringo guests in this video, as does Bruce Springsteen.

09-05-92 – **'Dame Edna's Hollywood' (USA)**

Act Naturally [with Dame Edna Everage]

00-05-92 – **Promo Video**

Weight Of The World

In an interesting video that features Ringo on a giant pair of weighing scales, 'Weight Of The World' scraped to No. 74 in the UK charts but wasn't a hit in the USA. It is taken from the critically-acclaimed 'Time Takes Time' album, which, despite being his first in 9 years, failed to chart.

27-05-92 – 'The Arsenio Hall Show' (USA)

Weight Of The World

13-07-92 – 'Live From Montreux', Casino, Montreux (Switzerland)

I'm the Greatest / No No Song / No Time [Performed by Burton Cummings] / Girls Talk [Performed by Dave Edmunds] / Rocky Mountain Way [Performed by Joe Walsh] / I Can't Tell You Why [Performed by Timothy B. Schmit] / Shine Silently [Performed by Nils Lofgren] / Bang The Drum All Day [Performed by Todd Rundgren] / Don't Go Where the Road Don't Go / Yellow Submarine / Desperado [Performed by Timothy B. Schmit] / Lysistrata [Performed by Todd Rundgren] / One World [Performed by Todd Rundgren] / Keep On Tryin' [Performed by Timothy B. Schmit] / Wiggle [Performed by Tim Cappello] / Black Maria [Performed by Todd Rundgren] / In the City [Performed by Joe Walsh] / You're Sixteen / Weight of the World / Walkin' Nerve [Performed by Nils Lofgren] / I Hear You Knocking [Performed by Dave Edmunds] / American Woman [Performed by Burton Cummings] / Boys / Photograph / Act Naturally / With a Little Help From My Friends

Ringo's 2nd All-Starr Band toured the USA and Europe from 02-06-92 to 06-09-92, and featured: Joe Walsh (The Eagles/James Gang), Nils Lofgren (Crazy Horse/The E Street Band), Todd Rundgren (The Nazz/Utopia/The New Cars), Dave Edmunds (Love Sculpture/Rockpile), Burton Cummings (The Guess Who), Timothy B. Schmit (Poco/The Eagles), Zak Starkey and Timmy Cappello. Peter Cetera (Chicago) left before the tour started.

06-09-92 – **'The Jerry Lewis Muscular Dystrophy Association Telethon' (USA)**

You're Sixteen

This was broadcast live from Caesar's Palace, Las Vegas.

00-09-92 – **Promo Video**

Don't Go Where The Road Don't Go

A terrific rocker from the 'Time Takes Time' album, the video features concert clips with a stop-motion effect.

21-10-92 – **'The Arsenio Hall Show' (USA)**

Don't Go Where The Road Don't Go / Act Naturally

16-04-93 – **The Earth Day Concert, The Hollywood Bowl, Hollywood (USA)** – *PAUL McCARTNEY*

See the PAUL McCARTNEY section for more details!

18-04-93 – **'Ringo Starr: Going Home' (USA)**

I'm The Greatest / Yellow Submarine / Boys / Weight Of The World / You're Sixteen / Don't Go Where The Road Don't Go / Photograph / Act Naturally / With A Little Help From My Friends

An excellent concert/documentary special made for the Disney channel, the concert sequences were taped in The Empire Theatre, Liverpool, on 06-07-92, with additional off-stage sequences in Liverpool on 29-09-92.

24-04-93 – **'Farm Aid VI' (USA)**

Something Wild / The Dark End Of The Street / She Makes Me Feel Good / If I Had A Boat / Farther Down The Line [All songs are with The New Maroons]

Heavily bearded, Ringo plays drums for this band, and clearly enjoys not being in the limelight himself and just playing.

26-06-93 – **'Music: Together For Our Children' (USA)**

Something Wild / The Dark End Of The Street [All songs are with The New Maroons]

This was taped in The University Of California, Los Angeles, on 23-06-93.

00-02-94 – **Promo Video** – *R.A.D.D.*

Drive My Car

See the PAUL McCARTNEY section for more details!

23-06-94 – **Friar Park, Henley-on-Thames (UK)** – *THE THREETLES*

See the PAUL McCARTNEY section for more details!

Maureen Starkey, Ringo's first wife, died on 30-12-94.

27-06-95 – **The Budokan, Tokyo (Japan)**

Don't Go Where The Road Don't Go / I Wanna Be Your Man / It Don't Come Easy / The Loco-Motion [Performed by Mark Farner] / Nothing From Nothing [Performed by Billy Preston] / No Sugar Tonight

[Performed by Randy Bachman] / People Got To Be Free [Performed by Felix Cavaliere] / Boris The Spider [Performed by John Entwistle] / Boys / You're Sixteen / Yellow Submarine / I'm Your Captain" [Performed by Mark Farner] / Honey Don't / Act Naturally / Back Off Boogaloo / Groovin' [Performed by Felix Cavaliere] / Will It Go Round In Circles"[Performed by Billy Preston] / Good Lovin' [Performed Felix Cavaliere] / Photograph / No No Song / With A Little Help From My Friends

Touring Japan and the USA from 02-07-95 to 28-08-95, Ringo's 3rd All-Starr Band starred: Randy Bachman (The Guess Who/Bachman-Turner Overdrive), Mark Farner (Grand Funk Railroad), Billy Preston, Felix Cavaliere (The Rascals), John Entwistle (The Who), Zak Starkey and Mark Rivera. Nils Lofgren and Clarence Clemons attended rehearsals, but left before the tour started due to Bruce Springsteen reforming The E Street Band.

30-05-97 – 'Ringo Starr and His Fourth All-Starr Band', Pine Knob Theatre, Detroit (USA)

It Don't Come Easy / Act Naturally / The Devil Came From Kansas [Performed by Gary Brooker] / Show Me The Way [Performed by Peter Frampton] / Sunshine Of Your Love [Performed by Jack Bruce] / Shooting Star [Performed by Simon Kirke] / Boys / Baby I Love Your Way [Performed by Peter Frampton] / You're Sixteen / Yellow Submarine / A Salty Dog [Performed by Gary Brooker] / Norwegian Wood (This Bird Has Flown) [Performed by Peter Frampton] / Theme From An Imaginary Western [Performed by Jack Bruce] / Conquistador [Performed by Gary Brooker] / I'm The Greatest / No

No Song / I Feel Free [Performed by Jack Bruce] / All Right Now [Performed by Simon Kirke] / I Wanna Be Your Man / Do You Feel Like We Do? [Performed by Peter Frampton] / White Room [Performed by Jack Bruce] / A Whiter Shade Of Pale [Performed by Gary Brooker] / Photograph / With A Little Help From My Friends

Ringo's 4th All-Starr Band toured the USA from 28-04-97 to 07-06-97, and Europe and Russia from 07-08-98 to 05-09-98, and featured: Peter Frampton (The Herd/Humble Pie), Gary Brooker (Procol Harum), Jack Bruce (Cream), Simon Kirke (Free/Bad Company), Mark Rivera, and, in 1998, Scott Gordon. Dave Mason (Traffic/Fleetwood Mac) left before the tour started. This performance was issued on DVD.

16-05-97 – **'In The World Tonight' (UK)** – *PAUL McCARTNEY*

Beautiful Night

See the PAUL McCARTNEY section for more details!

00-12-97 – **Promo Video** – *PAUL McCARTNEY*

Beautiful Night

See the PAUL McCARTNEY section for more details!

00-06-98 – **Promo Video**

La De Da [with Paul McCartney]

Ringo's first new single in 6 years, this actually charted in the UK too, albeit at only No. 63, and it didn't chart in the USA. The parent album, 'Vertical Man', got to No. 85 in the UK and No. 61 in the USA. Taped in S.I.R. Studios, New York on 09-05-98, and in Times Square on 10-05-

98, this entertaining video also features brief clips of Paul recording his backing vocals for the song.

15-06-98 – 'The Tonight Show' (USA)

La De Da

17-06-98 – 'The View' (USA)

La De Da / Photograph / With A Little Help From My Friends

28-06-98 – 'VH-1 Storytellers' (USA)

With A Little Help From My Friends / Back Off Boogaloo / Don't Pass Me By / It Don't Come Easy / Octopus's Garden / Photograph / La De Da / King Of Broken Hearts / Love Me Do / With A Little Help From My Friends (Reprise)

Taped on 13-05-98 in The Bottom Line, New York, 'Photograph', wasn't included in the TV broadcast, but was issued on an official DVD release of the show. Most fans would prefer to see Ringo do tours like this, but unfortunately he is more comfortable with the 'All-Starr Band' format. His version of 'Love Me Do' is on 'Vertical Man', though it's not as artistically successful as the great performance of 'I Call Your Name' from 1990.

03-07-98 – 'Live With Regis and Kathie Lee' (USA)

La De Da

This was taped on 14-05-98.

15-07-98 – 'The National Lottery Live' (UK)

La De Da

07-09-98 – 'The Jerry Lewis Muscular Dystrophy Association Telethon' (USA)

Octopus's Garden

11-09-98 – 'Hard Rock Live' (USA)

Photograph / La De Da / I Was Walkin' / Love Me Do / With A Little Help From My Friends

This was taped at Sony Music Studios, New York, on 17-06-98.

10-10-98 – 'Wetten Dass' (Germany)

La De Da

20-10-98 – 'The Late Show With David Letterman' (USA)

Back Off Boogaloo

21-10-98 – 'Live With Regis and Kathie Lee' (USA)

Back Off Boogaloo / Photograph

Following the 'Vertical Man' promotion, Ringo formed a 5th All-Starr Band, and toured the USA from 12-02-99 to 29-03-99, this time with: Todd Rundgren (The Nazz/Utopia/The New Cars), Gary Brooker (Procol Harum), Jack Bruce (Cream), Simon Kirke (Free/Bad Company) and Timmy Cappello, with occasional guest Ginger Baker (Cream/Blind Faith). Joe Walsh left before the tour started, but later played on some songs at select shows. Later in the year, Ringo released the Christmas album 'I Wanna Be Santa Claus', but it sold poorly, and no promo videos were made for any of the songs.

19-05-00 – 'The Late Show With David Letterman' (USA)

With A Little Help From My Friends

This was taped on 18-05-00. From 12-05-00 to 01-07-00, Ringo toured the USA with the 6th All-Starr band, which consisted of: Dave Edmunds (Love Sculpture/Rockpile), Eric Carmen (The Raspberries), Jack Bruce (Cream), Simon Kirke (Free/Bad Company) and Mark Rivera. Billy Squier, Ray Davies (The Kinks) and Billy Preston left before the tour started.

22-08-01 – 'Ringo Starr & His New All-Star Band', Rosemount Theatre, Chicago (USA)

Photograph / Act Naturally / Logical Song [Performed by Roger Hodgson] / Cleveland Rocks [Performed by Ian Hunter] / Back Off Boogaloo / I Wanna Be Your Man / You're Sixteen / Yellow Submarine / Things Can Only Get Better [Performed by Howard Jones] / Lucky Man [Performed by Greg Lake] / Give A Little Bit [Performed by Roger Hodgson] / No One Is To Blame [Performed by Howard Jones] / No No Song / It Don't Come Easy / The Glamorous Life [Performed by Sheila E.] / Take The Long Way Home [Performed by Roger Hodgson] / All The Young Dudes [Performed by Ian Hunter] / Don't Go Where The Road Don't Go / With A Little Help From My Friends

Touring the USA from 12-05-01 to 01-07-01 (coincidentally starting and finishing a year to the day since the previous tour), Ringo's 7th All-Starr Band featured: Roger Hodgson (Supertramp), Ian Hunter (Mott The Hoople), Howard Jones, Greg Lake (King Crimson/Emerson, Lake and Palmer), Sheila E. and Mark Rivera.

2001/1989-1999 – **Promo Video**

Yellow Submarine

To promote the triple live All-Starr Band album 'The Anthology... So Far', a couple of specially compiled videos were made.

2001/1989-1999 – **Promo Video**

With A Little Help From My Friends

Another video to promote 'The Anthology... So Far'.

29-11-02 – 'Concert For George', The Royal Albert Hall, London (UK)

Photograph / Honey Don't / For You Blue / Something / All Things Must Pass / While My Guitar Gently Weeps / My Sweet Lord / Wah Wah [all songs are with Eric Clapton, Dhani Harrison, Billy Preston, Jeff Lynne and others, and from 'For You Blue' onwards, with Paul McCartney]

Ringo was probably closer to George than any of the other Beatles, and, in typical Ringo fashion, makes light of what was already a surprisingly upbeat event, even saying to the audience at one point 'Thanks for the jelly babies'! After his own 2 songs, he joins the rest of the band in backing others, including Paul.

See the PAUL McCARTNEY section for more details!

00-03-03 – **Promo Video**

Never Without You

Ringo's new album, 'Ringo Rama', predictably didn't chart in the UK, and got to No. 113 in the USA. Taken from the album, the video for 'Never Without You' features Ringo and his band in an empty theatre, with shots of him sometimes playing the drums while singing this very good song.

13-03-03 – **'The Tonight Show With Jay Leno' (USA)**

Never Without You

13-03-03 – **'Live With Regis and Kelly' (USA)**

Never Without You / With A Little Help From My Friends

21-03-03 – **'Good Morning America' (USA)**

Never Without You / With A Little Help From My Friends

25-03-03 – **'Total Request Live' (USA)**

Never Without You

25-03-03 – **'Late Night With Conan O'Brien' (USA)**

Never Without You

02-04-03 – **'Last Call With Carson Daily' (USA)**

Never Without You / With A Little Help From My Friends

24-07-03 – **'Tour 2003', Casino Rama, Orillia (Canada)**

It Don't Come Easy / Honey Don't / Memphis In Your Mind / How Long [Performed by Paul Carrack] / Down Under [Performed by Colin Hay] / When I See You Smile [Performed by John Waite] / A Love Bizarre [Performed by Sheila E.] / Boys / Don't Pass Me By / Yellow Submarine / The Living Years [Performed by Paul Carrack] / Missing You [Performed by John Waite] / The Glamorous Life [Performed by Sheila E.] / I Wanna Be Your Man / Who Can It Be Now? [Performed by Colin Hay] / With A Little Help from My Friends

Ringo's 8th All-Starr Band, who toured the USA from 24-07-03 to 07-09-03, starred: Colin Hay (Men At Work), Paul Carrack (Ace/Squeeze/Mike and The Mechanics), John Waite (The Baby/Bad English), Sheila E. and Mark Rivera. This show was issued on DVD.

01-08-03 – **'Good Morning America' (USA)**

Boys / Who Can It Be Now? [Performed by Colin Hay] / With A Little Help From My Friends

This was broadcast live from Bryant Park, New York.

16-06-05 – **'The Late Show With David Letterman' (USA)**

Choose Love

17-06-05 – **'Good Morning America' (USA)**

Photograph / Choose Love / Yellow Submarine

This was taped in Bryant Park, New York.

19-06-05 – **'CBS This Morning' (USA)**

Choose Love

28-06-05 – **'The Late Late Show With Craig Ferguson' (USA)**

Choose Love / I'm The Greatest

29-06-05 – **'The Early Show' (USA)**

It Don't Come Easy / Choose Love / I'm The Greatest

This was taped on 20-06-05.

05-07-05 – **'The Tonight Show' (USA)**

Choose Love *(This was taped on 04-07-05)*

25-08-05 – **'Soundstage Presents... Ringo Starr' (USA)**

It Don't Come Easy / Octopus' Garden / Choose Love / I Wanna Be Your Man / Who Can It Be Now? [Performed by Colin Hay] / Don't Pass Me By / I'm The Greatest / Give Me Back The Beat / Memphis In Your Mind / Photograph / Back Off Boogaloo / Yellow Submarine / Act Naturally / With A Little Help From My Friends

This was taped in The Genessee Theatre, Waukegan, on 24-06-05, and issued on DVD in 2009.

00-09-05 – **Promo Video**

Fading In Fading Out

With a video filmed on stage and in a musical instruments shop, 'Fading In Fading Out' is one of Ringo's best latter day recordings. It's from the 'Choose Love' album, which failed to chart.

00-11-05 – **Promo Video** – HURRICANE RELIEF

Tears In Heaven

A charity record, Ringo makes a brief cameo, along with Elton John, Steven Tyler, Ozzy Osbourne, Phil Collins and many others.

16-07-06 – **'Live 2006', Mohegan Sun Arena, Uncasville, CT (USA)**

It Don't Come Easy / What Goes On / Honey Don't / Everybody Wants You [Performed by Billy Squier] / Free Ride [Performed by Edgar Winter] / A Love Bizarre [Performed by Sheila E.] / Boys / Don't Mean

Nothing [Performed by Richard Marx] / She's Not There [Performed by Rod Argent] / Never Without You / Yellow Submarine / Dying To Live [Performed by Edgar Winter] / Right Here Waiting [Performed by Richard Marx] / Ramblin' On My Mind / Performed by Billy Squier] / Time of the Season [Performed by Rod Argent] / Frankenstein [Performed by Edgar Winter] / Photograph / Choose Love / Should've Known Better [Performed by Richard Marx] / The Glamorous Life [Performed by Sheila E.] / I Wanna Be Your Man / Rock Me Tonite [Performed by Billy Squier] / Hold Your Head Up [Performed by Rod Argent] / Act Naturally / Memphis in Your Mind / With A Little Help from My Friends

Ringo's 9th All-Starr Band toured the USA from 14-06-06 to 20-07-06, and this time featured: Billy Squier, Richard Marx, Edgar Winter, Rod Argent (The Zombies/Argent), Hamish Stuart (The Average White Band/Paul McCartney's 1989-1993 touring band) and Sheila E. This show was issued on DVD.

00-08-07 – **Promo Video** – *PAUL McCARTNEY*

Nod Your Head

See the PAUL McCARTNEY section for more details!

00-12-07 – **Promo Video**

Liverpool 8

Ringo has upset a few people in recent years by his off-the-cuff remarks about Liverpool, but this song shows his real feelings for the place. An excellent song with an even better video (complete with

Beatles footage), the 'Liverpool 8' album that it's from got to No. 91 in the UK and No. 94 in the USA.

11-01-08 – 'The CBS Early Show' (USA)

Liverpool 8 / Boys / With A Little Help From My Friends

This was taped in St. George's Hall, Liverpool, for US TV broadcast.

14-01-08 – 'GM TV' (UK)

Liverpool 8

21-01-08 – 'The Late Show With David Letterman' (USA)

Liverpool 8

Ringo was due to perform 'Liverpool 8' on 'Live With Regis and Kelly' on 22-01-08, but walked off the set when he was told that the song would have to be cut short.

24-01-08 – 'The Late Late Show With Craig Ferguson' (USA)

Photograph / Liverpool 8 / Boys / With A Little Help From My Friends

25-01-08 – 'Larry King Live' (USA)

Photograph / Liverpool 8

25-01-08 – 'Live At The House Of Blues' (USA)

Photograph / With A Little Help From My From Friends

03-02-08 – 'Private Sessions' (USA)

Liverpool 8 / With A Little Help From My Friends / Photograph / Boys

08-02-08 – 'The Rachael Ray Show' (USA)

Liverpool 8 *(This was taped on 22-01-08)*

02-05-08 – **'Off The Record With Ringo Starr' (USA)**

Liverpool 8 (acoustic) + parts of Ticket To Ride, Come Together and Back Off Boogaloo

02-08-08 – **The Greek Theatre, Los Angeles (USA)**

Medley: With A Little Help From My Friends - It Don't Come Easy / What Goes On / The Stroke [Performed by Billy Squier] / Free Ride [Performed by Edgar Winter] / Dream Weaver [Performed by Gary Wright] / Boys / Pick Up The Pieces [Performed by Hamish Stuart] / Act Naturally / Yellow Submarine / Never Without You / I Wanna Be Your Man / Who Can It Be Now? [Performed by Colin Hay] / Photograph / Oh My My / Medley: With A Little Help From My Friends - Give Peace A Chance

Touring the USA, Ringo's 10th All-Starr Band featured: Billy Squier, Colin Hay (Men At Work), Edgar Winter, Gary Wright (Spooky Tooth), Hamish Stuart (The Average White Band/Paul McCartney's 1989-1993 touring band) and Gregg Bissonette (The David Lee Roth Band). This show was issued on DVD.

04-04-09 – **'Change Begins Within: Live At Radio City Music Hall' (USA)**

It Don't Come Easy / Boys / Yellow Submarine / With A Little Help From My Friends [with Paul McCartney] / Cosmically Conscious / I Saw Her Standing There [The last two songs are with Paul McCartney, Sheryl Crow, Donovan, Eddie Vedder, Moby, Ben Harper, Paul Horn,

Angelo Badalamenti, Betty LaVette, Jim James, and The TM Choir]

See the PAUL McCARTNEY section for more details!

28-05-09 – 'A Sideman's Journey' (UK)

I'm In Love Again [with Paul McCartney and Klaus Voorman]

This was taped in Paul's Hog's Hill Mill studio on 19-05-08.

00-11-09 – **Promo Video** – *PETER KAY'S ANIMATED ALL STAR BAND*

Children In Need Medley

A UK No. 1 charity record, Ringo's voice makes the briefest of cameos in this animated video.

12-01-10 – 'Late Night With Jimmy Fallon' (USA)

I Wanna Be Your Man / Walk With You / The Other Side Of Liverpool / With A Little Help From My Friends

In 2010 Ringo released another album, 'Y Not', but, surprisingly, no promo videos were made for any of the songs, though it still got to No. 58 in the USA. Rehearsals of 'The Other Side Of Liverpool' and 'Walk With You' circulate from this performance.

13-01-10 – 'The Daily Show With Jon Stewart' (USA)

Walk With You / With A Little Help From My Friends

18-01-10 – 'The Jay Leno Show' (USA)

The Other Side Of Liverpool

23-06-10 – **Press Conference, Niagara Falls (USA)**

The Other Side Of Liverpool / Boys / With A Little Help From My Friends

From 24-06-10 until 20-11-11, Ringo and his 11th All-Starr Band would do several short tours of the USA, Europe and South America, and this time starred: Wally Palmer (The Romantics), Rick Derringer (The McCoys), Edgar Winter, Gary Wright (Spooky Tooth), Richard Page (M. Mister), Gregg Bissonette (The David Lee Roth Band) and Mark Rivera (some shows only).

02-07-10 – **'Live From The Artists Den' (USA)**

Photograph / Walk With You / I Wanna Be Your Man / The Other Side Of Liverpool / It Don't Come Easy / Boys / With A Little Help From My Friends

This was taped in The Metropolitan Museum Of Art, New York, on 20-01-10.

07-07-10 – **Radio City Music Hall, New York (USA)**

Birthday [with Paul McCartney]

Paul was the big surprise special guest at this 70th birthday bash for Ringo, with even Yoko in the audience looking in shock! Ringo also performed a few songs, but to date no professionally filmed footage has surfaced.

09-10-10 – **Haskolabio, Reykjavik (Iceland)**

Give Peace A Chance / Happy Birthday [both songs are with Yoko Ono, Sean Lennon and Olivia Harrison, and are sung on what would've been John Lennon's 70s birthday]

This was broadcast by the website 'lifeandimynd.is' on 12-10-10.

01-06-11 – **Press Conference, Dunsfold Aerodrome, Cranleigh (UK)**

Boys / Freedom [Performed by Edgar Winter] / Broken Wings [Performed by Richard Page] / With A Little Help From My Friends

This performance was broadcast live on Muzu.TV.

04-06-11 – **Ukraine National Palace, Kiev (Ukraine)**

It Don't Come Easy / Honey Don't / Choose Love / Hang On Sloopy [Performed by Rick Derringer] / Free Ride / Talking In Your Sleep [Performed by Wally Palmar] / I Wanna Be Your Man / Dream Weaver [Performed by Gary Wright] / Kyrie [Performed by Richard Page] / The Other Side Of Liverpool / Yellow Submarine / Frankenstein [Performed by Edgar Winter] / Peace Dream / Back Off Boogaloo / What I Like About You [Performed by Wally Palmar] / Rock and Roll, Hoochie Koo [Performed by Edgar Winter] / Boys / Love Is Alive [Performed by Gary Wright] / Broken Wings [Performed by Richard Page] / Photograph / Act Naturally / Medley: With A Little Help From My Friends - Give Peace A Chance

00-09-11 – **Promo Video**

Think It Over

A nice version of the Buddy Holly classic, the video shows Ringo singing the song in a recording studio. It was recorded for 'Listen To Me', a Buddy Holly tribute album, and also appeared on 'Ringo 2012'.

12-11-11 – **Credicard Hall, Sao Paulo (Brazil)**

It Don't Come Easy

00-01-12 – **Promo Video**

Wings

'Wings' is a song that Ringo first recorded for 1977's 'Ringo The 4th', and while that version has the edge vocally, this new version is better overall. Ringo doesn't appear in the animated video, though it's still enjoyable enough. It is from the album 'Ringo 2012', which got to No. 181 in the UK, and No. 80 in the USA.

30-01-12 – **The Troubadour, Hollywood (USA)**

Wings / With A Little Help From My Friends

31-01-12 – **'The Late Late Show With Craig Ferguson' (USA)**

Wings / I Wanna Be Your Man

01-02-12 – **'Late Night With Conan O'Brien' (USA)**

Wings / Act Naturally

13-06-12 – **Press Conference, Toronto (Canada)**

Boys / I Saw The Light [Performed by Todd Rundgren] / Evil Ways [Performed by Gregg Rolie] / Rosanna [Performed by Steve Lukather] / Broken Wings [Performed by Richard Page] / With A Little Help From My Friends

In 2012, Ringo would form the 12th All-Starr Band, who would stay together until 2016, and, from 14-06-12 to 02-07-16, would do several short tours of the USA, New Zealand, Australia, Japan and Latin America. The line-up was: Steve Lukather (Toto), Gregg Roliie

(Santana/Journey), Todd Rundgren (The Nazz/Utopia/The New Cars), Richard Page (Mr. Mister), Gregg Bissonette (The David Lee Roth Band), Mark Rivera (2012 to 2013 only) and Warren Ham (Bloodrock/Kansas/AD, from 2014 to 2016 only).

07-07-12 – 'Ringo At The Ryman', Ryman Auditorium, Nashville (USA)

Matchbox / It Don't Come Easy / Wings / I Saw The Light [Performed by Todd Rundgren] / Evil Ways [Performed by Gregg Rolie] / Rosanna [Performed by Steve Lukather] / Kyrie [Performed by Richard Page] / Don't Pass Me By / Bang The Drum All Day [Performed by Todd Rundgren] / Boys / Yellow Submarine / Black Magic Woman [Performed by Gregg Rolie] / Happy Birthday / Anthem / I'm The Greatest / Rocky Mountain Way [Performed by Joe Walsh] / You Are Mine [Performed by Richard Page] / Africa [Performed by Steve Lukather] / Everybody's Everything [Performed by Gregg Rolie] / I Wanna Be Your Man / Love Is The Answer [Performed by Todd Rundgren] / Broken Wings [Performed by Richard Page] / Hold The Line [Performed by Steve Lukather] / Photograph / Act Naturally / Medley: With A Little Help From My Friends - Give Peace A Chance

This show was issued on DVD.

00-01-14 – **Promo Video**

I Wish I Was A Powerpuff Girl

Like a bad trip, in this animated video, a bearded Ringo 'appears' in a short yellow dress and with a pink ribbon in his hair. Bizarre in the extreme!

20-01-14 – **'The Lifetime Of Peace and Love Concert', The El Ray Theatre, Los Angeles (USA)**

Photograph / Boys / With A Little Help From My Friends [The last song is with Eric Burdon, Jeff Lynne, Gary Wright and others]

09-02-14 – **'The Night That Changed America: A Grammy Salute To The Beatles' (USA)**

Matchbox / Boys / Yellow Submarine / With A Little Help With My Friends [with Paul McCartney] / Hey Jude [with Paul McCartney, Jeff Lynne, Dhani Harrison and others]

See the PAUL McCARTNEY section for more details!

00-03-15 – **Promo Video**

Postcards From Paradise

The 'Postcards From Paradise' album reached No. 157 in the UK compared to No. 99 in the USA, and this semi-animated video is for the title track.

21-06-16 – **'Ringo Starr In Person', The Foelling Theatre, Fort Wayne (USA)**

Matchbox / It Don't Come Easy / What Goes On / Kyrie [Performed by Richard Page] / Medley: Hello It's Me - Bang The Drum All Day [Performed by Todd Rundren] / Don't Pass Me By / Yellow Submarine / Oye Como Va [Performed By Greg Rolie] / I Wanna Be Your Man / Hold The Line [Performed by Steve Lukather] / Photograph / Medley: With A Little Help From My Friends - Give Peace A Chance

This was broadcast on 26-03-17.

00-09-16 – **Promo Video** – *RINGO STARR and ALL STARS FOR UNITED NATIONS*

Now The Time Has Come

A various artists charity record, Ringo is the main singer, and he is also featured prominently in the video.

00-09-17– **Promo Video**

Give More Love

Largely a straight performance video, this is the title track for Ringo's album of the same name. It failed to chart in the UK, and got to No. 128 in the USA.

From 02-06-18 to 29-09-18, Ringo toured Europe and the USA with his 13th All-Starr Band, starring: Steve Lukather (Toto), Colin Hay (Men At Work), Gregg Rolie (Santana/Journey), Graham Gouldman (10cc), Gregg Bissonette and Warren Ham (Bloodrock/Kansas/AD). At the time of writing in spring 2019, Ringo is touring Japan with his 14th All-Starr Band, featuring all of the above with the exception of Graham Gouldman, who is replaced by Hamish Stuart.

Ringo, like Paul, shows no signs of stopping just yet!

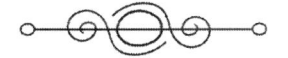

Peter Checksfield

BIBLIOGRAPHY

1964 – A Cellar Full of Noise – Brian Epstein (Souvenir Press)

1968 – The Beatles: The Authorised Biography – Hunter Davies (Heinemann)

1981 – Shout! – Philip Norman (Elm Tree Books)

1985 – Call Up The Groups – Alan Clayson (Cassell Illustrated)

1986 – The Beatles Live! – Mark Lewisohn (Harper Collins)

1993 – Hit Parade Heroes – Dave McAleer (Hamlyn)

1996 – The Complete Beatles Chronicle – Mark Lewisohn (Bounty Books)

1997 – Paul McCartney: Many Years from Now – Barry Miles (Martin Secker & Warburg Ltd)

1998 – Best of the Beatles: The Sacking of Pete Best – Spencer Leigh (Northdown Publishing)

1998 – Get Back: The Unauthorized Chronicle of the Beatles' "Let it be" Disaster – Doug Sulpy (St Martin's Press)

1998 – Revolution in the Head: The Beatles' Records and the Sixties – Ian McDonald (Pimlico)

2000 – The Beatles Anthology – The Beatles (Chronicle Books)

2001 – Eight Arms to Hold You: the Solo Beatles Compendium (44 1 Productions Inc)

2001 – The Beatles After The Break-Up 1970 – 2000 – Keith Badman (Omnibus Press)

2005 – John – Cynthia Lennon (Crown Publishers)

2006 – The Unreleased Beatles – Richie Unterberger (Backbeat UK)

2007 – The Beatles Off The Record - Keith Badman (Omnibus Press)

2007 – Wonderful Today: The Autobiography – Pattie Boyd, Penny Juror (Headline Review)

2009 – A Hard Day's Write: The Stories Behind Every Beatles Song - Steve Turner (MJF Books)

2009 – John Lennon: The Life – Philip Norman (Harper)

2009 – The British Invasion – Barry Miles (Sterling)

2009 – The Mammoth Book of The Beatles – Sean Egan (Robinson)

2012 – The British Television Music & Light Entertainment Research Guide 1936-2012 - Simon Coward, Richard Down, Chris Perry (Kaleidoscope Publishing)

2013 – Man on the Run: Paul McCartney in the 1970s – Tom Doyle (Polygon)

2013 – Pan's People: Our Story – Babs Lord, Ruth Pearson, Cherry Gillespie, Dee De Wilde, Simon Barnard (Signum Books)

2015 – Ringo: With a Little Help – Michael Seth Star (Backbeat Books)

2015 – Tony Sheridan: The One The Beatles called 'The Teacher' – Colin Crawley (CreateSpace Independent Publishing Platform)

2016 – From a Storm to a Hurricane: Rory Storm & The Hurricanes – Anthony Hogan (Amberley Publishing)

2018 – Finding The Fourth Beatle: The 23 drummers who put the beat behind the Fab Three – David Bedford (Tredition)

WEBSITES

www.beatlesarchives.com

www.beatlesbible.com

www.beatlesource.com

www.beat-magazine.co.uk

www.bootlegzone.com

www.georgeharrison.com

www.imdb.com

www.johnlennon.com

www.missingepisodes.proboards.com

www.oneforthedads.org.uk

www.paulmccartney.com

www.petebest.com

www.recordcollectormag.com

www.ringostarr.com

www.sirpaul.ru

www.thebeatles.com

www.the-paulmccartney-project.com

www.tv.com

www.wogew.blogspot.com

If you enjoyed this book, you might want to post an honest review on Amazon.... and you may also want to read 'CHANNELLING THE BEAT! (The Ultimate Guide to UK '60s Pop on TV)'!, and 'LOOK WOT THEY DUN! (The Ultimate Guide to UK Glam Rock on TV in The '70s), available now from Amazon & all good book stores!

Photo by Heather Carter

ABOUT THE AUTHOR

An acknowledged expert in his field, Peter Checksfield is the author of the acclaimed 'CHANNELLING THE BEAT! (The Ultimate Guide to UK '60s Pop on TV)' and 'LOOK WOT THEY DUN! (The Ultimate Guide to UK Glam Rock on TV in The '70s). He has also contributed to 'Record Collector', 'Now Dig This', 'Fire-Ball Mail', and various websites. His interests include collecting rare music TV footage, walking, cycling and local history. He lives near the coast in Kent, UK, with his partner Heather.

www.peterchecksfield.com

peterchecksfieldauthor@gmail.com

Printed in Poland
by Amazon Fulfillment
Poland Sp. z o.o., Wrocław